PRAISE FOR MARIA GRACE

Who hasn't thought Pride and Prejudice could use more dragons?

I've INHALED this series ... a well-written, well-researched, feel-good series ... this series is perfect.~***Kristen Lamb, WANA International***

I found it wicked brilliant!~***Jorie Love a Story***

I followed Ms. Grace down that rabbit hole as she truly held me captive. ~ ***Roofbeam Reader***

Leaves me in awe and delighted to have found it. ~***Ramblings of a Traveling Bookworm***

I was *still* surprised by how well this concept worked. .... It's by turns clandestine and tense, and playfully silly, and I found myself weirdly invested.~ ***The Book Rat***

Published by: RBF Books

Wrighting Old WRongs

Copyright © December 2023

Maria Grace

All rights reserved including the right to reproduce this book, or portions thereof, in any format whatsoever. The characters and events portrayed in this book are fictitious or are used fictitiously. Any similarity to actual persons, living or dead, events or locales is entirely coincidental and not intended by the author.

For information address author.MariaGrace@gmail.com

Author's Website: **RandomBitsofFascination.com**

DEDICATION

For my husband and sons.
You have always believed in me.

Chapter 1

OCTOBER 28, 1815

Sir Frederick Wentworth pulled his writing desk in his third-floor quarters at the London Blue Order offices closer to the window to catch the final rays of morning light. Larger than any shipboard accommodation he had dwelt in, it was the sort of room one might find in any of the better clubs in London. Commodious enough to fit a comfortable bed, a similarly comfortable chair by the fireplace, with a lined basket for Laconia, a modest press, and a writing desk that doubled as a dressing table, with a matching chair. The white walls made it seem a little larger, which helped as it had also gained the clutter typical of his landside accommodations. It was nothing to the suite of rooms the Dragon Sage enjoyed, but then, he hardly needed that much space, or attention, drawn to himself and Laconia. Especially now.

It would not be long before the sun hit its zenith, bathing his room in shadow. He used to be able to write in dim light, but recently, well-lit spaces suited the task better. Reading glasses might be in his future. Near future, if Laconia were to be believed. All things considered, glasses would probably be preferable to squinting and struggling to get letters and books at the right distance for reading. And there was little question that his future held a great deal of reading.

And writing. Starting with a letter to Anne back in Lyme. He dropped into the chair near the desk. Both he and the chair groaned as he reached for his writing slope on the floor beside the table legs.

Last night, he had rewritten his will in light of Anne's pregnancy. Thanks to Kellynch's insistence, the estate and his title would go to the baby, son or daughter. So long as the child lived, Anne would not be homeless. Their marriage articles provided for a jointure for her, funded by the dowry the Blue Order had provided. So, even if the child did not survive, Anne would still have means. Hopefully though, the Order would agree to his proposal that, should the worst happen, an additional sum would be added to fund her jointure. That would improve her comfort in the wake of loss.

Admiral Croft had agreed to step in whenever the law required a man's authorization, but Anne's wishes and decisions would be respected in all things. There were few men Wentworth could trust with such responsibility. Sophie had made an excellent choice in the man she had made his brother-in-law.

Now, he needed to tell Anne all the details and that the Ministry of Keeps held the paperwork for safekeeping. Copies were being prepared for both her and the Crofts and would be delivered by Blue Order courier as soon as they were ready.

Dear, practical, level-headed Anne would appreciate knowing those matters were handled—even as her heart broke knowing why such preparation was necessary.

As did his.

It was not as if he had not prepared this sort of document before. More than once, while he served in the Navy. But it was different then. Everything was different then. War among men, horrific as it was, was not like war with dragons. Yes, it was a grim job, but this was a different manner of grim. Magnified and intensified far beyond his expectations.

He had a family now, a child to bring up. Or he would soon. A home, a proper home, to return to. And there was the dragon to Keep as well.

Yes, everything was different now

He opened his writing slope and removed a sheet of paper, and edged the slope into the remaining swath of sun.

My dearest Anne,

Although I have not yet left London, you know where my latest mission will take me. I will not insult your intelligence by laying out all the complications and trials that may ensue from performing my duty. You are well aware of such things.

"Mrrrow." Laconia step-slithered in through an opening in the wall near the fireplace. Not an official corridor in the Blue Order offices, to be sure, but it was a poorly kept secret that many of the smaller dragons passed through hollows in the walls to traverse the buildings. Such pathways were also the thoroughfare through which much of the trade in gossip passed. No doubt Laconia had been gathering intelligence.

"What have you learned? I imagine you have been in some interesting places, considering the amount of cobwebs and dust adhering to your fine coat." Wentworth set his pen aside.

"Pray get the brush and help me remove it. I do not prefer the taste of cobwebs, and they stick to my whiskers with the tenacity of a seaman lashed to the mast in a storm." Laconia ran his thumbed paw over his whiskers and glanced at it. He sneered at the sticky traces tangled in his toes.

"Of course." Wentworth leaned his hard wooden chair back to reach into the top drawer of the little press in the corner near the fireplace.

Laconia stretched out his front catlike half and his long serpentine body and tail in the sliver of sunshine on the wooden floor. Black fur and scales shimmered in the fading sun. Such a handsome creature.

"So much dust and fluff." Wentworth sat on the floor beside him and brushed long strokes with the direction of his fur.

"Indeed, it was quite worth it, though." Laconia offered his be-webbed paw for the brush. "Our departure will be delayed by several more days."

"Another letter to be drafted? From whom this time? The entire Council? Londinium himself?" Wentworth grumbled under his breath and stared at the ceiling. "Does each ministry wish to register its own complaints? I am wondering if they want anything to be done at all."

"I suppose all those are possibilities in time. Remember the cold-blooded often move more slowly than the warm. But the current distraction is the Sage's unorthodox departure."

"Is it, now?" Wentworth returned to brushing the top of Laconia's head. Dusty webs dangled from his tufted ears. "Someone's scales are in a bunch because she did not follow protocols in taking her leave?"

"It was the draconic equivalent of stomping off and slamming the door behind her." Laconia's thick serpentine tail swept across the floor, bouncing against Wentworth's knee.

"You must agree though, all things considered, it was not unwarranted."

"Perhaps not, but it is unprecedented."

"Does anything about the Dragon Sage have precedent?"

"I suppose it depends upon where you look to identify precedent." Laconia turned to lick the shoulder Wentworth had just finished brushing. "No other dragon in the kingdom would treat Cowent Matlock so. He is ... distressed."

"Dare I ask what that might look like?"

"You will want to give him a wide berth. As I understand it, he was so angry he actually spurted flame in the Council Chambers. He was so humiliated! To lose control like a mere drakeling! Poor form indeed. Even now, he is still hiccupping flames here and there." Laconia sniggered under his breath.

"I do not understand why he should be concerned where the Sage goes. He does not control the movement of the other officer dragons, does he?"

"No, he does not. But the Sage is ... special. Unpredictable in so many ways, and he does not like what he cannot predict."

"The matters in the Archives?"

"That is indeed part of it, but I think there is more." Laconia curled his tail under him and sat upright. "He can cow the other dragon officers—all the dragons of England save Londinium himself—by sheer brute force. His dominance is uncontested. But because the Blue Order laws forbid harm to warm-bloods, apart from self-defense, there is a limit to the force he can exert while dealing with the Sage. She alone can stand in defiance, and there is little he can do."

"I never thought of that. So, in a sense, his dominance over her extends only as far as she will accept it?"

"Essentially, yes. So, she can challenge him in ways that no one else can."

Well, that was a different way of understanding things. "Did Cowent Matlock realize this when she was appointed as Sage?"

"I think not. But she was not nearly so challenging then. She has come into her own since her appointment, and I expect Matlock may regret the Council's decision now."

Wentworth pressed a fist to his chest. "You do not believe they will—"

"Remove the Dragon Sage?" Laconia turned to look at him. "Absolutely not. That would be tantamount to admitting he and the entire Council had made an error in judgement. Something warm-blood leaders might do on occasion, but no dragon is ever going to do. That would destroy their dominance—"

"They need to be infallible to lead?"

"No, just not admit that they are fallible. And no, you do not need to pontificate your opinion on that matter. It is what it is, and when it involves dragons of that size, one must simply accept what it is and move on." Laconia chirruped as though that settled matters.

"As you say. Except of course, we are not actually moving anywhere." Wentworth set the brush on the edge of the bed and settled his legs tailor-style.

"That will change. No doubt in the most inconvenient way possible."

That was always the way with dragons. Wentworth sighed. Three sharp raps at the door penetrated the silence. "Come."

The door opened enough for Sir Edward Dressler, Lord Physician to Dragons, to peer inside. The morning's final sunbeam glinted on the bald top of his head. "Am I interrupting anything?"

"No, pray come in." Wentworth stood and pulled the desk chair toward the worn, stuffed leather chair near the fireplace. "Do sit down. I did not realize you had returned to London already."

"Last night, to be honest. But with all the hullabaloo going on, it seemed a good idea to check in as soon as possible." Dressler settled into the chair and pushed his thick glasses higher on his nose.

"Have you any calming draughts for major dragons? From what I hear, there may be a need for it."

"Would that I did. Sadly, I have anything but that. Between what we have learned from Scarlett about the snapdragons—you recall her, yes? The red cockatrix who had been allied with Lady Elizabeth's kidnappers—and the recent findings in the Archives..."

"You have heard of them, too?" Wentworth's eyebrows climbed high enough to wrinkle his forehead.

"Every minor dragon in ten miles is twittering about them. But then, the news is far too interesting to remain contained. Granted, I do not know how much of the gossip is to be relied upon. I admit some of it seems too much to be believed. Dragonbane? I consider it a work of fiction."

"Have not heard about that." Wentworth leaned back and scratched his temple.

Laconia snuffed and flicked his tail, suggesting he knew as well.

Dressler rolled his eyes. "I am sure you will. Supposedly there are writings that talk about an airborne poison to which firedrakes are susceptible. The substance has been dubbed 'dragonbane' by those who are carrying the word, and there is a mad rush to identify what the substance is. Personally, I believe it is hogwash. I would surely have found some record of such a thing in my research by now. And I assure you I have done a great deal of research over the years. I do not believe there is any such weapon that can be brought to bear against—"

"The dominant dragons in England? I can see why there would be a great deal of interest in it though. All things considered, it must be an appealing holy grail to some."

"Absolutely, and that worries me. I will meet with the Council soon to determine what the official position on the matter will be. And what I am to do about it ... unofficially."

"Did the Council actually see the documents or did they just hear about them?" Wentworth asked.

"Their secretaries heard the gossip and brought it to them." Laconia's whiskers twitched in disapproval.

"Is there no privacy in these offices?" Wentworth glanced back at his writing slope. Best remember to keep it, and his correspondence, locked up.

"Precious little, and extreme measures must be taken to ensure it." Laconia looked at him meaningfully.

Like writing on a child's slate with another while an entirely different conversation was taking place as he and the Dragon Sage had been forced to do. "What do you expect from your meeting with them?"

"A lot of temper, spleen, and bad behavior." Dressler's laughter was forced and hollow. "It is a difficult and sensitive matter, to be sure. The news from Scarlett should be much better received, though."

"What can you tell me of that, or is it privileged information?" Wentworth asked.

"It has not been deemed so. I can discuss it, at least for the moment. Considering her part in the Dragon Sage's rescue, the terms of Scarlett's captivity at Briarwood Sanctuary for bird-types are generous. So, she has been amenable to assisting us. Scarlett identified several individuals involved and the meeting points used in their illicit trade in dragons and their body parts. It is the clearest information we have yet received. I am hopeful this will yield some progress in that investigation."

"That is excellent news." Wentworth rocked back on the back legs of his chair. "Have you any new word on Kellynch's condition? Anne has been writing regularly, to be sure, but—"

"A professional opinion is always appreciated. I understand." Dressler's lips turned up in a wry smile. "To be honest with you, I have never tended a major dragon with the extent of wounds that Kellynch has endured. Those sorts of interactions between large dragons are so regulated, that they are nearly unheard-of these days. So much blunt trauma, it is difficult to comprehend the extent of the internal damage that Kellynch may have suffered. His recovery is going to be a lengthy one. Anne is a faithful nurse, though, and if anyone can comfort him through this, it will be her."

"So, you believe he will pull though?" Pray, he said yes. A single weight removed could mean everything.

"I am optimistic."

Thank heavens! "What of Kellynch's temper? Prior to his reassignment to Kellynch-by-the-Sea, he was prone to some frightful tantrums."

"That is putting it diplomatically." Laconia muttered and licked his paw.

"Few of us are kind and patient when we are recuperating," Dressler said.

"While that may be the case, a man's tantrum is nothing to a dragon's." Wentworth suppressed a shudder. That was a memory he would prefer not to relive.

"You and Lady Wentworth will need to be patient as he mends and regains his strength."

"He will make a full recovery, then?"

"I have no way of predicting that. But I left Mr. Gillingham at Kellynch-by-the-Sea hoping to provide as much support as possible. We have a messenger assigned between us, and I receive reports on the progress every other day or so. There is little more that we can do."

"Perhaps a calming draught for my wife, who has to endure Kellynch's temper while I am called away." Poor, patient Anne.

"That is not unreasonable. I will include such a receipt in my next exchange with Gillingham."

Chapter 2

November 1, 1815

Kellynch was in good hands. Kellynch was in good hands. Anne pressed the heels of her hands to her temples and chanted the mantra again. Kellynch was in good hands. The vicar's widow, Widow Martin, was right. Kellynch was behaving like a spoilt child and if Anne did not take the upper hand soon, she would find herself overrun with the petulant dragon's demands.

She turned her back to the sharp breeze sweeping across the cliffs, bringing the salty taste of the waves below. The sun struggled and failed to bring warmth with its sharp beams. She shielded her eyes and glanced across the ocean. Beautiful and cruel. When one knew what lurked beneath those waters—splendid and terrifying dragons—it could never look the same again. Kellynch often talked about the ocean and how much he missed swimming freely there. His injuries kept him to his sea cave these days. Injuries inflicted by those sea dragons.

Mr. Gillingham—apprentice to Sir Edward, Lord Physician to Dragons—had proven himself adept at changing Kellynch's dressings and providing him with adequate distraction to temporarily forget the discomfort he suffered. Kellynch preferred her presence, but upon learning of her delicate condition, Wentworth had all but forbidden her from taking the treacherous cliffside trail down to the sea cave and had taken it upon himself to explain the decision to Kellynch.

Not unexpectedly, Kellynch did not like it. And he took every opportunity to express his displeasure about that, often moaning of the guilt she would feel if he were to die in her absence. At times, he sounded just like sister Mary.

Things had been going so well with him, at least until he was so grievously injured in the Battle of Lyme Bay. Had he expected to enter that conflict and escape unscathed? It genuinely seemed like he had. It was the sort of hubris one might expect from a dragon.

Especially one that had been previously wronged so deeply by his Keeper, and yet seen his complaints resolved with unprecedented favor.

As much as Anne had benefited from the Blue Order's generosity, it was still a little hard to believe. A coastal estate, both she and Wentworth with the rank of Keeper, a baronetcy that would pass to a daughter if there was no male heir, not to mention that Kellynch was permitted to keep the gold pilfered from the wreck of the Merchant Royal. One might imagine that would be enough to guarantee his good spirits, but Anne could hardly be so fortunate.

Kellynch would always remember his feelings about Sir Walter Elliot, the disgraced baronet who lost both his estate and his reputation in his fall from grace. Though he never came right out and said it, the entire situation humiliated Kellynch and left him exceptionally sensitive to any perceived slight.

Like Anne not personally tending to his recovery.

A loud caw overhead sounded like Balen. She flew the territory daily and brought reports to Kellynch that helped him feel he was still in charge, even though he had not the strength nor endurance to check the territory himself. It was a kindness not without its rewards.

Balen appreciated the excuse to stretch her wings and to monitor things herself. The territory might belong to Kellynch, but she felt her own responsibility over it as well. Much as Anne did.

How lovely it was to have such a sympathetic Friend.

Balen landed several yards away. The most unusual cockatrix in all of England, she had been called. And it was not a compliment. Whereas most greater cockatrix were stunningly beautiful, with ornate feathered head ruffs and splendid long tails, Balen was none of those things. With spindly legs, she stood nearly as tall as Anne. She resembled a stork with a stocky heavyset build, covered in deep grey feather-scales rather than soft feathers. Instead of lengthy and sharp, her bill was stout and heavy, shaped like a shoe that ended in a formidable downward hook. Her broad wings allowed her to fly fast, with great endurance. She was built for practical usefulness, not looks.

And she was Anne's Friend.

"I am afraid I have bad news." Balen squawked.

"What is happening in London?" Anne strode to her side.

"The Dragon Sage has left London without so much as a take leave from the Council Dragons. Wentworth is delayed yet again. And he has sent with me a copy of his updated will." Balen ducked her head to tap the sturdy leather satchel strapped to her chest with her beak.

The word "will" hit with far greater force than it should have. Anne dropped gracelessly to sit on the rocky ground. "Have we not already endured enough?" She pressed her hand to her not-yet-bulging belly. "It is not fair."

"No, it is not. But dragons have little sense of fairness. The bigger and more powerful one is, the less those smaller than one matter. And the dragons involved are the biggest in all of England." Balen laid her wide beak on Anne's shoulder and extended her wing to shelter Anne from the wind. "Has Kellynch been difficult?"

"Since I am not tending to him, he finds Mr. Gillingham's ministrations insufficient. He feels he deserves to be tended by the Lord Physician himself." Anne pressed her cheek to Balen's cool, smooth beak. She smelled like fish and salt water. "I understand he is uncomfortable, and that being injured is an insult to his pride. But it is not as though he has lost dominance in the region. I do not understand why he acts as if that is the case. It is more and more difficult to justify his ill temper every day."

Balen's shoulders drooped. "I am afraid the rest of the news I bring is going to make things even worse."

"Worse?" Anne gulped in a breath lest the tears that were always so near the surface these days escape. "Truthfully, the only thing I can imagine to make this worse is if my father showed up on my doorstep."

"I thought you would want to know before he did."

"No." The gravel slipped under her feet as she clambered to stand, her hands trembling. She stared at Balen who only blinked with that somber expression she usually wore. "Pray, tell me you are joking." She had to be. She had to.

Balen pulled her neck back and cocked her head. "Why ever would I do that?"

"No. It cannot be. He has not the funds to travel from Bath."

Balen clapped her beak and shook her head. "The house he let was struck by lightning and the roof caught fire. The storm put it out before the house was consumed, but it is not habitable right now."

"Why is he here? He knows Kellynch wants nothing to do with him."

"As I understand from the fairy dragon gossip, the Bath office was supposed to dispatch a message to Mr. Wynn at Lyme to pass on to you at Kelynch-by-the-Sea, requesting assistance. But the message went awry and someone decided they were supposed to send your father and sister to Lyme, instead of the message. So, they did not actually pay for their coach fare. I would not be surprised if once this all gets sorted out, the Order deducts it from his stipend."

"How is that possible? I do not understand. I thought the Order office in Bath was supposed to keep watch on him and see that he did not run into trouble." Anne paced along the trail, fists pumping at her sides.

"Your father has not made many friends in Bath, warm- or cold-blooded. I expect it was not difficult mischief to manage, and someone is quite glad to have him off their hands." Balen was not one to mince words.

"I dislike the notion that such a thing might have been intentional. That suggests ... things that I prefer not to believe are true." Anne struggled to force air through her tight chest. "If they set foot on Kellynch-by-the-Sea, Kellynch will declare it unforgivable."

"I spoke with the carriage driver bringing them here and convinced him to take them to the Royal Lion Inn in Lyme proper, instead. If the driver takes the route I suggested, they will not cross into Kellynch's territory at all."

"Brilliant thinking. Truly brilliant. Thank you." Anne gulped several deep breaths. "The rooms there should do nicely for them, though I know they will complain bitterly at the privations their limited budget requires."

"The Order should be made to foot the bill for their accommodations, since it is their error that has brought them here."

"I agree. I shall have to discuss the matter with Mr. Wynn, who will not be pleased about it. But first, it seems prudent that I go to the Royal Lion and prepare them for their guests."

BALEN, WITH ALL HER consideration and foresight, had already called down to the stables and suggested their driver, Jonty Bragg, prepare the coach and meet them up on the cliffs. Perhaps it was intrusive, but it was the sort of considerate thing Anne might have done under similar circumstances. And given the exhaustion of early pregnancy, it was a welcome relief not to scurry up and down the local hills.

Balen was a most considerate Friend.

Bragg handed her out of the carriage near the front door of the three-story white inn, where a sign of a gold lion wearing a crown on a red standard greeted her. Perched on Broad Street near Drakes Way, the inn offered a view of the shore and the ocean, if one could be bothered to enjoy it.

Balen had assured her that her father's coach was still several miles away, so she had time to make arrangements with the innkeeper for accommodations before they arrived. A portly, friendly looking man, just as an innkeeper should look, he seemed pleased to send a maid scurrying to ensure his two best rooms were prepared for occupancy.

She had settled the last of the details when the worn, somber-looking coach bearing her family rolled up. The driver handed them out. Elizabeth's complaints about the journey and Father's dissatisfaction at the quaintness of the inn tumbled in through the Royal Lion's street-facing windows.

Anne smiled an apology at the innkeeper and stood near the front door. Thankfully, the front hall was empty but for her and the innkeeper. With a low, beamed ceiling, paneled walls, and several comfortable hall chairs, the warm, welcoming space did not deserve the company about to violate it.

The door flew open and Father marched in. Impeccably dressed in dark coat and breeches, but covered in a light layer of road dust, he had not changed since her last encounter with him. His face was flushed and screwed up in an expression of petulance and disapproval. Behind him, Elizabeth fought to brush wrinkles out of her dusty pelisse skirt, oozing displeasure from every pore. Travel did not agree with them unless they were going to London for the season. Then it was tolerable. But since, at this time of year especially, there was no one to see or be seen by at Lyme, everything about it and the journey to get there would be unsatisfying.

"Anne?" Father stammered, jaw dropping in a decidedly inelegant expression.

"Whatever are you doing here?" Elizabeth folded her arms, which usually was the prelude to a tantrum. "What are we doing here? The driver had instructions to bring us to—"

"I gave orders that we should be taken to your home." He huffed as though that settled matters.

"I have made arrangements for you to have accommodations here," Anne said. How easily that placating tone she always had used with Father came back.

"Here? Here? No, I have no intention of in staying in such a place when my daughter lives not three miles away." He somehow managed to lift his head and look down at her all at the same time.

"You know that is not possible, and no, I will not discuss the matter."

"It is that awful husband of yours, is it not?" Elizabeth's eyes bulged like a horse about to throw its rider.

"Don't you say nothing about the baronet, Miss," the innkeeper said, in a low steady voice that had a hint of warning to it. "He be well-respected around here and the locals will not take well to you speaking ill of him."

"How dare you speak to me that way! He is my brother-in-law, and I will speak of him in whatever way I so choose." Elizabeth tossed her head and looked aside.

"Then do not be surprised if the locals choose not to do business with you. Loyalties run strong in Lyme, you should know. It does not do to cross them." The innkeeper crossed his meaty arms over his chest.

"You did not write to us of your plans, Father. Kellynch-by-the-Sea is not prepared to accommodate guests right now. It is fortunate that a near neighbor saw you on the road and alerted us to your visit. I imagine you would like some refreshments?" Anne turned to the innkeeper. "Pray, have their luggage sent to their rooms."

Father rolled his eyes and nodded at the same time. He would condescend to take such things, though they would not be to his standard.

"There is a private room in the pub. I will show you there and have a tray sent." The innkeeper led them through a low door to the back of the building. They passed through a well-proportioned dining room with several small tables and two large ones. Wide windows poured scant afternoon sun in to reflect off the mirrors and polished brass throughout the wood-paneled room. He led them through another narrow door to a small, white-painted room, lit by a single window. Most of the space was occupied by a narrow rectangular table that might have seated six if absolutely necessary, but probably better accommodated four.

Anne sat at the table at the seat nearest the window and gestured for Father and Elizabeth to join her. "How were your travels?"

The innkeeper shut the door behind him as he left them.

"Perfectly ghastly. We have been all day in that carriage with scarcely any stops for comfort." Elizabeth perched on her seat, hinting that it might not be worthy to receive her. "I do not understand why we could not find other accommodation in Bath. I am certain there were other houses to let there."

Father glared at Anne as though it were her fault.

"I am sure it has something to do with the unique financial position you are in—"

"Do not be vulgar, Anne," he all but snarled. "That is not the sort of thing discussed in polite company."

Since when were Father and Elizabeth polite company? "What has prompted your visit?"

"I imagine you already know. But since you ask, a fire has made our house uninhabitable. We need other accommodations," he said.

"But why come here? I am certain there are those who could have assisted you in Bath." Anne clenched her fist under the table.

"We were not satisfied with the living arrangements there. I have little reason to expect they will do any better for us now." He glanced at Elizabeth, who nodded vigorously.

"I insist on having a say in the house this time. That place we were in was terrible!" Elizabeth pressed her hand to her chest.

"We need something fitting to the station of a baronet."

"Need I remind you of your station?" Anne whispered as a serving girl entered with a tray.

The girl set several platters on the table and a tea service and walked out as slowly as possible, at least until Anne glared at her. No doubt there were many who wanted details about the baronet's unexpected arrival.

"I am a baronet!" He slapped the table.

"Who lost his family lands through mismanagement and debt. You are fortunate to have the living that you do." Not that he would understand her explanation any better this time than he had the countless times before.

Elizabeth leaned forward, whispering, "It is not enough for anything. I could not purchase a new gown for this season! Have you any idea how humiliating that is?"

"Do you have anywhere to wear a new gown?" No, that was not an appropriate thing to say, but who could blame her?

"I should, and that is also humiliating. We are so bored. Can you imagine, we have received no invitations, attended no concerts, had no socializing at all. It is too much to be borne." Elizabeth dabbed the corner of her eye with her handkerchief.

"Go talk to the ... bankers, Anne. They will listen to you. You can tell them I have learned my lesson and will live in moderation now. There is no need to continue this farce of a punishment." He folded his hand.

"You do not understand, do you? From whence do you think your money comes? You have no land, no investment, no savings. The little living that you enjoy is a gift, not a right." Anne laid her open hands on the table.

Father drew a breath, a long deep one that would inevitably fuel many arguments.

"No. There is nothing more, and if you abuse what you are given, even that will be taken from you. The life you once had is gone forever. You must learn to appreciate what you have."

"Why do you not take us in as any good sister would do? Really, it is too cruel. I am sure it is the doing of Lady Russell. She always thought far too well of you," Elizabeth said.

"Lady Russell is dead, of influenza."

"I am sorry, I did not know." Elizabeth had the small decency to blush. "But now that you are free of her influence, you may—"

"No, I may not. I cannot invite you into my home. It is simply impossible."

"No, it is not. You are being stubborn, Anne." He snorted like Kellynch did when he was not permitted his way.

"You know that is not true. You know precisely why it is and how it is entirely of your making. I will see what can be done. I will call upon you when I know something further. Do not come to Kellynch-by-the-Sea." Anne stood.

"Why are you such a selfish, ungrateful creature, Anne?" Elizabeth jumped to her feet and leaned across the table. "If it were you suffering—"

"Stop. Stop right there. I will not listen to the fictions that you craft to make yourself feel better. Enjoy your meal and your accommodations. Good day." Anne pulled her shoulders back and marched from the room, straight to her coach, which waited outside.

Jonty Bragg helped her inside, where Balen waited.

"Are you all right?" Balen laid a lap rug over Anne's knees.

"It went exactly as one might have expected it to go. Tomorrow I will pay a call to Mr. Wynn and get this matter sorted out."

Chapter 3

November 2, 1815

Balen launched from Wentworth's windowsill, and he closed the window after her. Off to find a meal, she would return later for his response to Anne's missive. Chill air clung to him in her wake, reminding him of the distance between him and everything he held dear.

He sat at the narrow desk, head in hands. At least Balen brought news of home, closing that gap a mite. He opened the leather satchel that Balen had worn and removed a carefully folded letter that smelled of Anne. Lilac and lavender with a hint of bergamot—a blend the apothecary at Lyme made up for her. A little shop at the base of a hill, with a stork holding a mortar and pestle on the sign. One more place he would have to visit when he returned.

Sighing, he turned back to the letter. It was a mark of trust that Anne did not seal the letter—and that Balen probably knew everything Anne was writing about. Yes, it felt a little intrusive, but it also meant Wentworth could ask Balen for details Anne might not have included. Anne was usually so circumspect when she wrote. It could be difficult to discern her true feelings on a matter.

He opened the first fold.

My dear W,

Where shall I begin today? What a day it has been. You will forgive me, I hope, in that I shall wait to address the questions you asked and unburden myself by telling you what has happened.

Good Lord! That was tantamount to her saying disaster had struck! He spread the letter fully open on the desk.

You will not believe who nearly appeared on our doorstep. My father and eldest sister. With Balen's help, I was able to establish them at the Royal Lion before they trespassed on the estate. It takes little to imagine how Kellynch would have reacted to such a flagrant violation of his dominance.

Why would...

Apparently, a fire has driven them from their lodgings in Bath. Their house is not fit for habitation. They had thought to stay with us, but it goes without saying that is not possible.

And the surly baronet and daughter would do what they always did, turning to Anne to fix problems that were not her own. Wentworth slammed his fist hard enough to rattle the bottles on the dressing table-desk.

I need not detail their complaints and demands. They are what one would expect. I hate to admit it, I can scarcely believe I am writing these words, but I find myself lacking the wherewithal to manage their needs right now. Between Kellynch and reestablishing the Blue Order offices, and the day-to-day matters of the estate, finding lodgings for my father is beyond me. Do you think there is some office of the Order that might help?

What it must have cost her to write those words? Damn it all, he should be home, helping her with all this. Not watching at a distance while she endured temper tantrums from man and dragon alike.

The Order was responsible for this situation. Surely they could help. They would help, he would see to it.

His chair nearly fell backwards as he stood. He caught it just in time and shoved it under the desk. The Ministry of Keeps. At some point he had heard that Sir Walter's stipend was being funded through the Ministry of Keeps. That would be his starting place.

He locked Anne's letter in his writing slope—Anne would not want gossip about her father circulating through the offices. It was embarrassment enough being related to him at all.

Ah, well, one could not choose their relatives, could one? He headed down the innumerable stairs to the lowest level of the Order offices.

By rank and importance, Sir Carew Arnold, the Minister of Keeps, should have rated a moderate-sized, first-floor office along with the Historian and the Scribe. But the need to entertain major dragons consigned him to the courtroom level, lit only by torches and smelling of damp stone and dragon musk. His was one of the largest offices, but only because of the need to accommodate major dragons. The sparse, hard-wearing décor demonstrated that practicality. Table, chairs, bookcases, and a desk. Nothing decorative or soft, all echoing utilitarianism at its finest.

Sir Carew welcomed him in and gestured to a seat near the enormous limestone table that dominated the office. The far side of the table ended near a dark dragon tunnel entry—a major dragon could hardly have fit through the doorway the warm-blooded used. Intentional or not, its looming presence dominated the room, reminding all of a major dragon's power.

"Good day, Sir Frederick. What has brought you today?" The slight man, with his shock of white hair, deceptively mild tone, and hunched shoulders, took a seat near Wentworth. A pair of bookcases behind him bowed with the weight of the journals and ledgers.

"Thank you for taking time to meet with me. I know you are busy—"

"You seem to be the only one in the Order who believes that." Sir Carew snorted, a touch of his legendary temper rearing its head. "You are right, I have five meetings scheduled today to hammer out Keep disputes, so please, get to the point quickly."

So many disputes? Who would have thought? That was a detail the Order clearly preferred to keep discreet. "Of course, I will be as brief as I can. You are already aware of the intricacies of our situation with Kellynch and the new Keep."

"Painfully aware." Sir Carew reached back to the bookcase and pulled out a volume without looking. "Give me a moment to look up all the details." Somehow it seemed like he was only doing that for show, that he would be able to recall it all from the top of his head.

Wentworth quickly described the situation Anne laid out in her letter.

"That man had the audacity to attempt to cross into Kellynch's territory? Pendragon's breath and bones! Does he have a death wish?" Sir Carew slapped the book and a little cloud of dust rose.

"Not at all. Sir Walter has some firm expectations about what his life should be like." Wentworth glanced at the ceiling and shook his head.

"He should consider it fortunate that he has a life at all. It is lucky for him that the carriage was diverted away from the estate, and he did not trespass. If you will look here," Sir Carew shoved the book at Wentworth, his wrinkled finger pointing to several lines in the middle of the page. "The stipend agreement, from which Sir Walter draws his living, clearly states that he is not to trespass on Kellynch's territory ever again. Doing so will nullify the financial agreement. What is more, you need to make certain your wife understands that offering any financial support to her father also will nullify the agreement."

Wentworth squinted and stared at the indicated lines. How had he not realized that language was in the estate charter? Not that he objected to having a concrete reason to refuse Sir Walter any favors, but still...

"You were unaware of these stipulations?" Clearly, Sir Carew did not approve of Wentworth's ignorance.

"I was certain I had studied the charter thoroughly."

"This is not the charter. It is a supplemental document to which the charter refers that sets out the provisions for the living allotted for Sir Walter." Sir Carew muttered something disagreeable under his breath. "The court should have reviewed it with you."

"I am quite certain they did not." Wentworth folded his arms over his chest and met Sir Carew's glare with one of his own. "I pay a great deal of attention to the language of such orders."

Sir Carew blinked several times, several thoughts and opinions crossing his face. "I am sure you do. Nonetheless, the language is there. As a consequence of the damage done to the Kellynch estate, Sir Walter can have no material help from anyone or anything connected to Kellynch or his territory."

Of course, that made sense, however unhelpful it was. "What then of Sir Walter's current crisis? Cannot the Order assist him in finding an alternative living situation?"

"Absolutely not. He is responsible for those arrangements."

"But the Order set up the situation in Bath. He assumed—"

"He is a self-serving ignoramus, taking for granted anything that he might use to his advantage. That was a singular event. Since the house has become uninhabitable, we can have our solicitors apply to take back the unused portion of this quarter's rent, which would give him some funds by which to reestablish himself. But more than that is entirely upon him. Just as it would be for any other man in England."

"I am not sure either he or his daughter is capable." Anne had always managed such things for him.

"Forgive my bluntness, but the only reason Sir Walter was provided that living was to maintain control over him and prevent him exposing Blue Order secrets. If it appears he is any danger to the Order because of his inability to manage his own affairs, he will be dealt with, and to put it as delicately as possible, the alternatives are not pleasant to consider. I am afraid all I can suggest is that your wife make clear to him the realities of his situation and what the consequences will be. For our part, all the Order will do is ensure he is carefully monitored. At the first sign he is a danger to us, we will be forced to act. Without hesitation."

"I see." It was not the first time Wentworth disliked a command-level response, and it probably would not be the last.

"It might not be the answer you wished for, but there is nothing more in my power to do for it." The edges of Sir Carew's voice softened.

"Understood." Which of course was the right thing to say, but in no way to be understood that he was going to leave Sir Walter to his own devices.

Laconia step-slithered in from the dragon tunnel and sprang to the tabletop. "You are wanted by the Council." He did not bother to voice the implied order.

"Thank you for your assistance, Sir Carew." Wentworth stood and bowed. "I should not keep the Council waiting."

"No, definitely not. I hope you are able to find a satisfactory solution to your wife's situation. I hope the Order does not need to act on this situation."

"Of course. Good day." It was not a good day at all, and it was looking to grow even worse now. Wentworth hurried out.

How convenient that the Council chambers were on the same level as the courtroom and Sir Carew's office. An unwelcome convenience when one needed time to adequately shift one's mind from warm-blood protocols to cold-blood ones.

The torchlit passage at the far side of the courtroom stank of dragon musk and brimstone. So, Laconia was not exaggerating. Matlock had been pushed to flaming outbursts. Wentworth had dealt with angry officers in the past and knew how to handle them. But none of them could burn him to cinders in a fit of spleen. That was the sort of thing one ought to remember and tread lightly.

He paused at the doorway to tug his coat straight. Hopefully, his thoughts would follow suit. He glanced down at Laconia, who nodded his readiness and rapped at the door. "Wentworth to see the Council, as directed."

"Come!" The word rumbled through Wentworth's chest and he pushed the door open.

Dunbrook caught sight of Laconia and roared, "That half-wyrm is not needed!"

Laconia turned on his tail and shot out, fur and body pouffed.

Unnecessarily rude, but definitely not the time to comment on that. Wentworth dropped to the floor to make the appropriate gestures of greeting.

"Rise and approach." Matlock snorted, wisps of smoke rising from his snout. He rose to his full height, imposing height. His blue-green hide dulled in the torchlight, but his orange eyes glowed, angry, dangerous.

Not the note he wanted to start the conversation on, but good to know where things stood. He took several steps into the hazy, dimly lit, cavernous space. How odd that they would not choose a lavish chamber fitting their rank for their meetings.

"You are aware of the Dragon Sage's departure?" Dunbrook huffed fetid breath Wentworth's way. The largest and sternest-looking drake anyone had ever seen, his deep stony grey face appeared chiseled into a permanent scowl with a voice to match.

"It has recently been explained to me. I had no foreknowledge nor any participation in it." Sometimes a little offense was the best defense.

The look Chudleigh shot at Dunbrook suggested Wentworth was right. The amphithere rose high on her serpentine tail. Her body was long and slender, covered in striking jade green scales. With a rattle of feathers, she unfolded her wings iridescent with multicolored feathers. The feathers continued along her shoulders and up her head, giving the impression of an elaborate woman's headdress. Bright, intelligent blue eyes sparkled in the candlelight, examining, judging them.

"So, you do not know who traveled with her?" If anything, Dunbrook sounded more irritated.

"No, Barwin, I do not. Nor have I had contact with anyone related to the Sage or the Historian or the Scribe."

Dunbrook's lip curled back and he growled. "I imagine you claim not to know where Bede is, either, then?"

"No, sir, I do not. I understood her to be doing work in the Darcy House library."

"She is not there."

"I fear I cannot be of assistance to you in locating her." Thank heavens for Lady Elizabeth's foresight in not detailing her plans to him.

Dunbrook clawed at the stony floor, leaving gouges in his wake. "Have you been given any documents to transport?"

"I am not in possession of any documents from the office or the Archives, nor have I any expectation of that changing."

"Exactly assss I told you." Chudleigh slapped the floor with the tip of her tail.

"Remember your place, Barwines." Dunbrook's snort ruffled her showy head-feathers.

"Remember yourssss." She hissed in his face and extended her wings.

"Enough." Matlock stomped his front foot, a jet of flame punctuating his words.

Wentworth hopped back. One did not want to be too near a dragon at the end of his tether.

"We have no material reason to doubt Wentworth's word." Matlock glowered at Dunbrook, then turned the glare on Wentworth. "See that it remains so."

"You insult Kellynch by your accusation."

"He is not among my concerns at the moment. He should understand his place in the ranks, and if he does not, that will be his problem, not mine." Matlock opened his wings and flapped a great breeze at Wentworth.

Well, that was telling, was it not? Usually Matlock was much more politic, even with respect to a low ranking dragon like Kellynch. "Are your current concerns the reason my presence was demanded?" This was wholly the wrong time to back down from even angry dragons.

"Precisely," Matlock folded his wings over his back, though his tail still swept broad strokes across the stone floor. "Your orders have changed."

Wentworth did not need a meeting with the Council to have figured that out.

"I no longer need you to take a message to Cornwall."

Excellent. Then he would be off to Lyme within the hour. "If you will then excuse me—"

"You are not dismissed." Matlock's voice boomed off the walls like falling rocks. "Your services are still required. You will accompany me to Land's End."

"I am unclear what you will need from me, then." Matlock had staff and attendants of his own.

"You will report to General Yates this afternoon. At the Pendragon Knights' training ground."

"I do not understand."

"You need instruction in carrying the Dragon Slayer."

Chapter 4

November 3, 1815

It was convenient that the Blue Order office for Lyme had moved to an available cottage on the grounds of Kellynch-by-the-Sea. Prior to that, it had been in Mr. Allenden's shop, which was, for many reasons, less than ideal. Sometimes even the Blue Order had to make do with less-than-ideal circumstances, and everything related to Allenden had been less than ideal.

Even with the improvement in the office situation, not everything had been resolved. Instead of walking into town to collect her undelivered Blue Order correspondence, though, now Anne had only to traverse the estate. While it was an improvement, it still was not the way things were supposed to be. Those letters were supposed to be delivered by Blue Order courier to the manor and placed directly into her hands.

That courier would be Cypher, a dusky red drake with darker markings that resembled cryptic symbols, who served as the office secretary. The one who battled an ever-growing pile of work in a campaign she would likely never win. At least not while Mr. Wynn, Regional Undersecretary of the Somerset-Dorset region, was managing the reestablishment of the Order office in Lyme. Even though Jasper, Wynn's red and black drake Friend, assisted Cypher, meeting Wynn's standards kept both drakes fully occupied. Had a third been available, that one would have been at wits' end as well. So, Anne did what she could to ease the burden, regularly walking over to pick up her correspondence.

Mrs. Frankel, the short, sturdy, housekeeper for the Order office, with mounds of red curls peeking from under her mobcap, greeted her at the front door. Mrs. Frankel was a force of nature. A gale on two feet that, in some impossible feat of nature, left order rather than chaos in her wake. Exactly the presence the still-chaotic office needed since its hurried relocation from the back room of Mr. Allenden's shop. "Here for your correspondence, Lady Wentworth?"

"Yes." Anne peeked around Mrs. Frankel. The front room, the largest in the cottage, teemed with boxes, trunks, and stacks of ledgers and journals, obscuring the mismatched furniture within. "Good heavens, what has happened here?"

"Would you like to take a seat and have a bite while I tell you about it? I'm afraid it is quite the story. The kind that will probably leave you all prickly and irritated." Mrs. Frankel removed a pile of books from a worn upholstered chair and placed them on another nearby stack. She trundled a dozen steps to a plain-fronted wooden cabinet on the far side of the room, shoved a wooden box aside just enough that she could open the door and remove the familiar painted tin. She pried off the lid and carried it to Anne.

Clear cakes, marzipan, barley sugar candies, and Jordan almonds filled the tin. "It looks like you have recently refilled it." Anne took a clear cake and a cube of marzipan. On second thought, an extra clear cake might be necessary to maintain her composure if the story was as Mrs. Frankel described. She took a second one.

Mrs. Frankel nodded vigorously. "One must find comfort where one can, eh?" She scooped out several sugar-coated almonds, covered the tin, and made room on a nearby wooden chair. She plumped the ragged cushion and sat down.

"What storm blew all this in?" Anne asked.

"You're right there, quite the storm it was." Mrs. Frankel popped an almond into her mouth and stared out the window. "Were you aware that the Blue Order office in Lyme was once housed in a proper townhouse with access to the dragon tunnels?"

Anne shook away the prickles dancing along the back of her neck and shoulders. "I had no idea. Wentworth never mentioned that. At least I do not think he did. He resented the office Mr. Allenden maintained, but I never thought to ask him more about it."

"It was quite the tragedy, to be sure. There aren't many who want to speak of it even now." Mrs. Frankel pursed her lips into a peculiar frown. It seemed she did not want to discuss it either.

"What happened?"

"In short, and mentioning no names in particular, it seems that, unbeknownst to the Order office managing the facility, a visiting Keeper who was using the guest rooms had planned a tryst with another member there. Amid their entertainments a candelabra was knocked over and a terrible fire ensued. The building was heavily damaged and more than one death was attributed to the blaze." Mrs. Frankel stared out the window, purposefully not meeting Anne's gaze.

"Were you keeping house for the Order office then?"

"I was. Barely got meself and Mist out in time. She still has scars along her belly where she slithered over burning furniture to wake me. I sleep like the dead, you know, and it nearly killed me."

"She is a brave and loyal Friend. No wonder Balen thinks so highly of her."

Mrs. Frankel caught Anne's eye for a moment, then looked away again. "I hated moving it all to Mr. Allenden's shop. His wife hated snakes and could never accept Mist as anything but a snake. She was terrible to Mist."

"I am sorry, I wish we had known."

"Well, it is done and over now. Our little sorrows are not the point, though. You see, there was a fairly large cluster of wryms who were given leave to use a broken-down stone shed in the back garden of the townhouse as a lair. Some generations ago, they did a favor for the Lyme magistrate and that was how he repaid the favor. In the chaos after the fire, it seems the wyrms took it upon themselves to gather what was left of the Order documents and take them underground, into the tunnels to protect them."

"How extraordinary." Anne nibbled the corner of her clear cake—she needed a moment to compose her thoughts. Tart apple, with a crunchy crust of sugar on the top. "It seems almost too much to believe of wyrms."

"Indeed, it does. I would not have believed it myself but for..."

"But for what?"

"Does Mr. Wynn have to know?"

Anne winced. Skirting Blue Order protocols was not something Mr. Wynn tolerated. "Whatever you tell me, I will protect you and Mist. He can be a bit ... unreasonably particular." And that was putting it incredibly kindly. Even Balen found him nigh on intolerable at times.

"I trust your discretion, Lady Wentworth." Mrs. Frankel sighed, chewing her bottom lip. "I suppose it will all come out one way or another. As soon as we got set up here, boxes and bundles began appearing on the back doorstep. Slowly at first, but now so quick that Cypher and Jasper can't keep up."

"Appearing?"

"Yes. In the dark of night, they are delivered, with little trace of who brought them."

"And Mr. Wynn did not think to tell me?" Anne nearly dropped her marzipan.

"I once suggested he should, but he said it was not in the jurisdiction of the Special Liaison."

"I see he and I are of different opinions on the matter. I will discuss it with him. Soon." And since Kellynch was the ranking dragon of the region, her opinion would carry a great deal of weight. But no need to involve Mrs. Frankel in those matters. "How much is left to transfer from the dragon tunnels?"

"Mist has met with the wyrms several times and the situation is a bit complicated."

"Dragons are always complicated. What manner of complications are we talking about?" Anne took another bit of clear cake. Perhaps that would settle her increasingly uncertain stomach.

"That they are, that they are. As I understand it, this lot here," Mrs. Frankel gestured around the room, "represents less than perhaps a third of the material they have been guarding."

Merciful heavens! "How did we not know there was so much?"

"Mr. Allenden had no space and little concern for such material and, if he had been told about it, conveniently forgot. The scandal around the fire in the office was such that several important issues fell by the wayside."

Once the matter of the records was resolved, she would have to ask what other issues slipped from notice. But not today. "You mentioned complications."

"Yes, well, I have not spoken with them, of course. Not being an official of the Order, it seemed ill-advised to step into matters that are not my business. But Mist has become friendly with the wyrms and shares some of their concerns."

"And those concerns are?" Anne finished the clear cake. Good thing she had another one waiting in her hand.

"You realize Mr. Wynn is away right now, yes?"

"I thought he was off to Bath, was he not?"

"Yes, exactly. He is there to see about finally getting the repairs to the old Lyme office underway. Mr. Allenden, for reasons I can only speculate upon, was supposed to have supervised that, but..." Mrs. Frankel's lopsided frown seemed to weigh down her face as she cocked her head.

"Given his diligence on other matters, one should not be surprised."

"The wyrms have expressed concerns about being able to continue to occupy their lair during and after the renewal of the property. The Order is not always generous with the minorest of minor dragons, though."

Especially where Mr. Wynn was concerned. No doubt his attitude about Scarlett and the efforts to rescue her had gotten back to the wryms, considering that Anne had heard whispers about it all over Lyme. Little matter that he had eventually chosen to do the right thing, that he ever hesitated was a sore point among the local minor dragons, at least as Balen told it.

"Perhaps ... well, no, I am well overstepping my bounds—" Mrs. Frankel pressed her knuckles to her lips.

"Pray, do speak your mind. Unlike some, I do not think you need to be a major dragon or an Order officer in order to have valuable insight." Anne popped the entire marzipan cube into her mouth to punctuate the point.

Mrs. Frankel snickered. "One wonders if the Order would find themselves more generous if there was something in all these ledgers, and journals and books that the Order would consider valuable."

"I wish I could say you were wrong, but that is an excellent suggestion." Anne glanced around the room. "No one has had a good look at these volumes yet, have they?"

"Jasper has gone with Mr. Wynn to Bath. Much of this has arrived since their departure. Cypher has only started to catalog the material. It does not seem within the scope of my duties to read such documents."

"But I am under no such restriction." Anne ate the last of her second clear cake, stood and dusted her hands. "Where to begin?"

"Cypher has done some preliminary sorting on the materials, as I understand." Mrs. Frankel stood and surveyed the bookish landscape. "Let me see if I can remember what she told me." She picked her way through the piles.

How many volumes had they gathered in this room? And how was it no one realized they were missing? Was it all Mr. Allenden's fault, or was there something more afoot?

"It seems this section represents books from the libraries of deceased Order members. Some of them are quite old, I think. At one time, when an Order member died without dragon-hearing heirs, all the books in their libraries, such as they were, were left to the nearest Blue Order office, to be sorted and disposed of properly. Given the size of this pile, clearly that was not a priority for the office." Mrs. Frankel's open-armed gesture included better than half the room.

The Historian and the Scribe might be interested in those older volumes. Anne would need to write to them and ask.

Mrs. Frankel edged through a narrow game trail between stacks. "I think Cypher told me that these ledgers related to Order business and expenses for the Order-affiliated households. Several prominent members have owned seaside property here. And these—yes, this is what I was looking for." She pointed at three modest stacks near the cabinet that housed the lovely painted tin. "Cypher says these are journals, written by both warm- and cold-blooded Order members. She and Jasper agree, these are most likely to have unique and useful information."

"Excellent." Anne made her way toward the piles. "Would you put on a pot of tea? It seems I have my work cut out for me."

Mrs. Frankel ducked her head. Was that to hide the little smile turning up the corners of her mouth and dimpling her plump cheeks? Almost as if that was what she had hoped for in the first place. "Of course, Lady Wentworth. I shall be back directly. We can move these books into the records room for you. Unless you prefer the office—"

"No, I think I will avoid trespassing into Mr. Wynn's territory." One did not invite a dragon's wrath that way—not even a warm-blooded one's.

Mrs. Frankel nodded vigorously and picked her way to the kitchen.

Anne's fingers tingled as though someone had handed her a gift wrapped in a pretty box and tied with a ribbon. How long would it take to open it and discover the treasure within? She picked up as many volumes as she could carry and headed for the records room that doubled as a library.

At one time used as a bedroom, the cramped room now held bookcases along all the walls, and a pair of small desks, set facing each other, with matching chairs. Candlesticks with candles burnt low suggested late nights of work—Cypher and Jasper? Probably. Everything was orderly, despite a fine layer of dust that never seemed to bother the dragons much. Mr. Wynn's office generally resembled the aftermath of a ship in a storm, rather like Wentworth's office—an environment she preferred not to surround herself with.

She set the stack on the closest desk and settled into the hard chair. Her skirt caught on a scratch on the edges of the seat. Dragon talons, no doubt.

A quick pass through the journals to identify the ones most likely to be helpful. Perhaps bring them back to the house to read at her leisure. There she would dive in and study the treasures the wyrms brought.

Or at least what she hoped would be treasures, not merely dry lists of mundanery that would help her sleep at night, but little else.

Mrs. Frankel strode in with a tea tray that included a plate of sandwiches and laid it on the opposite desk. "Can't have you going hungry in your condition, now can we? I'll bring in the rest of the books."

"Thank you." Anne reached for a sandwich of sliced ham and cheese on a sturdy brown bread, neither dainty, not elegant, but since her appetite was neither dainty nor elegant, at the moment, it was both fitting and well appreciated.

The topmost volume of the stack was bound in red cloth that had faded to a fragile pink. Mice, or maybe rats, had nibbled the edges of the cover. She suppressed the shudder and took another bite of sandwich for the distraction. Between Laconia, Corn, and Wall, rodents were a thing of the past in Kellynch-by-the-Sea, and if she had her way, it would continue.

No title page. It went straight into spidery handwriting covered with pen splotches and the occasional paw print—cat, not tatzelwurm, as they lacked thumbprints. Lists, so many lists. It seemed it was an entire book of lists. Well, that was not likely to prove very insightful, was it? She perused the next three volumes that seemed to be written by the same hand, with the same splotchy pen. All similarly gripping and brimming with perceptive observations. Anne rolled her eyes and freed another sandwich from the plate.

"I was afraid of that." Mrs. Frankel strode in with a fresh stack of journals. "You've made such quick work of those I imagine you ain't finding much."

"Not yet. But you have brought me fresh hope." Anne reached for the top of the new pile.

"And there's a few more where that came from as well." Mrs. Frankel winked and left.

Anne took another bite and opened a journal with a faded blue leather cover. The Order still issued those journals to its members for keeping estate records. This might be interesting. Was there a name attached to this volume?

She scanned the first several pages. No, no identifying clues yet, but there, what was that?

Merciful heavens, yes! It said "sea dragons!"

Chapter 5

November 4, 1815

My dearest Anne,
Pray forgive the delay in writing to you. I can only imagine the misery your father and sister have brought with them into Lyme. I petitioned the Minister of Keeps to see what might be done, and he is adamant that there is no help to be found in his office. Your father is responsible for finding his own situation. That the Order handled his arrangements in Bath was a unique favor and not to be taken as the way of things going forward.

Moreover, even if we were of a mind to do so, to offer them financial relief of any kind would nullify their living. Even their trespass on Kellynch's territory will do so. I hate to add to your burden this way.

Captain Harville's younger brother is a solicitor in Lyme. We have exchanged favors in the past. I will write to him immediately and ask for his assistance. He manages the arrangements for many properties and may be able to find an appropriate situation for them. Cypher knows his Friend and can put him in touch with you. I will continue pursuing other avenues of assistance here.

Wentworth laid his pen aside and leaned his face into his hands. If only Sir Walter were the worst of his concerns. How was he to tell her of the new nature of his mission and what it might mean for them? How could something be worse than the memory of his time in Chesil, the enormous sea drake's belly? He swallowed hard, the fishy-acidic taste of the experience lingering on his tongue.

One did not carry the Dragon Slayer blade lightly. It was not an honor, but a terrible burden that marked one for life. If one did not have to fulfill its purpose, none would even recognize it had ever been a possibility. Only the dreadful nightmares would remain. If he was forced to wield it, though, he would die or he would become the most hated man in England—at least as far as dragonkind went—and the stigma would follow his family for generations.

It was difficult to say which fate was worse.

General Yates, Grand Cross of the Knights of the Pendragon Order, had never married for that reason. Only rarely showed his face when dragons were present. Executioners were never welcome in good society.

Darcy had carried the blade more than once and loathed to talk about it. In each instance, he avoided using it. In the first case, Lady Elizabeth had intervened and rescued Baby Pemberley. In the second, Cornwall had yielded to the Council's authority, and in the last, the dragons of Pemberley Keep had rallied around little Pemberley to defeat Bolsover's challenge.

He was a ridiculously lucky man.

Surviving the Navy had likely consumed all Wentworth's luck. And even if it had not, luck was not the thing one should count on. Especially when one had dependents.

Something he had never worried about before. How different his world was now.

He raked his fingers through his hair. His will had been prepared, anticipating different circumstances. But this? Where to even begin? Who would even understand such things? How did one prepare one's affairs to leave his family despised among the cold-blooded?

Darcy. He understood the weight of Wentworth's orders. If anyone knew how to prepare for such a thing, it would be him.

Another letter he would have to write this evening, after he finished Anne's. For now, he had an appointment with General Yates.

Longer ago than anyone cared to remember, the Pendragon Knights' training facility had been carved out beneath the royal armory, a significant distance from the Order offices. It was a place few wanted to admit existed, much less encounter on their regular business. Rough, poorly lit dragon tunnels were the only way to reach it. No direct, above-ground access existed, as much to keep out the curious as to protect the secrets that lay within. A space best kept out of sight and out of mind.

Wentworth paused at the door and stared at the lock. The blackened iron seemed to absorb the faint torchlight, drawing it into the dangers that lay behind it. Damn it all.

Procrastinating would not change things. If anything, it would annoy General Yates, Grand Cross of the Pendragon Order. Annoying one's training officer was never a sound strategy. Wentworth pulled the dragon-headed key from his pocket. Cold, with a spot of rust at the tip. He thrust it into the lock.

Clack.

The door swung open. Damn. Foolish, to be sure, but he had hoped that it would not.

He stepped in to face a huge, mostly circular room half the size of the Blue Order courtroom. A central arch rose twenty feet above him, a dark void overhead. Even without the courtroom's soaring ceiling, sound lost its way in the gloom above. With a barely smooth floor, and all other surfaces rough-hewn at best, it might well have been a secret cavern, used by a clandestine society for secret meetings.

Which was, in fact, precisely what it was. Funny how strictly form and function walked hand in hand, even in a place such as this.

Flickering torches along the wall stank of an oily residue, a smell that mixed with the stale air strangely devoid of dragon musk, creating something unique, a displeasure all its own. He headed toward a doorway beside a narrow wooden bench. Not an escape, but a changing room where he could trade his coat and cravat for a muslin shirt and trousers better suited to sweaty, dirty work.

Clothes changed, Wentworth slipped out of the changing room and studied the life-sized dragon models, or rather dragon-part models, slumped and lifeless around the edges of the room. The firedrake's head, covered with ragged leather, seemed to call to him with its blank, painted eyes. It bared carved yellow fangs, honed to piercing points. He could almost hear the snarl that would have gone with that expression. It was the sound Cornwall had bugled in the courtroom the day Darcy had been the one carrying the Dragon Slayer.

He drew his elbows tight to his sides, fists tight, shoulders tensed. That sound, that visceral impulse to run for one's life, never looking back, burned itself on his soul, changing him forever. Were there even words to describe it? No, not in his lexicon, at least. The dark impressions and instincts would remain unspoken, despite the Sage's urgings that he commit them to paper.

He glanced over his shoulder at the collection of weapons near the dressing room door. Each carefully fitted into a worn wooden rack, all had been considered Dragon Slayers at one point in time. A spiked mace, several tall halberds, a crossbow, and a battle axe, all formidable weapons. The flail seemed out of place, as did the clubs, but perhaps, against large minor dragons, they might have been useful. Distasteful notion that.

Nearly a dozen swords, standing proud in a dedicated rack, caught his attention. The oldest was said to have been carried by Pendragon himself in the days before the Accords. The rightmost one in the collection Darcy had wielded, and Wentworth would soon carry. He flexed his aching hands in and out of fists.

It was not as if he had never carried a sword. He had, and used it in battle, kept himself alive that way. It was a brutal, bloody, very personal business. One saw the face of his enemy at the end of his sword, the bloodlust, the terror, the wide-eyed surprise as they died. He could no longer consider swordplay a sport, the way many gentlemen considered fencing. It would never again be less than life or death to him now.

Perhaps that was why he took up archery when he found himself in need of sport. Developing a proficiency that did not relate to bloodshed or personal violence had been most satisfying.

Still, when he had taken up his sword, it had been against a sworn enemy, not one who was supposed to have been his ally.

"You done staring yet?" Everything about Yates was large and square, his jaw, his shoulders, his face. A carved marble effigy climbed off a knight's tomb, with about as many social graces as one might expect from such a creature.

"It is a noteworthy collection." Wentworth shook out his hands and strode toward Yates. What dark corner had he been hiding in?

"Each weapon marks an improved understanding of the Pendragon Order. A situation that should never have happened, but did, that was then used to improve and strengthen the Accords." Yates clasped his hands behind his back, like a senior officer lecturing midshipmen.

"That is an interesting way to look at the situation."

"It is not just words, Wentworth, it is the truth." Yates gestured to the sword rack. "Pick up the current Dragon Slayer."

The command was going to come, eventually. No more procrastinating. Wentworth steeled himself and took the sword. The horrible weight ached in his hands. Everything about the sword differed from what he knew.

Or did it?

"I can tell by your look. You have realized it is a sword. Larger, perhaps heavier than you have known before. A different balance perhaps, but just a sword. A sword used against an enemy you have never faced, a war you have never fought. Your proficiency is there, your blood, your bones know how to wield it." He clapped Wentworth's shoulder. "Not like others I have taught who thought sport fencing was wielding a sword. They required a great deal more training."

"I hope there weren't many of those." The longer he held it, the less foreign, the less intimidating it felt. It should not be that way. This was a Dragon Slayer—

"No, there weren't." Yates folded meaty arms across his chest. "Now tell me, what do you feel, what do you hear, holding that?"

"The sword speaks? That is an unusual ability in a piece of sharpened steel."

Yates rolled his eyes and snorted. "Not the sword. You. Your spirit, your conscience. What does it say?"

What a revoltingly intimate question from a man he barely knew, barely wanted to know. Wentworth grunted.

Yates drew another sword from the rack. "I asked you a question, I expect an answer." He brandished the weapon at Wentworth.

"One I do not choose to answer." Wentworth raised the sword, instinct taking over, wresting control from his will.

"I do not recall giving you a choice." Yates swung his weapon in a broad, showy arc. A move meant for emphasis, not a real threat. Not yet.

Wentworth parried. "You are in no position to make such a demand."

Yates freed his blade from the parry, stepped back, and shifted his grip. There would be no more demonstrations. He was ready for a skirmish. "I am your commanding officer."

"How do you figure that?" Wentworth adapted his stance to balance the Dragon Slayer's length.

Yates adjusted his grip—odd. "Have you forgotten, baronet means a perpetual knighthood? You are one of the Pendragon Knights." Three quick forward steps. Thrust.

Wentworth skittered back out of the way, but did not drop his guard.

"You did not realize, Sir Frederick, that you are answerable to the Grand Cross of the Pendragon Order?" Yates swung again.

Wentworth parried. The clank of steel on steel rattled through his bones, echoed off the walls. "It seems like the sort of detail that should have been clearly communicated."

Yates rushed at him, swords still locked. "It seems like you are getting sloppy attending to details, Captain."

"Retired, I might remind you."

"Un-retired as soon as you accepted your title." Yates jumped back and leveled his sword.

"When I accepted this mission, more likely." Wentworth slipped to his right. Yates was weaker, less accurate on that side. "Not that there was much opportunity to refuse."

"A Pendragon Knight cannot refuse." A powerful, two-handed swing from Yates's shoulder.

Caught against Wentworth's sword. "Another detail that might have been good to know."

"Would it have made a difference? Would you have turned down an estate and a Keepership?"

"Another question too personal to answer." Wentworth shoved Yates back.

"What does that sword say to you?" Yates closed and kicked Wentworth in the shin.

Was that supposed to throw him off balance? Had Yates forgotten Wentworth's experience? Real conflict did not abide by gentlemanly rules. Wentworth spun on his heel and swept Yates's foot from under him.

Yates bounced to the floor, then back to his feet in a single motion. "What does it say?"

"Nothing, the damn blade does not speak." Wentworth blinked sweat out of his eyes.

Yates rushed at him again, pushing him back against the wall. "Yes, it does."

Wentworth elbowed him back. "This is foolishness! Utterly unnecessary! Not the way a civilized man behaves." Wentworth ducked away from the wall and into open ground. "If you think this is preparation for dealing with a dragon you are an imbecile."

A wild grin replaced Yates's scowl. "Better, better. What else?"

What manner of madness was this? "Why are you so set upon bloodshed? What purpose do you think this is going to serve?"

Yates spun away and lowered his blade. "And that is the pertinent question."

Wentworth half dropped his sword. It would not be beyond Yates to use this as a ploy ...

"You have asked the question. You must understand." Yates gestured to the sword rack and put his own back. "Disarm." He picked up a stained, ragged towel from the bench and threw one to Wentworth.

"What are you talking about?" Wentworth dragged the musty cloth over his sopping face.

"If you do not understand why you must do what you are called to do, you will die. The dragon will see the hesitation, the weakness, and that will be the end. You see, that is what major dragons do best, probably the minor ones too, but I've never crossed swords with one to prove it. The big dragons are masters at spotting weakness in their opponents and seizing opportunity when it arises. We have to think it out, decide our next move, even if only for a split second. They are faster in this arena, so much faster and that bare moment is enough to give them the advantage. When you know why you must prevail, truly know it in your bones, then you might have a chance."

"Is this what you told Darcy?"

"No. He knew why he had to carry the Dragon Slayer. You don't."

"What are you talking about? I understand my mission. To protect Matlock from Cornwall."

"Idiot." Yates spat on the floor and dropped onto the bench. "Do you really think the Cownt needs your protection?"

That question Wentworth had been avoiding.

Damn.

"Ignoring the obvious, just as I expected." Yates pointed at the bench beside him until Wentworth joined him. "I have not been told this, but trust me, I know this. Matlock means to bring Cornwall to heel, one way or the other. If he leaves the matter to Chesil, who would be all too glad to do it, it would be considered an act of war against the Blue Order."

"War? You mean the start of an actual dragon war?" Wentworth could barely speak the unthinkable.

"Yes. If Chesil acts against a member of the Order, there is no choice. So, it cannot happen. If Matlock has to put Cornwall down, you are there to ensure it happens."

Wentworth sprang to his feet and threw the towel to the floor. "When was bloody Matlock going to tell me that?"

"Why do you think he sent you to me?"

"He's not man—ah—dragon enough to tell me himself?"

"A dragon, especially a dominant one, does not admit he entertains the possibility of defeat. Damn creature cannot say such a thing." Yates picked the towel off the floor and flung it at Wentworth. "Assuming Matlock injures Cornwall, you stand a fighting chance of surviving the encounter."

It had been a long time since Wentworth had found sailors' invectives quite so useful. Good thing he had a vast supply to bring to bear. He needed every single one and repeated several for good measure. "You realize, though, a bloody sword will not do a whit of good when Cornwall takes to the water?"

That stopped Yates, jaw agape, suddenly out of words. He blinked several times.

Oh, that was far too satisfying.

"What are you blathering on about? What does a firedrake have to do with the water?"

"So, there's something you don't understand about the situation." Wentworth coughed out a gallows laugh. "Cornwall has been learning to swim, you see. And if the worst happens, he will undoubtedly head into the water well knowing that there's naught I can do to him there. What better way to exert dominance even when injured?"

"Damn and bloody hell. That makes things different. Don't discount me so soon, though. That fact only changes things a wee bit." Yates crossed to the other side of the weapons rack. "Seems like we may need to bring this back, after all." He handed Wentworth the crossbow.

And so the Order would claim his favorite sport as well. Damn.

Chapter 6

November 4, 1815

Anne's elation upon discovering 'sea dragons' in the newly discovered journal soon cooled to irritation. No, that was putting it far too mildly. Something more akin to indignation, resentment, or even fury.

How wrong it was for the journal-writer to tease with something so significant, only to dissolve into their own opinionated diatribe about the existence—or lack thereof—of the creatures.

It was too much to be borne. Anne slammed shut the once-promising blue journal and left. Mrs. Frankel tsk-tsked and offered another clear cake—which she took—on her way out the door.

Only for the day, though. Her sense of duty alone required her to return to those journals, unless Cypher or Jasper volunteered to read them in her stead. She would not ask them to take on the task. They were both so busy as it was. But should they volunteer, then, of course, she would agree.

Anne returned to the manor, exhausted, frustrated, and annoyed at the world. So, she did the only thing possible. She wrote a letter to Wentworth. Dear Balen was pleased to take it directly to London.

Balen was such a faithful companion and Friend. It was hard to believe she had never had a Friend before Anne. How many fools had overlooked her for her plain looks and even plainer manners? She was all that was good and right with the cold-blooded world. It was Anne's privilege to be counted Friend to her and to Laconia as well.

Knowing she would soon hear from Wentworth, and that their correspondence would be safe from prying eyes, eased her heart just enough that she easily fell asleep, something that happened less and less often these days.

THE NEXT MORNING, SHE took tea and toast in the dressing room next to the chambers she and Wentworth shared when the Order was not demanding his presence elsewhere. As usual, where Wentworth was concerned, the room was cluttered with stacks and piles on most of the horizontal surfaces. His dressing table. The top of both dressers and the press. There was barely enough room for a tea tray on the small table by the window, beside a precarious pile of books. Two sea chests in the corner contained more disorder within. So much for the myth that sailors were tidy by necessity.

Morning sun streamed through the window's crisp white curtains. Traces of sea breeze blew in through the edges where the window did not quite close properly, bringing the perfume of salt and sea inside. Funny how easily she had grown accustomed to the smell. And the clutter. She had never thought that possible, but she had grown accustomed to the chaos. And to the one who had created it.

And she missed him. As busy as she was, one might think she would welcome fewer demands on her time and energy. And one would be wrong.

But there was nothing to be done for it, but endure. Endure and write many letters. And be grateful for Balen's help.

Corn and Wall, the tatzelwurmlings, tumbled in through a small opening between the wall and fireplace. Corn, with his white ears and blue eyes, slithered in first, tripping over his front feet and rolling onto the worn carpet near Anne. He righted himself and licked at the white fur on his shoulder as if to say, 'I meant to do that.'

Green-eyed Wall twitched his little black nose through the hole, checking what lay beyond the hollow in the wall one last time before he gracefully step-slithered in. He twitched his whiskers at Corn, an expression of disapproval, though he would never come out and admit it.

The hole by the fireplace was the sort of thing Wentworth would have seen fixed immediately upon their taking possession of Kellynch-by-the-Sea, but the wyrmlings, and Laconia, their sire, declared it too useful to be repaired, so it remained. While passages through the walls were handy for catching errant rodents that tried to invade the manor, they were also convenient for hearing gossip and moving about unnoticed.

Kellynch had named the wyrmlings himself, cocking a snook at Dug Cornwall, who had finally faced his comeuppance at the Blue Order court. It was not enough to simply let the court rule against his nemesis. Kellynch had added insult to injury. Luckily, the wyrmlings adored Kellynch so much that they embraced the joke as well. Such a funny relationship those three had—what other major dragon had minor dragon Friends?

Well, it could be considered that Vicontes Pemberley did as well, considering the way they flew with her in defense against Bolsover. Was that why Kellynch admired her so?

"What brings you here so early in the day?" Anne asked. "Do you not usually spend the morning in Kellynch's company?"

"He is disagreeable today." Wall wound himself around her feet, going clockwise.

"So very disagreeable." Corn wrapped himself around her in the other direction.

Anne bent over to pet both their heads. "Do not tell me he ordered you away?"

"Oh, no, nothing like that. He is never that disagreeable." Wall sat back on his tail and looked up at her, blinking somberly.

"And we would not believe he meant it even if he did." Corn chirruped.

"And yet you are here this morning." Anne broke a slice of buttered toast and offered each one a piece.

"We thought we might help him. He wants to see you." Wall took the toast and held it between thumbed paws as he crunched on it.

Corn ignored the toast and rose on his tail paws on her knee. "You must go right now. Hurry!"

"Is the need really so urgent I cannot have my toast first?" Anne reached for her teacup.

"No, it is not." Wall glared at Corn. "Break your fast. You will need your strength for meeting with him."

That did not bode well. "Has he another list of grievances?"

"Yes. But he is not being unreasonable." Corn's serpentine tail slapped the carpet.

"Is that true, Wall?"

"This time he is correct."

"I confess that is not what I wanted to hear." Anne leaned back and reached for her teacup. "In which lair is he?"

Corn rose still higher. "In the sea cave."

Of course he was. Anne squeezed her eyes shut. "He realizes I promised Wentworth that I would not go down to the sea cave whilst he was gone."

"Kellynch does not approve of that demand." Corn tried to glare at her, but he had not perfected the expression and only managed to look silly.

"Kellynch does not understand how difficult, even dangerous, the path to that sea lair is for me. Especially now." She laid a hand on her belly.

"He is not pleased about that either." Corn snorted and tossed his head.

"I do not recall asking his opinion on the matter." Anne pushed herself up and stood. She needed to move. "Why should the birth of an heir to the estate trouble him?"

Wall paced along the floor beside her. "An heir should be a good thing. I have tried to tell him so. But our Laird is prone to jealousy. He fears you will neglect him in favor of your spawn. He believes that you not visiting the sea cave is evidence of that already beginning."

"Oh, merciful heavens." Kellynch really was like a petulant child. "I understand his displeasure, but I will not break my promise to my husband, unless life and limb are in danger. And clearly, they are not. Mr. Gillingham has been attending him daily, overseeing his recovery."

"Mr. Gillingham takes excellent care of our Laird." Wall rubbed against her ankle.

Corn spring-hopped onto her chair. "But Kellynch does not like him."

"And he has a good reason for that, I suppose?" Anne rubbed her temples.

"Kellynch wants you," Corn said.

"If he wants me so very much, then pray tell him, I will be happy to visit him in the dragon lair attached to the manor. I can attend him there in safety, and give him all the attention he desires." Well, perhaps not all the attention. That might not be humanly possible. But it would be enough that Kellynch would take notice.

"He says the path there is uncomfortable," Corn's tone edged into the persuasive range and Anne glowered until he hunched back. That was not a habit she would tolerate.

Wall stopped and stared at Corn. "And I told him if it was important to him, he could manage the discomfort easily." Poor little fellow, so annoyed.

"Kellynch can be determined and set in his ways, can he not?" Anne said.

"You should not disagree with him." Corn harrumphed and turned his back on her.

"I will disagree with him when he is clearly in the wrong. If he wants Lady's attention so much, a minor inconvenience in the service of her safety is not that much to ask." Wall pressed his side against her legs.

"Will you not try for his sake, Lady?" Corn looked over his shoulder at her. "It would mean a great deal to him."

"And if I should slip and fall on that trail, what then? Would he be satisfied to see me lose the babe I carry, or even life and limb myself?"

"Well, no, I do not think he wants that." Corn hunched a bit.

"Of course not, Lady. He is not so cold as that," Wall said.

"Then tell him I will meet him in the official lair later this morning and will stay with him there as long as he desires. If that does not motivate him to ascend the cliffs, then I have nothing else to offer him."

Corn snorted and sniffed. "He will not like it. I will tell him, but he will be angry." He spring-hopped off the chair and disappeared into the wall.

"Of course he will have a show of temper at first, but I think he will decide a minor discomfort is worth the time with you." Wall purred against her ankles.

She scratched his chin. "You are a splendid fellow. You might be able to convince him toward that conclusion a little more quickly than your brother suggests is possible."

"Of course, Lady. I will see to my Laird's best interests." Wall disappeared into the wall.

AN HOUR AND A half later, Anne made her way through the dragon tunnels from the house to the nearby lair, pausing occasionally to set her candle on the floor and make note of maintenance that still needed to be done. A few rocks in the way here, a floor needed smoothing there. A bit of widening in a few spaces, not really that much, and Kellynch could comfortably navigate the tunnel to the manor's cellar. It might not be the most comfortable journey for him, but it would probably please him to be in the house proper.

Tomorrow she would give the orders to make it so. Hopefully by then, Kellynch's temper would be mollified and he would join her there.

When she reached the lair, she lit several torches with her candle and placed them in their holders carved into the wall. She added a thick pillow to the wooden stool kept there to accommodate warm-blooded visitors.

On the whole, the lair was not unpleasant, surprisingly roomy, even comfortable, with a well-smoothed stone floor and similarly even rock walls. Larger than his previous lair near Kellynch Hall, this one had been essentially dry. But the Order had enlisted the help of local wyrms to create a spring-fed pool in the far corner in which Kellynch could lounge. He could not get to the ocean from the pool, which was a profound disappointment, but he had the sea cave for that, so he was content.

Intriguing. Was it possible the wyrms Mrs. Frankel mentioned were the same who had helped dig out the pool? That was something to investigate.

She pulled the stool near the pool and sat down. Sometimes, like now, the quiet in the cavernous space rang profound. Just her breathing, the soft lapping of the pool, and the odd crackle from the torches. Sounds which disappeared into the background under normal circumstances demanded one take notice and attend them. Cool and soothing, peaceful.

Unlike the dragon who would soon visit.

She sighed. Would Kellynch actually deign to visit with her here, or would he turn intractable about not getting his way? The outcome was no more certain than a game of fish.

Anne hated playing fish.

She glanced at the watch that hung off the fob at her waist. An hour, she would give him an hour. That was certainly long enough to be kept waiting in the cold, damp lair, on a stool which would make her back ache.

Fifteen minutes. Twenty. Half an hour.

There was no smell of green in the air—the lair was totally dark unless there were warm-blooded visitors. How did Kellynch and the tatzelwurms get around in total darkness? One of those questions she might never have answered.

Wait, what was that?

Scraping, rasping, something on stone. Dragon hide. Nothing else would make that noise.

So, the wyrmlings had been successful, at least enough to rouse Kellynch from his sea cave. What his temper might be when he arrived would be another issue altogether. But it was progress.

She smelled him first. Rotten fish and pungent acid, mixed liberally with dragon musk. She gulped back bile. Casting up her accounts, even if she was with child, would not impress him.

Kellynch slithered past her, a cold, presence drawing close. Fifteen, maybe twenty feet long and thick, two large men might barely be able to join hands around him, though his body got thinner towards his tail. Long and legless, like a snake, his squared off head, toothy and shaggy, and a bony ridge along his back marked him as a wyrm. Spinal ridges lined his back growing smaller towards his tail.

His eyes glistened red in the low light, then he turned aside, not deigning to acknowledge her.

Was that a cut direct, in dragon parlance, or something less?

His sides were still discolored—bruised, Mr. Gillingham said. And his sluggish movements lacked the regal grace and bearing he usually carried. If a slithering dragon could limp, that was how he moved. He had too much pride for that to be affectation. Poor creature really suffered.

Kellynch slipped into the spring-fed pool at the back corner of the lair and curled into something resembling a comfortable position. "So, you have deigned to visit me." He rested his chin on a large rock near where Anne sat.

"I hardly think that fair. It is you who have decided a visit from your Keeper is worth preserving her safety." So that was how it was going to be with him.

"That is unfair. I am the estate dragon and I am due—"

She folded her arms over her chest and straightened her spine. "Kellynch, if all you want to talk about is what you are due, I shall send Cypher to you so you can dictate a list of complaints to present before the Blue Order. Perhaps you can find satisfaction with them."

"They owe me a debt." The tip of his tail slapped the pool, sending a small splash against her skirts.

"For which you have been well compensated. I will not have this conversation with you again. I am sorry you are uncomfortable. We are doing the best we know how to do to relieve your suffering. Your continuing disagreeable temper is not helping at all."

"What is not helping are the continued impositions upon me and my territory." He raised his chin and looked directly into her eyes.

"Imposition? What do you mean? I understand the circus was dreadful, but we talked about that at length, and you agreed it was a needful burden to eliminate a significant danger to the Order."

"Then, with no discussion, you moved the Order office into my territory without so much as a by-your-leave-Laird."

"To host the office is an honor and a privilege, adding to your status. It is an honor to you and I enjoin you to remember that."

"That does not change the fact it should have been discussed with me first." He flicked his forked tongue at her. "I resent the lack of recognition that the territory is mine."

Anne closed her eyes and counted. Seven…eight…nine…ten. "You make an excellent point. We should have discussed the matter with you. Wentworth and I are both new to the intricacies of Dragon Keeping and failed to recognize the respect due you. We will do our best to pay better attention to that in the future."

"Truly?" His eyes grew wide.

"Yes. We made a mistake, unintentional though it may have been. But it was thoughtless and should not happen again."

"Then why is that man in Lyme?"

'That man' always meant her father. It had been too much to hope word of that had not reached him. She probably had Corn to thank for that. "Your territory does not include Lyme proper."

"The Order promised he would stay away from me."

"I have kept him away from you. As soon as I learned he was coming, I directed him away from Kellynch-by-the-Sea to take lodgings at the Royal Lion. You have had no interactions with him. And he did not pass through your territory."

"But he is here and I want him gone. Lyme is too near for my liking." Kellynch splashed again, a little bigger this time.

"For mine as well. But the house he let in Bath was damaged by fire and he has no place to go at the moment. I am working to find other arrangements for him as quickly as I can, but it is going to take some time to accomplish. I do not want him here any more than you do."

"It is an affront to my dignity for him to be permitted so close to my territory."

"I do not understand, but I would like to." Something in Kellynch's tone made it necessary to add that.

"His presence makes it look like I am not strong enough to chase him off, which is the right and proper way for a dragon who has been wronged to behave—short of eating him, of course, which would also be appropriate."

Oh, that made sense, in a draconic sort of way. "Does it make you uneasy that you find it difficult to patrol the estate lands to ensure that he does not trespass?"

"Yes, it does." His whiskers drooped. How much did it cost him to admit even that level of weakness?

"I have a thought, a way that we might help with that." Hopefully, this was not a terrible idea. "On Pemberley estate, where Vikontes Pemberley is not yet able to manage all the boundaries, she has organized the local minor dragons to assist her with the process."

"But there are so few minor dragons here—"

"Yes, but I know of a local cluster of wyrms who need a new lair. They remained loyal to the one who helped provide their current lair for decades and they might even have been the same ones who dug the pool for you. I expect they would offer you the same fealty if you were to designate a place for them on your territory. Who better to help you keep watch over your borders than a grateful cluster of wyrms? And to be emulating the vikontes in estate management, what a mark in your favor as well."

"That is an interesting thought, indeed." Kellynch pulled back and cocked his head. "I will need some time to consider it."

That he did not reject it outright was actually an encouraging sign.

"Now, brush my spinal ridge, it itches. The brush is over there."

Chapter 7

November 8, 1815

One advantage of having been a sailor meant Wentworth could avoid the roads and sail back to Lyme. A modest-sized sailing ship, with minimal crew, and he could get home in half the time a carriage would take, and, perhaps more significantly, less time than it would take Matlock to travel the dragon tunnels.

Wentworth wanted to spend every moment he could find with Anne.

It was perfectly normal for a man to desperately want to be with his wife. Even if circumstances were anything but perfectly normal.

Not even remotely normal. No point in dwelling on that.

He shaded his eyes and stared into the wind at the approaching shoreline. Almost there. Almost. He pulled out his spyglass and looked again.

Was that her at the dock? By Jove, it was! His breath caught in his throat. What a stunning sight.

Must be Balen's doing—bless that creature from the tip of her deadly sharp beak to the points of her business-like talons. She was every bit as perceptive as Laconia and willing to assist where she could. He would trade a thousand beauties for a Friend of such character.

A small part of him struggled not to dive from the side and swim the rest of the way to shore. But memories of the Battle of Lyme Bay and the enormous sea drake Chesil kept him firmly on deck. Still, waiting for the vessel to dock was almost worse than risking the waters once again.

At last, the crew signaled readiness and Wentworth sprang from the sailboat's deck to the dock. He rushed to Anne, catching her up in his arms. She smelled of lilac and lavender as she buried her face in his shoulder. No, it was not proper, but pity the one who dared to comment on that.

He probably should say something. It was appropriate, after all, but he had lost the faculty of speech.

"I have brought the carriage to take us home," she whispered. "A cart will be here soon to take your trunk."

"You are a wonder, my dear." Wentworth wasted no time and was soon settled into the well-worn soft squabs beside her, and pulled the little white curtains closed across the side glass. The coach eased into motion under Jonty Bragg's sure guidance. He pulled her close, arm around her shoulder, and kissed her solidly.

"You are far more suitable than I was warned to expect of an old sailor." Her breath tickled his ear and the side of his neck.

"And that is precisely why I hurried home, to be suitable." He kissed her again, and she clearly did not object.

"How long have you before the Order claims you once again?" She sighed and leaned into him as she spoke.

"I expect Matlock to arrive tomorrow, by dragon tunnel. The next day at the latest,"

"But the tunnels go to the burned-out Order office. How will he come to Kellynch-by-the-Sea?"

"As I understand, there is still a guest lair there, in decent condition, that he intends to use. Kellynch's official lair would not be accessible to him even if he was of a mind to use it, and the sea cave even less so. Matlock is a far larger dragon." Larger, maybe not grumpier, but certainly far more powerful.

"Will he need to be attended whilst he is in Lyme?" Always practical and planning, that was his Anne.

"He might want to eat, but that is relatively easy to deal with. He is in no mood to hear complaints from any corner, though, so I doubt he will demand an audience with Kellynch. He may not even wish to speak with me. To be honest, I think he resents the idea of needing a second in this affair with Cornwall, and that is made worse by having to turn to a warm-blood to fill the position. He cannot risk being incapacitated before another major dragon. The impact on his dominance would be dangerous at best, and possibly catastrophic."

"You really think it will come to that?"

"What I would give to tell you no, but given our previous experience with Cornwall and Chesil's complaints, I am certain that no one will come away unscathed. Even the Order itself is in far more peril than all but a select few will accept."

Anne shuddered beside him. "Having seen Kellynch's state, I can hardly imagine what major dragons are capable of doing to one another."

"How is he?"

"According to Mr. Gillingham, he will surely recover. But I could have told you that. It will still be some time before Kellynch is all put to rights, but I do not think it will be long."

"Is he growing restive like your nephew did after his injury?"

"Yes, though that is not exactly the word I would use. Kellynch longs to demonstrate himself as dominant in his territory, all the while Mr. Gillingham keeps insisting that he rest. To be honest, I think Mr. Gillingham is on the cusp of outliving his usefulness here. Kellynch finds him more irritating by the day. And I just might as well."

Wentworth took her warm, small hand in his. "You do not sound as pleased with Kellynch's recovery as I might have hoped."

"Kellynch has slipped back into his cross and complaining ways. Everything has been displeasing to him. I finally resorted to suggesting he invite minor dragons to his territory so he could emulate young Pemberley, thinking that may satisfy his need to feel more dominant."

"There are few things a dragon enjoys more than feeling dominant. But I cannot imagine any of the local cockatrice would settle on Kellynch-by-the-Sea."

"Not cockatrice. While Kellynch feels comfortable enough with Balen, he is not fond of the smaller bird-types. He calls them too flighty." Anne chuckled. "I learned recently of a cluster of wyrms with a long history of loyalty to the Order who are likely to be displaced by the rebuilding of the old Order offices in Lyme."

"Really? I have never heard of them. But then again, reports of the destruction of the old office were sparing in detail."

"Wyrms being what they are, are you surprised that the Order speaks of them very little? Which I suppose might be some of the appeal for Kellynch. He always feels slighted by the Order—major wyrms get little respect, according to him. And I believe he is right. So, bringing some notoriety to a cluster of minor dragons that the Order has neglected holds a particular appeal to him. Or at least it seemed so the last time I spoke to him of it. I probably should have spoken to Mr. Wynn about it before I brought the idea to Kellynch—"

"Wynn? Why?" Wentworth tried, unsuccessfully, to keep the sneer from his voice. "We know his feelings about minor dragons. He would have had nothing useful to bring to the conversation."

"But if he feels I have taken something from the Order—"

"I think he is more likely to ignore the matter, unwilling to credit you with his relief that he does not have to deal with the issue himself." Wentworth turned aside to roll his eyes and laughed.

"I have missed that sound. I have missed you." She squeezed his hand hard.

"And I you. There is no way to predict what the next few weeks will hold. But today is ours, and I intend to make the most of it."

"You do, do you?"

"Indeed, I do. I hope you did not have any other plans, as I will be a tyrant and insist that you cancel every one of them." He swept her into his lap.

"How disappointing."

He looked at her in shock.

A brilliant smile bloomed as she giggled. "I was looking forward to insisting that you cancel every one of your plans in favor of what I have in mind."

"I have indeed married a brilliant woman."

THE NEXT MORNING, THEY dallied well past their usual sunrise waking, ignoring the demands of the world and the Order, even taking a full breakfast from the comfort of their cozy—if cluttered—dressing room. If only they could stay here and ignore the rest of the world.

Wentworth fed Anne a last bite of crunchy buttered toast and berry jam as a sharp rapping rattled the windowpane. A cockatrice bearing a satchel with the Darcy insignia perched on the windowsill.

"Blast and bother. I suppose there is nothing but to let him in." Wentworth grumbled and wrenched the ill-fitting window open.

A cold gust shoved the young male cockatrice, stumbling, into the room. Wentworth shut the window behind him. There was a storm brewing in Lyme Bay. Annoying and utterly fitting at this point.

"A message from Pemberly, Sir Frederick." The messenger bobbed his head respectfully.

"You were directed here from London?"

"Yes, that is why it took so long. Sir Fitzwilliam answered you directly, but did not realize you had been dispatched already."

"Of course. I am glad you were directed here and that some helpful dolt did not simply take the letter from you to keep until I returned," Wentworth muttered.

"Sir Fitzwilliam was very clear. The message was only to go into your or Lady Wentworth's hands. Shall I wait here for your response?"

"Yes, do. In the meantime, you may fish in the bay or go down to the kitchen for a meal."

"That wind is picking up something fierce." The cockatrice looked over his shoulder through the window. "The kitchen will be most agreeable."

Wentworth opened the door. "Downstairs, and to the back of the house. You will smell it."

The messenger cawed a 'thank you' and flew out.

"Dare I ask what correspondence you were expecting from Sir Fitzwilliam?" Anne asked, wrapping her shawl more tightly over her shoulders.

"It is a grim business, I am afraid." Wentworth opened the seal and quickly scanned the letter. He would read it in greater detail later. "Excellent. Beyond excellent. This is more than I could have hoped."

"What do you mean?" Her entire being, her voice, her posture, her expression had shifted, tight and guarded now, as if the wind had chased away all warmth from her soul.

He set the letter aside and took her hands in his. "You know my trip to Land's End may end badly, in several different ways."

"Yes, only too aware." Oh, the expression on Anne's face. She was trying to be brave, but such a circumstance!

"There are some ways that are worse than others, to be sure, and it is only right that I try to plan for every possibility. I owe you that. I owe our child that."

"We would expect no less of you."

Such a tragic compliment. His heart ached. "Matters are fairly clear if I do not return. The estate will pass to our heir. But if our heir does not survive, then—"

"I will have my jointure and will make do."

"Yes, and I know you can do that. But I hate the thought of you being alone in the world, even with Balen as a companion, especially if I must fulfill my duties as Matlock's second. So, I asked Darcy what arrangements he made for Elizabeth when he was tasked with carrying the Dragon Slayer. I will not belabor those details now, but he ends with this: If it should come to it, the Sage is prepared to offer you a position with her office, and the stipend that goes with it. A cottage on Pemberley will be made available to you and Balen, Laconia, Corn, and Wall if they so choose as well. Do not argue that you do not need such provisions. You are capable, and you do not need these arrangements. But I do."

She chewed her lip, the racing thoughts behind her eyes unreadable. "I cannot deny you anything. I am grateful that you have put so much consideration into all these arrangements. You are indeed the best of men."

"Better than your father, I hope, but hardly the best."

"You are to me." She kissed him far more properly than he would have liked. "Now, tell me, how can I help, how can I support you? What help can I offer?"

His first instinct was to brush aside her offer, but the look on her face! He could not deny her. "That is an excellent question. One that I know will not be satisfied if I simply say managing the estate in my absence, or even managing Kellynch, which is quite a feat in itself."

"Those are tasks that come with being Keeper, and you and I both share that title."

"True. I imagine handling your father's situation will hardly fit the need, either. Has Harville's brother contacted you?"

"Balen introduced me to his Friend yesterday. I will meet with him soon. And that is also not a service to you." She poked his chest with her finger.

"Dealing with your father in my stead is a favor to me."

"Pray do not be difficult." She tugged his lapels down with both hands. "I need to feel as though I am caring for you, just as you did when you wrote to Sir Fitzwilliam on my behalf."

"I am sorry, but I fear I lack the imagination necessary—"

"You lacking imagination?" She cupped his stubbled cheek with her hand. "I would hardly agree with that estimate."

He chuckled, kissed her palm, and pressed it against his face once more. "My darling, there is no need for more. You are my greatest support—"

"I know you feel that, but I want—I need to feel useful. Let me think." She pressed her head to his chest, his heartbeat a steady, welcome anchor for her thought.

He stroked her back, waiting. How precious a man who could endure a bit of silence.

"Wait, I have an idea." She grasped his hand. "There is every likelihood there will be injury of some kind while you are at Land's End. We have been tending Kellynch's injuries here, and I have some sense of what is needed to tend injured dragons. I will consult with Mr. Gillingham, and prepare a medical trunk with instructions, to enable you or whomever is representing the Blue Order at Cornwall Keep, to tend injuries suffered by both warm- and cold-blooded. Since I cannot be there to tend to them myself, the least I can do is see that the supplies and instructions are available for you."

"That is brilliant, Anne. I would have never thought of it, but yes, that would be most welcome. Definitely the type of preparation I would like to have."

"You are not saying that to placate me?"

"Not in the least. Until Kellynch's injuries, I would have never thought of rendering aid to a dragon. Even having seen it done here, it still did not cross my mind. But you are quite right. It is a sensible thing. Hmmm, there's an idea."

"I have got you thinking now? I can see it in your eyes… Yes!" A satisfied smile crept up her lips. "You are wondering if you should take Mr. Gillingham with you, since he seems to have worn out his welcome with Kellynch. Absolutely, yes, that is the right thing to do."

"I will never get over how you seem to know what I am thinking. Shall we approach him now?"

"Absolutely. I think he will be thrilled to accompany you. He has grown bored and impatient managing Kellynch. We probably ought to write to Sir Edward and obtain his permission, though."

"There is no time for that. Will you write to him and explain the situation?"

Chapter 8

NOVEMBER 10, 1815

"Out!" Cownt Matlock snarled. The noise rang through the underground guest lair beneath the burned-out Order office with the force of a winter gale. Bits of dusty cobweb fell from the ceiling onto her face as the growly echoes faded in the flickering candlelight.

Anne peeked at Wentworth beside her as she dug her heels in and forced herself to hold her ground. All good sense insisted that she run fast and far. Why was it that dealing with dragons often meant leaving good sense behind? Lady Elizabeth had taught her that backing down in the face of an angry dragon was the fastest way to lose their respect, and right now, she could not afford to lose any ground.

"How dare those creatures simply assume—" Whiffs of smoke rose from Matlock's nostrils. Only the greatest vexation could have him so close to losing control.

"They will trouble you no more, Cownt." Hopefully they would not make a liar of her. "I only just learned of their presence and was not aware that they were using the guest lair as their own."

"They should pay for their trespass." His tail hit the ground with a heavy, threatening thud.

Now was not the time to explain the situation and hope for understanding. Now was the time to get everyone to safety and wait for the storm—Cornwall—to pass. "Kellynch will see that they will not bother you again, Cownt." Hopefully bringing Kellynch into this would assure Matlock that someone understood the great affront he had suffered in finding lesser creatures in his domain.

Matlock's eyes narrowed and his voice deepened further. "Kellynch should have seen to the matter before I arrived."

"We apologize for your inconvenience." Wentworth stepped slightly in front of Anne, nodding toward the stairs.

This was how they agreed to manage the situation, no matter how much she hated to leave his side. He would distract Cownt Matlock with plans for their encounter at Land's End, while she saw the wyrms safely to Kellynch-by-the-Sea.

She backed toward the staircase, climbing upstairs backward. One did not turn one's back on an angry dragon. Convenient how that was one of the few parts of the building that had remained structurally sound after the fire.

Balen met her outside the cellar door. "I have gathered the wyrms. Not surprisingly, they are agitated."

"Not too agitated to listen to reason, I hope." Anne closed her eyes and drew the first of several long, deep breaths. Those should have steadied her, anchored her in the sense of safety above ground, but knowing the conversation that was likely taking place beneath her feet hardly allowed her to take comfort in anything.

"I cannot promise reason. We are dealing with wyrms, after all." Balen rustled her broad wings and shook her head. "But they will be open to whatever might spare their shaggy little hides from Matlock."

Wyrms were generally not considered sensible. They tried sensible creatures' patience. Balen was very, very sensible.

Balen led her to what had been a stone shed, now more a haphazard pile of rocks in the shade of a windswept tree. "The Keeper of Kellynch would speak to you." She scratched at the nearest rock, flexing her talons in what might be a not-so-subtle reminder that the wryms had best not continue testing her patience.

Anne stopped half a dozen steps away as dragon etiquette dictated. Several of the rocks in the shade-dappled pile quivered and the dirt nearby shook. Two shaggy heads popped out between the rocks. Leonine with their manes, short snouts, and fangs, the garden wyrms were covered with bits of dirt and leaf debris. Or maybe they were rock wyrms? The two species looked so similar it was difficult to tell.

"Lady Wentworth, may I present Gravel and Pebble, leaders of this cluster." Balen beckoned the wyrms out with her wing.

The two wyrms, one notably larger than the other, wriggled out from between the rocks and met near Anne, twining around each other as wyrm pairs were apt to do. Mottled in browns, greys, and black, their color made it difficult to tell where one ended and the other began. It certainly explained the legends of two-headed creatures well.

"Lady... Lady Anne." The larger wyrm, Gravel, stretched out and touching his chin to the floor. The smaller female did the same beside him.

She strode forward and tapped the back of their heads, hardly a natural gesture for her, but it was the right one, so she would accommodate it. "Cownt Matlock has ordered you away from this place. You should be grateful for his restraint in dealing with you. Your unauthorized use of the lair here violates numerous Blue Order rules, claiming territory not granted to you."

Gravel hissed and rose high on his tail, weaving back and forth. "The Blue Order did not maintain its agreement with us. The shed was assigned as our territory, but it has been left to fall to ruins. We kept the grounds as was agreed even after the fire. Does that not count for something?"

"You have done the Order a valuable service. Still, I cannot contradict the orders of the Cownt. You must leave this place and never dwell on Order office property again. He will not be moved on the matter. However, Kellynch, who holds the territory known as Kellynch-by-the-Sea, is prepared to accept you as minor dragons in his territory."

Pebble peeked around Gravel. "Kellynch, the marine wyrm?"

"He is a marine wyrm." Balen clacked her beak.

"More important, though, he is a laird and the dominant dragon in the territory," Anne said.

"Why would he accept us in his territory?" Gravel leaned back a little, as though trying to judge Anne's posture for truth-telling.

Anne made herself as big as possible, flaring her elbows and squaring her shoulders. "He is ready to increase his status as a landed dragon. He cannot increase his territory, but having minor dragons in his land increases his dominance."

"Having minor dragons increases dominance?" Pebble's head turned sideways as she asked. Wyrms tended to do that, as though thinking made them off-balance.

"Will many of us increase his dominance more?" Gravel rubbed cheeks with Pebble.

"How many are in your cluster?" Gracious, she should have asked that earlier!

"How many? Many?" Gravel seemed confused by the concept.

"I do not think these wyrms can count." Balen scratched at the dirt. "But I have counted at least two dozen in the cluster."

Anne fought to swallow her sigh. Two dozen they could accommodate. "I do not know if your numbers make a difference. But I know it will increase his status if you are willing to work for him, with him. As Vicontes Pemberley's minor dragons work with her."

"What sort of work?" Gravel edged back, wary. Beside him, Pebble hissed just loud enough to be heard.

"He must protect and patrol the ocean side of his territory. Your help keeping watch on his borders on land could be important. Is that something you are willing to do?"

Pebble and Gravel wrapped around each other, murmuring and muttering. It looked almost like they had to talk out loud in order to think. Finally, they stopped and turned back to Anne. "Must know more. Cannot risk angry Laird."

They might not be the wisest of dragons, but clearly, they were no fools. "Of course. He is ready to meet with you at his sea cave. If you are willing, Balen will fly ahead and announce you to him. He has promised you safe passage there and out again, regardless of the outcome of your discussion."

"Kellynch can be trusted?" Gravel asked.

It was not an unreasonable question, considering Kellynch was within his rights to eat any minor dragon who trespassed on his territory, and it was entirely up to him to define who was trespassing. "Kellynch can be trusted."

"I will bring Rubble." Gravel swiveled his head toward the pile of stone, swaying to and fro as though searching. "Pebble, stay with the cluster and keep them calm."

Pebble looked none too happy with the order. "Is best. Will stay."

Interesting. Who knew wyrms to have such foresight? Lady Elizabeth would want to know about this. "Excellent. Balen, if you will inform Kellynch to expect the wyrm representatives?"

"Lady is not to be there?"

"No, the sea cave does not agree with me, and I have other business to attend to here in Lyme. Balen will be with you, though, as my representative. You know her and can trust she will ensure your safety. Pray, excuse me." Anne nodded her head and turned away.

All told, she would have rather stayed with the wyrms.

Anne slipped out of the sunshine, into the dimly lit front room of the Royal Lion Inn. Old must and traces of food smells entertained her until her eyes adjusted and she saw the innkeeper striding toward her, past an older man pretending to read the newspaper on a well-used settee near the window. "Do you know if my father and sister are in?"

The innkeeper wiped his hands on his apron and muttered under his breath. Given his expression, it was probably language not suitable for a lady's ears. "...in their rooms..." He gestured toward the stairs. "How long do they plan to stay?"

"I am trying to determine that myself." Anne resisted the urge to pinch the bridge of her nose and smiled instead.

The innkeeper folded his meaty arms and wrinkled his face into a serious expression. A very warm-blooded way to establish dominance.

Good heavens! Perhaps she really was spending too much time with dragons!

"There are rumors that the Sir and his daughter are under the hatches." The innkeeper glanced toward the stairs.

The man with the newspaper snickered softly.

"Excuse me?"

"Not apt to bleed freely. No longer swimming in lard. Low on blunt." He rubbed an imaginary coin between thumb and fingertips.

Newspaper man leaned a little closer.

She glowered at him as she forced her voice into a lower register and raised her chin. "You will be paid, sir."

"Is that to say you are guaranteeing their bill?" His right eyebrow climbed into his furrowed brow.

"If necessary, yes."

"Then, as to these demands..." He pulled a sheet of paper from an apron pocket and handed it to her.

Elizabeth's handwriting. Merciful heavens. A list of requirements for their comfort. Requirements. Anne pinched her temples. "The answer is no. What you supply is adequate, there is to be nothing extra."

"You planning on telling them that, Lady?" He laced his fingers and tapped his thumbs together.

"It appears I must." She sighed through gritted teeth. Gathering her skirts, she dragged herself upstairs, feeling two sets of eyes boring into her back as she went.

She paused at the top of the stairs. Best gather her wits, her patience, and all the ladylike composure she could find now. She forced herself to knock on the door to their suite.

The door opened and Elizabeth peered out. "Anne? Imagine that. You have come. Father, look! She has deigned to grace us with her presence." She backed up and opened the door, a questionable affectation of a gracious hostess at best. No sense identifying what it was at worst.

Anne had intended to ask after their health and happiness, but since Elizabeth's expression made clear what kind of answer she would receive, skipping that courtesy was definitely the better choice.

"Have you come to do your duty by us and release us from this purgatory?" Father looked up from the couch and the paper he was reading. By the looks of it, it was a letter, but who would write to him here?

"My duty?" So, this was where the conversation was to begin. Lovely. "Whatever do you mean by that?"

Elizabeth dropped into the overstuffed chair nearest him. "Do not be a dolt, Anne. You have played your role fully, establishing yourself as mistress of the local estate. You do not need to lord it over us any longer. We acknowledge your precedence, now invite us to stay with you and be done with this unseemly show." She leaned back and draped her graceful arm over her forehead, a long-suffering heroine from an epic novel.

The sort Elizabeth was not inclined to read.

"How many times must I explain to you? I cannot do anything of the sort." Anne stood between them in the center of the room.

Elizabeth peeked out from beneath her arm. "Cannot? Hardly. You mean will not."

"Such implacable resentment from you is despicable, Anne, truly despicable." Father tsk-tsked under his breath.

"If I were to invite you to Kellynch-by-the-Sea—and let us be clear here, I am not doing so—have you any idea of what it would cost you?"

"Cost us?" He dropped the letter and slapped the couch cushions beside him. "You cannot mean to say you would expect us to pay for the privilege? I suppose vails to the servants are an unpleasant reality, but knowing our circumstances I presumed you would provide those…"

Anne glowered.

"Stop this charade at once. I will not have it." He stood.

Anne folded her arms over her chest and leaned back so she could look down her nose at him. Awkward, but hopefully it made the point. "Have you read the documents that explain the circumstances of your stipend? Of the living which clearly you do not enjoy, but cannot function without?"

"We have been provided an insufficient sum each quarter. What more need I know than that?"

"To begin with, the reason you receive the stipend is to keep my and my husband's name away from the ill-repute you would gain if you were left destitute."

"You think very well of yourself now, Anne, if you think all we have is due to you." Elizabeth sat up straight and rolled her eyes.

"And living below our station does not already disgrace you?" Father asked.

"Your station is that of a disgraced gentleman who lived beyond his means and could not pay his debts. It would be unseemly for you to live above that station." Anne bit back a few other choice remarks.

Elizabeth gasped. "Anne! How can you say such a terrible thing?"

"The terms of the stipend include a clause which states that if you ever set foot on our land, and that would include visiting my home, or staying with us, you will forfeit all future moneys. Are you ready to give up your living for a brief sojourn at my home? And I say brief because Wentworth would see you forcibly removed from the house in short order."

"How could that beast do such a thing? He is your husband, after all. Would you allow him to treat your flesh and blood in such a fashion?" He turned a remarkable shade of red-leaning-toward-purple that clashed terribly with his blue-leaning-to-teal coat.

"You signed the agreement, Father. If you did not know the terms, that is not my fault. You put your name to the document. You have no right to complain now." Anne closed her eyes and drew several deep breaths. "In any case, that is not why I have come."

"So then why are you here?" Father returned to his seat.

"I have arranged to visit with a solicitor regarding finding you a new situation. I would find it useful if you would provide me a list of what you require—"

"Finally! We shall see ourselves in a proper place once again! Like Camden Place in Bath. Oh, that would be most agreeable. You will see to that, Anne, yes?" Elizabeth clapped like a schoolgirl.

Anne gritted her teeth. "You can no longer afford Camden Place or anything like it."

"But that is what we require." Elizabeth's voice climbed higher. "You said you wanted to know what we required—"

"If you cannot be realistic, you are of no help to me." Anne raised an open hand to her sister. "I will decide for myself what you need and you will live with that."

"I expect then to find ourselves in a barn with cows and pigs and chickens sharing our space!" Elizabeth whined.

"If you think that is going to bully me into giving in to your demands, you had best think again. You have no option but to live within your means now."

"You must see reason, Anne. Surely you can afford to be generous with us." He was using his long-suffering voice now.

How Anne hated that. "You cannot afford me to be generous. The terms of the living are clear. You can have nothing from Kellynch-by-the-Sea or the agreement for the living is null and void. It is even problematical if I pay so much as a single pence on your bill for the inn."

"You are making this up. Father, you would never have signed such a ridiculous document." Elizabeth turned to him, wide-eyed.

He did not reply.

"Need I make an appointment with the solicitor to go over the document with you?" Those words sounded more like a threat than Anne had intended. Then again, perhaps not.

"No. I have some vague recollection of the document." Father huffed and looked away. "Elizabeth, provide Anne what she has asked for. I am quite finished with this conversation." He stood and left the sitting room.

"What has gotten into you, Anne? How can you be so deucedly cruel to him? It is bad enough you parade your title and fortune around in a way that he cannot even enjoy. We should be able to enjoy our connection to you, you realize that, do you not? You are titled, that should be a joy to him, not a burden. Why have you taken that from him?"

"I have taken nothing from him or you. Have you forgotten I had no dowry when I wed because it had all been spent on your wardrobe?"

"So, I could marry well and then I would pay it back." How that logic made sense to Elizabeth was beyond comprehension.

"That has not happened. And it will not happen. So, which one of us has lost?" No, no, she should have kept that thought to herself. Anne knew better than to engage—

"I have. I am the elder sister and not married. You and Mary are. That is a cruel joke. Neither of you should have been permitted to marry before—"

"So, you would strip from me even that? I do not know what to make of you. You do not have to be so bitter. You could be happy for us."

Elizabeth sneered.

Enough, enough with such pointless talk. "So will you or will you not do as I asked regarding a new situation for you?"

Elizabeth turned her back and walked toward the window. "You will do as you please, no matter what I say."

"And you will be dissatisfied, no matter what I do." Anne let herself out.

Chapter 9

November 11, 1815

At dawn, Wentworth and Gillingham set sail for Land's End. Luckily, the lad was not the type prone to seasickness, though there was a touch of concern at first. But he had assured Wentworth he had prepared himself a useful draught in case the need arose. Had to give him credit for thinking ahead. It was a quality Wentworth appreciated in a man.

Not that he exactly appreciated the man at the moment. Wentworth would rather have journeyed to the dock in the carriage alone with Anne, than to be stuck in Gillingham's company. Courtesy and propriety be damned. That time should have been theirs, especially considering there was a fair chance there would be no more time for them, ever, after this morning.

Now was not the time to dwell on that. His best chance of returning whole was to focus on the job he had to do and nothing else. Not easy, but something he had practiced. So at least he had that resource to draw upon.

By tomorrow afternoon, they would be at Land's End, dealing with whatever awaited. At least one dragon would be dead, maybe more. And the Order might be at war.

He probably ought to take some time to think and plan further, but really, what was there left to consider? He and Matlock had talked the issue half to death while in Lyme. Then he and Laconia well and truly killed it when they reviewed matters again afterwards. Bless Anne for not asking him to rehash it all when he finally dragged himself to bed that night. She carried burdens enough. Those details would not lessen the weight she carried.

Blast it all. There had not been enough time with her. He had left her with written documentation of everything she might need in the event of his demise. That had been necessary. But there was so much he wanted to say, to do, so much time he simply wanted to spend with her and his child. And he had to settle for so little.

Resentment and its cousins threatened to settle into a neat battalion to lay siege to his mind and heart. But he cut them off and drove them into retreat. He would have to deal with them at some point. But now was not the time. Focus. Focus.

"Morning, Captain, sir." Gillingham strode up to the small sailboat's railing, tipped his head, and leaned on the polished oak, face into the wind.

Not that Wentworth wanted company, but all told, it was just as well. Gillingham's presence would help keep his focus where it should be. "You ready to take up a life at sea now, Gillingham?"

"It is an interesting notion." Gillingham swallowed hard, as though his lauded draught was not as effective as he'd hoped. "I hear ships' surgeons are kept quite busy."

"True enough. The Navy lost more men to accidents and disease than battle." No, those were things he did not want to think about either.

"So I've heard. I don't imagine there's much call for a physician to dragons shipboard, though."

"No, not so much." Wentworth sniffed. Few ships enjoyed dragon company. A few tatzelwurms, a cockatrice or two, but not much more than that. "I don't think Laconia ever experienced such a need the entire time we were at sea." He glanced toward the prow, where Laconia stood like a figurehead, scanning the horizon.

"He's quite a remarkable tatzelwurm." Thankfully, Gillingham ended the comment there. So many people used the compliment as an excuse to pontificate on the perceived shortcomings of the species. At least the boy had some sense of decorum.

Water slapped at the hull as the bow cut through the sea, sending a fine spray onto Wentworth's face. He missed the feel and taste of salt on his face and wind in his eyes while on land. Maybe that was why Lyme felt so homely to him. To him and Kellynch. "What do you make of Kellynch's condition? I barely got to see him, Matlock had me so occupied."

Gillingham looked over his shoulder and caught Wentworth's gaze. "You made a rather compelling argument for me to join you. Cownt Matlock is the second most important dragon in the kingdom, after all."

Wentworth's forehead knit. "You mean to suggest you would have left if Kellynch were in danger?"

Gillingham's eyes went wide. "No, hardly. I suppose I should not jest about such serious matters. Pray, forgive me. I rely upon levity when dealing with issues of great import." He chewed the side of his cheek and returned his gaze to the sea. "Kellynch was grievously injured, to be sure. And we have little experience ministering to such injuries—major dragons rarely come to actual blows any more. But the training and knowledge provided by Sir Edward was more than sufficient to the task. Kellynch is now in the disagreeable part of the recovery process where he feels well enough to complain, but not well enough to return to his usual duties."

"It seems the sort of period in which he would be apt to linger."

"It is not uncommon for that to happen. With men or with dragons. I think there are those who enjoy being waited upon and cared for a little more than they should."

"An apt description of Kellynch. Such a curmudgeon. Takes so little to rattle his equanimity. Are all draconic patients like that?"

Gillingham nodded, lips wrinkling into a lopsided frown, more thoughtful than angry. "The larger they are, the more they are accustomed to having their demands met. That makes the biggest dragons the most difficult of patients."

"Have you treated many large dragons?"

"I would not say many, but the ones we have attended have been memorable. Dug Bedford was quite surly, you know. He had a history of tooth problems. The Dragon Sage herself, in her youth, helped create a dragon-sized tooth key which she used to remove a diseased tooth that was giving him no end of trouble. After that, he allowed Sir Edward regular access, convinced that the relief offered was worth tolerating the ministrations of warm-bloods. He gets a right grumble in the gizzard when his teeth ail him, you know."

It would be interesting to know if Dug Bedford would enjoy being described that way. Even more interesting to hear how the Sage herself described the experience. Perhaps he would ask her when next they met. "So how did you get yourself in studying with Sir Edward?"

Gillingham tipped his head and seemed to study the clouds. "That's a right tale, for certain. It weren't hardly my intention, you know. My father was the local apothecary and my uncle the local surgeon. So, the medical arts were the family trade, so to speak. I had thought to go off to study surgery, so I would follow my uncle about to assist him and help my father compound his potions for the shop when Uncle didn't need me."

"They were both Order members?"

"Indeed, never had Friends, though. Don't think their professions were open to having a Friend following them about. Oddly enough it was Bedlow, a little red drake whose Friend is an apothecary, who first gave me the notion to tend dragons."

"How was that?"

"Papa took me with him to visit Garland, down at Loxdale Green. Bedlow, the little red drake—well, not so little, about the size of a mastiff, I think. In any case, he had a run-in with a pack of genuine mastiffs and didn't come out the better for it. Using what my uncle had taught me with his warm-blooded patients, I patched him up. That got me to thinking, and I am told that is not always a good thing. But in this case, it was, as it ended up with me accepted into Sir Edward's school, and being on the way to making something of myself."

One could hardly fault a young man for wanting to do that. That was, after all, how Wentworth ended up in the Navy. "Do you find there is great call for your specialty?"

"That is a question I wondered about, myself—"

Laconia, black fur and hide glistening with sea spray, streaked across the railing and stopped between Wentworth and Gillingham, panting and breathless. Probably not a good sign. "I just spoke with Siren, matriarch of the Lyme Bay serpent-whales."

"I imagine the fact that she spoke to you and not to me is not a good sign, then." Wentworth stepped back from the railing and beckoned Gillingham to follow him to the bow.

"She regularly speaks to you?" Gillingham's jaw dropped.

"Often enough." Wentworth shrugged. "That she did not take the time to do so now suggests that matters are urgent. Shall I guess, Laconia?"

"I should think it obvious. Chesil awaits us, beyond the edge of the bay."

"Of course he does." Matlock had already had his share in the conversation. It was only proper that Chesil had the same right now.

"How would he know we were sailing out?" Gillingham asked.

"The same way most major dragons are aware of what goes on in their territories." Laconia licked his paw, a touch of scorn in his gold eyes. "There is always someone, often small and feathery, who wants to gain a big dragon's favor. They are always about to inform said dragon of what is going on. In this case, Chesil also has many small sea dragons bringing him news, as well. I think it is safe to assume that he knows or soon will know about anything happening in his territory."

Gillingham looked at Wentworth. "Is that true?"

"May I suggest, questioning a minor dragon's veracity in front of them may not be the best way to convince them of your respect." Wentworth allowed his tone to grow sharp. For a man who claimed to understand dragons, Gillingham's rudeness bordered on bite-worthy.

Laconia bared his fangs with the slightest hiss, mostly as a show of support for Wentworth. He typically turned his back and ignored such a fool.

"Forgive me, you are entirely correct. I apologize for my ill-chosen words. I did not mean to question you, Laconia, only to indicate my astonishment at the efficiency of draconic lines of communication." He bowed toward Laconia.

Laconia sniffed and flicked his tail, as much forgiveness as he was likely to offer. At least at this juncture.

"I suggest you step away, better yet, take yourself below deck. Chesil is not one to tolerate insults lightly. I will not risk jeopardizing our delicate relationship with him." Wentworth pointed astern. This was not what he needed to worry about now. Perhaps he should leave Gillingham on the ship when they reached

Land's End and send him right back to Lyme where the damage he could do was limited to annoying Kellynch.

Gillingham's shoulders fell, but he turned and trudged away. Better disappointed than dead.

"Do tell me that boy is not the idiot he seems to be," Laconia muttered.

"He is still a puppy. A knowledgeable puppy, but a puppy nonetheless. He really is not that bad—"

"Let me see you say that when he insults your intelligence to your face." Laconia's tail whipped.

"Foolishness is not limited to the warm-blooded young alone. Corn can be quite the jolly idiot, no?"

"And I can bite him and drag him away by the scruff of the neck if the situation warrants. Do you think Kellynch would tolerate the level of stupidity that fellow just demonstrated?" Laconia bared his considerable fangs.

"I grant you that." Wentworth pulled his spyglass from his coat and gazed at the horizon. "Any notion of what Chesil wishes to discuss?"

"Have you really any doubt?"

"I know he will want to discuss Cornwall, but have there been fresh developments at Land's End that I should be aware of, lest Chesil declares me an idiot?"

"You need not worry about that." Chesil slowly rose alongside the vessel. The deep green sea drake shared much in common with a major land drake. Four limbs, long neck and tail, lizard-like. But as he rose higher, the differences became obvious. His snout was long and flat, similar to a crocodile, and his neck very long. Sharp, yellowish, backward-pointing protrusions—horns perhaps—covered his face ahead of four deeper-yellow fin-like frills behind his skull that seemed to slick back for swimming. A spiked emerald-green fin ran down the length of his spine, all the way to his tail. Something in the tone of his voice finished the sentence with, '*I already consider you an idiot.*'

"Matriarch Siren brought your summons." Wentworth bowed to Chesil, willing his limbs to remain steady and his stomach not to bolt. Seeing Chesil would never stop being ... dreadful.

"I expected no less." Chesil's voice boomed like thunder across the sea, reverberating in Wentworth's bones. "You are finally on your way to deal with the trespasser."

"I am on my way to Land's End."

"It is about time. I expected it would be a higher priority for you."

"Dug Cornwall is a concern for the leadership of the Blue Order. I had to bring news of the troubles with him to them. It is the sort of news that had to be delivered face to face."

Chesil snorted. "I cannot imagine Londinium did not already know."

"I cannot speak to what the Brenin knew or not." What did Chesil know of Londinium? The remark seemed to suggest a level of unanticipated familiarity between the two. What could that mean? "As for the rest of the leadership, sometimes what one knows cannot be acted upon until that news is received through official channels."

"Now that they know, what will they do about it?"

"There has been considerable debate on that matter."

"Is that all Blue Order dragons do? Talk?" Chesil snorted out a spray, not unlike Matlock's puffs of smoke. Just what he needed, another angry dragon.

"No. But they weigh their actions carefully. Grand Dug Matlock is journeying to Land's End himself to confront Cornwall."

"They are sending their own representative? Interesting. They do not trust that Cornwall will listen to you?"

"What do you mean, interesting?" Wentworth fought to keep his voice steady. No doubt he smelled like fear, but at least he could avoid demonstrating it.

"You suggested that the Order embodied cooperation between cold- and warm-bloods. That all the terrestrial dragons of England would submit to its orders and those of its representatives. But your behavior suggests you do not actually believe that."

"Just because there is one poorly behaved actor, does not invalidate the Order as a whole. If anything, you should be reassured about the Order's commitment to see its principles followed, even by the highest-ranking among them."

"You have no place to tell me how I should interpret what I see. You have no idea of what has transpired, of what I know. I have little reason to trust the Order or its words."

"You have had dealings with the Order before? You are familiar with some of its leaders?" Bloody dragons' bones! There was something missing in all Wentworth had been told.

"It is no concern of yours."

"I beg to differ with you, Chesil. As a representative to both parties in the matter, it is of great importance to me and something that I should know. Tell me of your prior dealings with the Order."

"They have never seemed to be of much value." Chesil growled deep in his throat, a sound as much as a feeling that Wentworth registered in his ribs. "See that Cornwall is dealt with. By the winter solstice." Chesil disappeared under the waves.

Laconia bumped his head against Wentworth's shoulder. He was as unsettled as Wentworth about the exchange. "What do you suppose he is not telling us?"

"I think he knows Londinium personally." Wentworth rubbed his chin.

"And he does not seem to approve of him."

"No, and that, my Friend, worries me. I wonder whether Londinium respects Chesil."

"And how Matlock views both of them." Laconia mrowed. "I dislike the idea of being caught between the three of them."

"It explains a great deal of Matlock's temper, though." But what did one do with such information?

Heavy footsteps approached. "That is one bloody huge dragon," Gillingham gasped. "I know you said he was big, but somehow I never pictured how enormous that really was."

"You and most of the rest of the Order. They have no concept of how sizeable a problem we face," Wentworth muttered.

"I do not understand, though, Chesil is a sea dragon. As I understand, he does not like to be on land, is even less effective out of the water. Does not that lessen the danger to us?" Gillingham asked.

Laconia glowered and hissed. He was right. The young man needed to start thinking before he spoke. Best follow his own advice; Wentworth drew a long breath. "England is an island. Think about what that means. The sea is everything to us."

"Surely, he would not interfere with ships at sea. That would expose him, would it not?"

"Yes, it would. But he has little to lose from such exposure. Men are no threat to him." Was it really so difficult to grasp?

"But if dragons are found at sea ..." Gillingham's boyish features finally—finally!—registered some level of understanding.

"Then it is only a matter of time before the secrets of the Blue Order are revealed." No need to explain what that would mean.

Chapter 10

November 11, 1815

Anne and Balen stood in the doorway, watching the coach carry Wentworth and Mr. Gillingham to the ship that waited to take them to their fate. How could the skies be so bright and the wind so light and cheerful on such a dreadful morning? Even the local fairy dragons cheeped and chirped happy little songs entirely inappropriate to what was happening around them.

If Wentworth had been traveling alone, she would have joined him on the drive. But Gillingham's presence would restrain them to absolute propriety, which neither of them was up to. One day, she would stop resenting Mr. Gillingham for stealing these last few moments from her. Assuming Wentworth returned. If he did not, she might never forgive him.

But dwelling on it would change nothing.

"You know, I can fly to Land's End almost as quickly as I can to London." Balen said quietly, leaning into Anne's side.

Anne stroked the soft feathers between Balen's wings. "You know I do not like to burden you—"

"I have offered, you have asked nothing. I enjoy feeling useful."

"And appreciated."

"It is a new sensation, I admit." Balen clacked her beak with a soft snort. "Do you wish to walk?"

"Yes, very much so." Moving always helped shake the heaviness from her limbs. Though today it might take an exceptionally long walk to do so.

They took a path that led to the flower garden, now sleeping until spring. One day, she would make sure some plant would be blooming nearly every month. But for now, the brown, quiet ground seemed the place that would understand her heart and demand nothing from her. "I am still not accustomed to the seasons near the shoreline. They feel so different from inland."

"They are. For many reasons that are more obvious to one who flies than one landbound. But I do not imagine that is what you want to talk about." Balen stretched her wings to catch the wind, tipping her head back and closing her eyes as the wind ruffled her feathers.

"True enough. What does one talk about under these circumstances?" Especially when talking might shred the fine veil of self-control she had donned while dressing this morning.

"What was and what one remembers. What has happened now. What one fears. What plans one has in place against contingencies. What odds favor which outcomes."

Anne chuckled, though it made her eyes burn. "I am not sure I was asking for such a list. It is a good one, to be sure."

Balen looked up at Anne, her head half-cocked. "I thought not, but it seemed only right to offer an answer."

Anne swallowed hard and dodged Balen's penetrating gaze. "I dislike this. This having no idea of how things could go and what to expect. Waiting on news like a navy wife awaits a letter. We were too long apart for this to be tolerable now."

"Is it useful to know he feels the same?"

"I suppose. I wish it changed anything."

"It is a difficult thing to be tangled in the matters of large dragons." Balen walked a little faster.

Anne lengthened her stride to keep up. "It sounds as though Kellynch has assailed you with his latest complaint?"

"I have been staying out of his way."

"That seems prudent. He took deep offense that Matlock did not seek an audience with him, or even pass through his territory on his way to Lyme—despite the fact that the dragon tunnels do not actually cross into his territory." Anne shook her head. Vain, irritable creature.

"I would have thought it would have been a relief not to have to manage all the issues of propriety and provision for a personage such as Cownt Matlock."

"And yet he feels slighted, as if Matlock deemed him not worthy of an audience."

"I suppose that is to be expected. Though I, for one, am glad Cownt Matlock did not trouble us with a visit." Balen hopped over a rock in her path. "Have you any idea how many protocols there are attached to such an event?"

"The mind boggles. I expect it would be much like a visit from one of the royals." That was the stuff of Father's dreams, all the while knowing it was nigh on impossible. "Perhaps that was why Cownt Matlock chose to stay at the guest lair. Perhaps he was too preoccupied with business himself to attend to such things."

"That is quite the thought, is it not? A dominant dragon being too preoccupied for displays of dominance and asserting precedence. But there is some reason to believe that. Do you mind if I share the idea with Kellynch? It might help calm his offense." A breeze ruffled the feathers on the back of Balen's neck—or was that an expression of her current feelings toward Kellynch?

"Pray do. He needs all the cheer that might be brought his way. Between Matlock and the issues surrounding the wyrms, melancholy is knocking at his lair."

"I thought he and the wyrms had already come to an agreement. He would not be the only dragon whose status could improve with the arrangement." Balen stopped walking and stared at Anne. "Did he not approve their occupancy in his territory and were they not well pleased with both his offer and the possibility of finally being noticed by the Blue Order?"

"That is what happened. But why would we ever believe that so simple a discussion could have resolved so complex a matter?" Anne stared into the sky and pulled her shawl tighter. "Do you really imagine the Order would allow something that seems to be so straightforward to slip by them unfettered? No, no indeed."

"Dare I ask the nature of the trouble?"

"I dare say you will enjoy this. Enjoy in the broadest, most ironic sense of the word. You see, I have since discovered that the charter for Kellynch-by-the-Sea, unlike the charter for most dragon estates, contains no provisions for minor dragons in residence. You see, no one considered that there were minor dragons living in the area who might want to be part of Kellynch's new territory, or that Kellynch might be interested in having minor dragons in his territory. And because of the decidedly unusual circumstances surrounding the award of this territory, there are serious penalties in force around even minor charter violations." Anne forced a thin smile. "So, we must have the charter redrawn to make the provisions for minor dragon occupancy, and once we do, then our fine Mr. Wynn must give approval. Once that happens, then it must be sent to the Minister of Keeps, who may or may not give his final approval to the scheme."

"What utter nonsense. You do not plan to go through with all that, do you? Kellynch is not going to put up with so much delay. He is anxious to emulate the other major dragons of the Order, especially young Pemberley."

"Kellynch's patience is short and the wyrms seem adamant about wanting to be properly installed under the protection of a major dragon as soon as possible. I had not realized that was such a mark of status among minor dragons, particularly the lowest-ranking ones like the wyrms. Apparently, there are no small wyrms officially recognized as part of the estate in any place in England. Only the larger minor dragons are so established. Now that the possibility presents itself, they are anxious for the status." Anne shuddered. "It all feels like dealing with Father and Elizabeth. Anything for status and recognition."

"What are you going to do?"

"Clearly, I cannot expect the cluster or Kellynch to wait on the vagaries of the Order. As soon as Bragg has returned from the docks, he will take me to call upon Mr. Harville. He is authorized to manage charter documents for the Order, as well as property issues among the warm-blooded. How convenient that I will be able to attend to both matters in only one visit."

***

Mr. Harville's office was as far from Kellynch-by-the-Sea as one could be and still be in Lyme. The drive gave Anne time to think. Far too much time. Usually, she enjoyed that luxury, but for the next several weeks, at least, it was a hardship she would have to find some way to cheerfully bear.

Bragg handed her out of the coach at the front door of Mr. Harville's office. The freestanding building itself was made of white-painted stone that seemed too bright when the sun hit it. Black shutters flanked the windows and their flower boxes on the second story. Black trim framed the third-story windows. In many respects, it looked like most every other building in Lyme. Only the wee white drake, peering through the front window, identified it as an extraordinary place.

The dragon was no larger than a lady's pug, so dainty it seemed formed from bone china. A place where such a fine little creature felt comfortable had a great deal to be said for it. Tension she had not realized she carried sloughed away.

She rang the bell and a young clerk let her in.

"Lady Wentworth? Mr. Harville is expecting you. Please come this way." The clerk led her through a large sitting room, furnished with wooden benches, tables, and chairs with no cushions.

A few bore the marks of teeth and claws, which might easily pass as damage done by a dog. Was it possible that the cushions that might otherwise have been there had been chewed by a particular little dragon? The little drake in question scrabbled across the smooth hardwood floor and nearly crashed into her ankles.

"Alabaster, ye daft little thing. Don't go bothering the Lady." He scooped the little dragon into his arms, where she nuzzled the side of his neck. "You must excuse her. She is a dear little creature, for all that she trips over her own feet and tail."

"It is no bother, truly." Anne offered her hand for the drake to sniff.

The little dragon sniffed her hand and somehow wriggled her way into Anne's arms.

"Well, ain't that a strange thing? She don't normally do that with strangers." The young man studied her, head cocked, arms folded across his chest.

She stroked under Alabaster's chin. "I think she is sweet."

"You should see 'er with those she don't like. You'd think her possessed of the very devil 'imself." The clerk chuckled as they walked toward a half-open office door. "Lady Wentworth, here to see you, sir."

The spit and image of his brother, Wentworth's dear friend Captain Harville, the younger Mr. Harville stood and bowed. He was a slight, wiry fellow, probably strong in a way that did not look strong. Straw-colored hair had been styled back from his large blue eyes into a tousled arrangement that was supposed to be fashionable right now. His dark suit and shoes, while neat and well-fitted, were not as modern as his hair. Definitely more to him than mere style. That was comforting.

"I hope you will forgive my Friend for being so forward. I must say it is not like her." Mr. Harville pulled a chair near his heavy desk for her.

"I am glad she can so readily identify a Friend." She sat and settled Alabaster in her lap. The little drake grumbled contentedly. Had she been capable, she would have purred.

A large window admitted sunlight, while bookshelves and filing cabinets took up much of the remaining wall space. Granted, there were several stacks of paper and folios along the top of the desk. But all in all, Mr. Harville's office declared him a well-ordered man who knew his business, and would get things done.

"How might I be of service to you, Lady Wentworth? Your husband mentioned something about needing a property to let." He settled in behind his desk.

"Most definitely. But it seems that is not the only matter for which I will need your expertise. The charter documents for Kellynch-by-the-Sea need some significant revisions. We need to add provisions for minor dragons on the estate. Kellynch's situation is so singular that we do not wish to risk getting on the wrong side of the Order with these matters."

He stroked his chin. "Would these minor dragons by any chance be a cluster of wyrms who lived by the old Order offices?"

"Word has traveled so quickly?" That certainly could not make matters any easier.

"You see, I told you accurately." Alabaster poked her head up and wrinkled her nose at her Friend.

"It is not appropriate to assume one already knows a client's business," he said.

"Every minor dragon in these parts knows about Kellynch's talks with the cluster. I fear you will have to learn to tolerate a newfound popularity among the minor dragons of the region." Alabaster's tail tip flicked as she pressed into Anne's side.

"Indeed? I was given to believe that there were not many minor dragons in this region," she said.

"Not many compared to some locations, but enough. And we have all been waiting to hear what sort of Keep Kellynch-by-the-Sea would be. We have not had a major dragon installed in the region in quite a long time and many are waiting to learn how their lives are going to change because of Kellynch." Alabaster's shoulders drooped.

"What do you mean? I am still new to the business of dragon Keeping."

Alabaster ducked her head under Anne's elbow.

"It is all right to speak freely, my Friend. But if you prefer, I will try to explain."

Alabaster squeaked in Anne's lap.

"You will have to forgive my Friend. She does not like to speak of conflicts and contention."

"Are there conflicts among the local dragons I should be aware of?" Anne asked.

"Not that I know of. But that could change depending upon Kellynch. Styles of Keep management differ as much among dragons as they do among men. Do you know if Kellynch dislikes minor dragons in general?"

"He has two minor dragons, tatzelwurmlings Corn and Wall, whom he has known since their hatching and he considers his Friends. And he is a great admirer of young Pemberley, who is well known as a friend to minor dragons."

Alabaster sat up and gazed at Anne.

Mr. Harville offered a similar expression. "Well, that is most extraordinary, and very welcome indeed. I have never heard of such a thing."

"We do not keep it a secret, but it is not the sort of topic one finds many opportunities to discuss." Anne stroked Alabaster's soft back.

"Those tatzelwurmlings of his, how well trained are they?" he asked.

"What do you mean?"

"If Kellynch welcomes minor dragons, his territory is going to boast many small dragon visitors, seafaring bird-types, primarily. He will need help managing them and all the gossip they will be bringing. I would recommend you prepare his Friends carefully for their roles as his lieutenants. Come to think of it, that cluster of wyrms might be helpful as well."

Merciful heavens! "His lieutenants? But they are so young. And the wyrms, we hardly know them."

"Perhaps your Friend can help as well. As Liaison to the Blue Order, I expect you will have much more work than you ever expected simply keeping track of all the information that crosses the territory."

"Gracious! This was never what we anticipated. We thought this place was chosen for Kellynch because there were few other dragons about and the estate itself was not particularly significant."

"What major dragons consider to be significant is not the same thing as what is actually significant." He tapped steepled fingers together.

"Well, then, that makes my other errand, that of finding a property for my father and sister, all the more urgent." Alabaster nudged Anne's hand when she stopped petting.

"They are here in Lyme, staying at the Royal Lion?"

"Dare I ask how you know?" She clenched her left hand while petting Alabaster with the other.

"The innkeeper's complaints have been loud and widespread." Alabaster said. "Most of the local shopkeepers have heard about him and been warned to refuse him credit. You will be happy to know that the innkeeper has not spread the word that you have promised to cover your father's debts, though."

"That is good of him." Anne huffed under her breath.

"Forgive me if this is very personal, but it is actually quite pertinent." He shifted a stack of papers to the side. "Is it true that your father and sister were forced from their home because of a fire?"

"It seems you have specific knowledge of their situation. Have they been talking about those details such that it has become part of the local gossip?"

"No, not in this case." He opened a folio and removed something that looked like a map. "So, I am correct, there was a fire?"

"To what does this question pertain? Do you have reason to suspect they set fire to their own accommodations?"

"Not at all, far from it." He started and blinked hard. "It is a delicate matter, one requiring the utmost discretion."

Discretion. Anne swallowed against the constriction in her throat. "Whatever could you mean, sir?"

"Your father and sister were in the vicinity of Bath, yes?"

"They were."

He spread the map on his desk. "As you can see, this map represents the southwestern counties of England, from Cornwall to Somerset and Dorset."

"I suppose you are going to explain to me the meaning of those dates pinned to what appear to be dragon Keeps within those counties?"

"Quite astute, Lady Wentworth. Most of those are dragon Keeps, though a few are homes of Blue Order members, with or without Friends." He tapped the map. "At each one of these locations, on the indicated dates, there has been a fire."

Anne leaned closer and peered at the map. "So many? I know fire is not exactly an unusual occurrence, but still, it seems notable."

He slid a small piece of paper and pencil toward her. "If you would, add the date of the fire your father and sister suffered. An approximate date is fine, if you do not have the exact detail."

Anne jotted down the information and handed it to Harville, who pinned it near Bath on the map.

"I imagine you have already compared the number of recent fires affecting Blue Order members to the number of fires affecting the dragon-deaf in the same regions?" she asked.

"Indeed, we have. When one considers how few hearers there are in the population, it seems that fires are occurring three to four times more frequently on Blue Order-connected properties. I am gathering dates from other regions right now to determine whether or not this is a localized phenomenon."

"You think the fires are deliberate, then?"

"We have reason to suspect so, and worse still, we suspect the culprits may be cold-blooded."

Anne gasped. "Dragons may be doing this? But do not the Accords—"

"Forbid dragons from harming humans except in the case of self-preservation? Yes, absolutely. But in the quest of dominance and influence, such things may be forgotten, especially when it is so difficult to determine how a fire came to be in the first place."

"What you suggest is—"

"Most serious, and exceedingly dangerous, and I would not blame you at all if you wish to walk away and pretend you have heard nothing of it." He waited, eyes fixed on Anne, but she did not respond. "If you are willing, there is a favor I would ask of you."

"You want me to ask my father and sister for more details surrounding the fire they suffered?"

"I suppose it was not difficult to guess. As persons specifically not in high esteem with the Order, it seems especially interesting to understand the situation."

That was a chilling thought. "I must see about assigning some cockatrice guards around the Red Lion, just in case. Then I will discuss the matter with them."

Interesting how he did not even mention the fire that destroyed the Lyme office, despite there being a pin to represent it. Did he suspect more about that than he was willing to say?

Chapter 11

November 12, 1815

Wentworth's ship docked at the small port near the Cornwall Keep. Secluded and maintained by the Blue Order, it saw little traffic save the local seafaring cockatrice and fairy dragons in the nearby woods. Even so, the lack of activity there set Laconia's fur on end and Wentworth's nerves on edge.

Theirs was the only ship at the dock, which might have explained some of the lack of activity. Since it was not a commercial venture, why would it be manned apart from actual arrivals or departures? Or if a storm was on its way and precautions needed to be taken. But the sun shone brightly, cutting through the brisk, chill wind, unhampered by clouds or any other threat of weather.

Wentworth and Laconia, with Gillingham close behind, debarked and scanned the shore for activity as waves lapped rhythmically against the short wooden dock.

A messenger had been sent from the ship at dawn to notify the Keep of their impending arrival, so there should have been someone there to meet them. They might not have been dignitaries, but a luggage cart and driver would have been appropriate. Were they being intentionally ignored or was something more serious afoot?

Not a little ominous, all things considered.

A loud caw sounded overhead.

"I dare say that is our greeting committee. Come along, Gillingham." Wentworth waved for him to follow as he strode down to the end of the dock and behind a large stone storage shed with a sagging wooden roof.

A scrappy-looking grey cockatrice, wearing a Blue Order insignia on his harness, landed near the shed, two long steps away from the men. "Sir Frederick?"

"Yes. You have been sent from Cornwall Keep?"

"Yes, sir." The cockatrice scraped the rocky ground with his talons as he edged back, eyeing Laconia as prey watches a predator. "I have been sent to tell you that you are not welcome on the Keep. Cornwall has not forgotten your offense to him, and you are not to set foot on his territory."

Laconia growled softly.

"All things considered, I am not surprised." Wentworth's face screwed into a frown, and he huffed. "Even so, to turn away an official messenger from the Order..."

"I was told to expect you to say such a thing and to respond by reminding you that a dragon is sovereign in his Keep. He has as much right to keep you out as Kellynch does to keep out Sir Walter." The cockatrice bobbed back and forth as if bowing as he slipped back several more steps.

Laconia bared his fangs and hissed.

The cockatrice jumped back.

"Do not be stupid. I do not eat messengers." The scowl on Laconia's face disagreed with his sentiment.

"Just what I would have expected him to say." Wentworth glanced at Gillingham, whose slack-jawed look of surprise might have been amusing under other circumstances. "Very well then, we will have to make do with other accommodations. Is there an inn nearby?"

"I am not supposed to offer you any assistance. However, my flight back to the Keep will pass directly over the local inn. I cannot be responsible if you choose to follow me that far. But do not trespass on Cornwall's Keep." The cockatrice glanced over his shoulder, as though looking for eavesdroppers.

Interesting, most interesting. Loyalties so divided that the messenger would take such a risk. "Fly on, then, and we will be attentive to your path." Wentworth waved the messenger on.

The cockatrice launched and circled overhead until they got their bearings, then flapped toward the nearby village.

"Is this sort of thing common, sir?" Gillingham panted as he struggled to keep up with the cockatrice.

No matter how slowly it flew, Laconia would be the only one of them to be able to keep up.

"I hardly know, myself. I am much more familiar with the workings of diplomats than of dragons." Wentworth struggled for breath. "I am hardly surprised, though. We did not part on good terms, Cornwall and I. It is inconvenient. Especially as I am supposed to ensure a guest lair is readied for Matlock on the Keep."

"Matlock is expected." The cockatrice circled overhead and cawed. "A lair Cornwall considers suitable for him has been prepared."

Lovely. Cownt Matlock was already put out with the substandard arrangements in Lyme. Another inferior lair would do nothing to help his already caustic disposition. "Matlock will demand my presence for an audience. Is there a place where I might meet with him away from the Keep?"

"That information will be dispatched as necessary." The messenger stopped circling and flew on.

"Understood." Wentworth frowned. Standing as a pawn between the two dragons now? How much more interesting could this become? No, strike that, he did not want to know.

The cockatrice came to rest on the roof of a modest, two-story building, which had clearly weathered its share of storms, and waited there until Laconia arrived. Then he took off toward the Keep. Doubtless Cornwall would not welcome the news of their arrival—hopefully he would not take it out on the messenger.

Wentworth and Gillingham slowed from their jog to a brisk walk the rest of the way to the inn.

"Sir Frederick?" The innkeeper, a weathered man with a leathery face and deeply tanned arms revealed by pushed-up sleeves, greeted them at the door. "My Friend heard tell that you might be looking for a place to stay." He glanced at Laconia and nodded.

Good, they had no need of a place that would not welcome Laconia as well. "Your Friend would be quite correct. My companions and I need accommodations whilst we conduct our business here."

The innkeeper's face folded into something halfway between thoughtful and concerned. "I have only the one room available right now, will that do?"

"We will be grateful for it." Less than ideal, but he had endured far greater privations than cramped quarters with a sound roof overhead and solid walls around him.

Gillingham looked a little uncertain, but said nothing. Did he object to sharing quarters, or was he keeping quiet in hopes that no one would think to send him to sleep in an outbuilding of some sort?

"Can someone be sent for our things?" Wentworth asked.

"Me boy is out with the cart getting supplies right now. Don't expect him back before tomorrow. I'm afraid you will need to make your own arrangements." The innkeeper folded his arms, his posture suggesting that they had best not ask if he himself would assist.

"I will tell the crew," Laconia said as he spring-hopped off.

Odd. Interesting. What was he concerned about? Something about the whole situation left Wentworth with an itch in the back of his mind. One that seemed all too active recently. "If you will show us to the room, then, we will sort out the luggage presently."

The innkeeper nodded and ushered them inside. The front room was dark and dank, with several small tables near a smoke-blackened fireplace and a few worn chairs near the window. An abandoned pewter tankard and plate on the far table suggested that such meals as were available would be taken here.

The innkeeper opened an unobtrusive door, hung at such an angle it seemed it might not open. But it did, revealing a narrow, uneven staircase. He plodded upstairs, no doubt assuming they would follow. The stairs ended in a short, cramped hall lit by a single window on the left. Two doors to the right and one at the end made up the only landmarks in the space.

He led them to the last room in the hall. "Here you go. Your meals, morning and evening, are included in the rate." He wrenched the doorknob and shoved the door open with his shoulder. It squealed against the doorframe in protest.

A slim window, matching the one at the end of the hall, dressed with dingy, once-white curtains, lit the room. A bed, a chair, a dressing table, and a small press, all worn and askew, fit inside only because there was no fireplace. It was only November, so the innkeeper would probably not have permitted a fire if there had been a place for it, in any case. Again, not the worst place he had ever experienced.

Given Gillingham's expression, though, he had probably expected something more.

"Right then, it will do. We must be off to see about the luggage." Wentworth closed the door and led the way down the stairs and out the door. "Gillingham, come along."

Gillingham paused outside, looking about as though to find his bearings.

"Not what you expected, eh?" Wentworth started toward the dock.

"I cannot say that it is." Gillingham leaned close and whispered. "Does something seem strange to you?"

"It does. Look lively and stick close." Wentworth glanced over his shoulder. What did he expect to find? Only an empty street lined with a few worn buildings and fewer people, nothing suspicious or dangerous.

Laconia met them at the dock. "There is a problem."

"Dragon's bones! What now?" Wentworth dragged his hand down his face.

"Just before I arrived back here, your luggage was just put on a cart to be taken to the Keep's manor house." Laconia's tail slapped the stony ground.

"Oh, bloody hell." Wentworth muttered as he stood.

"They have not been gone long." Laconia pointed down the road with his nose. "They had a donkey cart, and the said that it did not seem the creature was inclined to get anywhere quickly. You should be able to catch them with little effort."

"Up for a bit of a trot, Gillingham?" Wentworth did not wait for an answer, but took off with Laconia by his side.

To his credit, Gillingham merely grunted, then kept pace a step behind as the village disappeared behind them.

In a few minutes, Wentworth made out the cart on the road ahead, approaching a dark thicket of trees, oddly resembling a miniature dragon woods. Thick, old trees with branches that met and arched over a narrow trail, much like woods surrounding the old Kellynch estate. The cart stopped abruptly, the donkey braying loudly.

There was nothing more certain than a donkey spotting danger. Damn it all.

The cart driver jumped down and spotted Wentworth and Gillingham. "You there? What you want?" With one hand, he reached behind his seat.

No doubt he had a firearm concealed there.

"No harm, sir, no harm." Wentworth slowed and raised his hands. "The trunks you are carrying—I suspect you have been given incorrect information. They belong to us, you see, and though we had thought we would stay on the Cornwall estate, we are in fact staying at the local inn. We merely want to have our things."

"How do I know these are actually yours?" the driver shouted as he slipped a blunderbuss from behind his seat.

"We aren't far from the dock, drive back there and ask the sailors who unloaded the trunks. They will tell you who I am." Wentworth pointed toward the village.

"I don't like it none. Irregular, it is…" the driver's voice trailed off as growls and barks—not from any dog Wentworth had ever known—exploded from the thicket's shadows. "What the bloody hell?"

The hair on the back of Wentworth's neck rose—only dragons growled like that. What the bloody hell, indeed.

Laconia rose on his tail and sniffed the air. "Dragons."

The donkey brayed and took off at remarkable donkey-ahead-of-a-crisis speed, the cart bouncing and clattering behind. Few understood just how fast a frightened donkey could run. And when a donkey started running, a wise man should follow close behind.

The cart driver was a wise man.

But men who dealt with dragons often demonstrated questionable wisdom.

"What do we do?" Gillingham edged close to Wentworth. Laconia positioned himself in front of them both.

"That sounds like drakes, big ones. We sure as hell can't outrun them. I fear I did not come armed for this." No, the dragon-slaying crossbow was still stowed under the false bottom in one of the trunks departing with the donkey.

"Isn't that unfortunate for you." A grey-green head appeared from the thicket, quickly followed by the rest of a large minor drake.

Thick and square, with bony knobs around its eyes, this was a drake designed for a fight. Its massive shoulders bowed out its front legs like a bulldog's as it slipped into the sunlight. Easily three times the size of a bulldog and no doubt much stronger, this was not a creature to ignore.

"What is the meaning of this?" Wentworth boomed in his best officer's voice. "You have not been threatened. Why are you threatening us? It is clearly against all the rules of the Order."

A yellowish drake of similar build and stature scurried out on the other side of the road. "I feel threatened, what about you?" Was it snickering?

"Quite threatened indeed." The grey-green was definitely laughing.

"You cannot prove a threat. Do you want to forfeit your lives for a moment of sport?" Wentworth searched the woods behind the dragons for more. The scent of dragon musk was too strong for only two minor dragons.

"I see no one around. Who do you think would turn us in? The driver only knows he heard a pack of dogs growling in the woods." The grey-green drake licked his lips.

"I will report you." Laconia puffed out his chest and whipped his tail.

"The little half-wyrm thinks he can escape us." The yellowish dragon crouched to pounce.

"We will be missed. There will be an investigation," Gillingham shouted.

"Spoken like the cowardly spawn you are." The dragons crept closer.

Yes, as Wentworth expected, two more bulky drakes appeared out of the woods behind them. "I am a Pendragon Knight and he, the apprentice of the Lord Physician to Dragons. We will be missed."

"Anyone could say those things. There is no proof. You look more like a snack than a knight." The grey-green dragon's top lip curled back.

"And you look like an interesting pair of boots." Never reveal fear to a dragon.

"That one has a bit of snap. Ain't many who talk back to death." The yellowish dragon ended the word with a hiss.

Laconia hissed back.

"If the Order does not hunt you down, Kellynch will." Wentworth pulled his shoulders back and flared his elbows. He needed to be big.

"And Chesil will not appreciate it either," Gillingham added. "I expect he would send his own forces against you. Probably keep you alive until he could do the deed himself."

"Chesil? What has he to do with matters on land?" Yellow pulled his neck back, eyes widening.

He was aware of Chesil. Good, that was helpful.

"What do you know of Chesil? That is not a name well known amongst the Order." Green backed up half a step and glowered at Wentworth.

"Kellynch, the dragon I Keep, is Chesil's vassal, assigned the Lyme Bay territory within Chesil's territory. We have had many dealings with Chesil. I am under orders from him as well as the Blue Order."

"I heard tell there was such a man." A ruddy dragon from near the trees stopped well behind Yellow.

"If you are he, tell us, what happened during the Battle of Lyme Bay?" a brown dragon near the thicket demanded.

Promising. "I believe the detail you are interested in is that I was swallowed by Chesil and later cast up on the beach by him."

"Who was on the beach to witness the event?" The grey-green dragon snarled.

"Myself, his wife and her Friend, a greater cockatrix who resembles a large-billed stork," Laconia said.

"That is what the cockatrice said." The ruddy dragon's tail slapped the leaf-littered ground, stirring up a cloud of dust and dry leaves.

"The story is not known among warm-bloods. We should believe him." Brown backed away another step.

"I did not ask you." Green hissed. "Why should we care if he is connected to Chesil? What has he to do with us? We are part of Cornwall's Keep."

"You are affiliated with Cornwall, you say?" Wentworth asked. What might it mean if they were?

"We are permitted to reside on his Keep." Yellow's voice lost its deadly edge.

"What is your role, then? Are you guards on his lands?" That could actually be quite problematic. A cart coming from Cornwall's Keep could be construed to be an extended part of his territory, therefore under his Keep's protection.

The grey-green dragon growled and stomped—not nearly as impressive a gesture when the ground did not rumble like it did when Matlock stomped. "You question us?"

"Indeed, I do." Wentworth raised open arms to shoulder level. "Cornwall has assigned you to protect the security of the Keep?"

"We do not need to be. We have taken up the duty of our own volition." Green threw back his head and roared as though he thought himself quite large and important.

By Jove! These dragons were no more than rogues, like highwaymen operating under their own authority.

Now was not the time to back down. He sucked in a deep breath, enough to shift to his on-deck-in-a-storm tone. "And all of you are willing to risk being taken apart, one joint at a time, when the Order or Chesil discovers what you have done?"

"There will be no evidence." The green one crouched and crept closer.

"There you are wrong." Gillingham pointed to the thicket. "There was a harem of fairy dragons near the dock. Their male has an injured tail. I promised them I would tend to him after we settled in. Two juveniles were sent to keep watch and remind me of my promise lest I forget. If you look, you can see them there, high in the tree."

"No one listens to fairy dragons." Yellow followed Green, closer and closer.

"The Dragon Sage does." Wentworth said.

"You have connections with the Dragon Sage?" The ruddy dragon skittered back.

Green looked over his shoulder and glowered at the smaller, retreating dragons. "Coward! Even if he knows her, she cannot touch us here."

"She led the Council in ruling against Cornwall, in favor of Kellynch. Do not underestimate her reach." Wentworth opened his arms further.

"Spoken like prey trying not to die." Yellow's long forked tongue flicked toward them.

"You heard them!" Gillingham cried, hands cupped around his mouth. "You heard their threat! Be off now, to Lyme and tell the Undersecretary what you have seen. Quickly!"

Two yellow and black creatures launched from the top of the trees, toward Lyme.

"They will never make it. They will be in a cockatrice belly before they reach Falmouth." A gob of spittle dripped from Green's fangs.

"Perhaps. But how many more from the harem might be here in these woods waiting to carry the tale?" Gillingham stretched his arms wide and waved them at the woods. "Think of how much status and dominance it would give a mere fairy dragon to be the one to carry the word that brings you lot down."

"I will not risk my hide to give status to a fairy dragon." The ruddy dragon disappeared into the thicket. The brown one followed without comment.

Green and Yellow stared at each other, twitching, grunting, and tongues flicking.

"Later." Yellow hissed. "Later. We will hunt them later."

Green grumbled and growled.

"How much more pleased will Cornwall be to know that we have tormented, tortured them with the knowledge that they are being watched?" Yellow tried to laugh, but the effort was far less threatening than he probably hoped for.

"That would please him." Green twitched his brow ridges. "You have bought yourself another day. Enjoy watching over your shoulder and fearing the dark. I will relish the opportunity to pick apart your bones and suck out the marrow."

The dragons disappeared back into the woods.

Bloody hell.

Chapter 12

November 13, 1815

Filial duty or not, had there been anyone she could have sent to the Red Lion in her place, Anne would have gladly done so. One might hope that Father and Elizabeth would be pleased that she brought word of potential new situations for them. Mr. Harville proved far better connected than she expected and had a surprising number of possibilities for them.

How she had learned to hate, hate, hate that word, especially from Father's lips—Mr. Harville was not Mr. Shepherd, the solicitor Father had relied upon for decades. Father disliked and distrusted suggestions that did not come from Mr. Shepherd. And of course, Elizabeth agreed.

But since Shepherd was neither a member of the Blue Order, nor a particularly good solicitor, his services were no longer sought. One more offense in Father's long list of grievances toward the Order. One more thing Anne would refuse to discuss with him.

At this rate, the list of things she refused to discuss with him would be longer than the list she would by sometime tomorrow afternoon. She pressed her temples and sighed.

Still, though, the possibility of a home in Exeter, Southampton, or Portsmouth, all larger than their situation in Bath, might be enough to shake off some of their sourness. Even if the houses were not as grand as Camden Place.

Maybe.

Perhaps.

One way or another, she would see.

Jonty Bragg handed her down from the coach and opened the inn's door for her. Impassive and proper, as his dark features always were, even he sported a furrowed brow and lines beside his eyes. Likely set there the last time she visited and Father tried to commandeer the coach and Jonty's services without her permission. Poor man. There would definitely be an envelope of appreciation waiting for him at the end of this ordeal.

The innkeeper, still portly, but now lacking his previously warm and friendly demeanor, shuffled up a moment later, rolled his eyes, and pointed upstairs. Just as well. She really was not in the mood for idle conversation, in any case.

Best not dawdle on the steep staircase. She might lose her resolve altogether, given a few extra moments to contemplate her fate. Anne knocked on the door.

Elizabeth let her in. She was dressed to entertain company—but who could she possibly hope would appear? What possible point in keeping up appearances in a place like Lyme where they knew no one? "It is only Anne, Papa." She turned up her nose and led Anne into the stuffy sitting room, which sported a few too many pieces of furniture, and far too little taste.

"I do not suppose you have brought any manner of good news with you, have you?" Father did not look up from the newspaper he pretended to study. It was not open to the society pages. He read nothing but the society pages.

"It is possible that I might."

"Is it too much to hope for that it is news of an end to this nonsense, and we will be reinstalled to our rightful home?" Elizabeth suddenly seemed quite animated.

"I will not dignify that with an answer." Anne perched on the chair farthest from them both, a stiff, overstuffed affair upholstered in a slippery, shiny red-flowered chintz.

Interesting. Father rolled his eyes and looked away from Elizabeth. Had he come to accept the finality of the Council's judgement? That alone would be progress, small progress, to be sure, but it would be something.

"There is no need to be rude, Anne. We are the ones suffering here, with no home, no friends to receive us, and nothing to do. No shopkeepers will honor our credit. Even the innkeeper has muttered that it is only because of Kellynch-by-the-Sea's promise that he tolerates us here. Really, it is quite awful. You should be considerate of the boredom and the indignity we suffer."

And Elizabeth should be cognizant that they had brought it upon themselves.

But that was not going to happen. "I called upon a local solicitor, Mr. Harville, the brother of Wentworth's friend from the Navy."

"What use could a solicitor from Lyme be to us?" His face wrinkled as though he were sucking a bad lemon.

"As it happens, he is well informed as to your unique situation, and acts as an agent for a considerable number of properties."

"But is he competent? Should the name of Elliot be trusted to such a man?" Elizabeth stood between Anne and Father, looking from one to the other. "Can you be certain he is not acting in his own interest, seeking to connect himself with the name of Elliot, to profit by association?"

It was hard to tell which was stronger, Anne's urge to slap her own forehead or simply slap Elizabeth. Instead, she clutched the portfolio in her hands more tightly. "You are entirely welcome to seek out your own situation without my help. Pray feel free to do so. It will save me a great deal of time and trouble."

Father grumbled. "We may as well see what this Harville fellow has to offer. I suppose it cannot hurt."

"If you insist." Elizabeth sat on the settee beside him.

Anne ground her teeth and forced something that hopefully resembled a smile onto her face. "I was surprised to find he had connections with half a dozen potential situations for you. Each with their own unique merits and limitations, of course."

"I do not approve of limitations," Elizabeth muttered.

"None of us do, I think." Patient, she had to be patient. "What advantages and limitations did your situation in Bath have?"

"It was not in Camden Place, nor even near it. The location was quite demeaning." He turned away from Anne's challenging gaze.

"It was inconvenient from the local shops." Elizabeth sneered.

"What of the house itself? Were there any aspects you liked?" Anne tried not to grimace in anticipation.

"The roof did not leak," Elizabeth said. "And the fireplaces were not smoky, except for one upstairs. There were an adequate number of windows."

"Thank you, that is most helpful." Actually, it was not, but it was a polite thing to say.

"There was a bit of a garden behind the house which you thought had potential for flowers or some such." Father's brow creased, and he blinked several times. Recalling that seemed challenging.

"Potential, yes, but little else." Elizabeth sniffed. "It was a small little place, overrun by weeds and several scraggly trees. There were those odd little birds, colorful ones, that had rather a pretty song."

Fairy dragons? Great merciful heavens! "You never mentioned those. I would love to hear more."

"What of them? They were pretty in the summer, they seemed to enjoy the flowers. But they got into the attic as soon as the weather turned, and we had a bother of a time getting rid of them."

No! No, no! "Getting rid of them?"

"We borrowed several cats and that seemed to sort out the issue well enough." Elizabeth turned to him. "But then we had troubles with those dogs. Do you recall that?"

"Dogs?" Anne glanced at Father, who would not meet her eyes. She clenched her left hand into a tight fist. "What happened with dogs?"

"There was this pack of hounds that plagued us. From the time we brought in the cats until the fire drove us out, there were dogs watching us, constantly. So bold, too! There were times they would dash into the house, creating as much havoc as they could. I have never seen such a thing. When I would try to walk out, they would follow me. It was eerie, like they knew what they were doing, as though they were organized and planning something." Elizabeth rubbed her upper arms briskly. "I know that is utter nonsense, to be sure, but the feeling was difficult to ignore."

"It sounds very … uncomfortable …" Anne stared at Father, who simply frowned and avoided her gaze. Surely, he had known the nature of those dogs and what their presence might mean. How could he not have told her?

"What of the houses your Harville fellow recommends?" he asked, eyes downcast.

"Yes, of course. Perhaps we should start by location. There is one in Exeter, two in Southampton, two in Portsmouth, one near Bath, and one in Weymouth. Have you a preference for any one of those places?"

Three sharp knocks on the door made her jump. Elizabeth opened it.

Jonty Bragg peeked in. "Lady Wentworth, you are urgently needed at Kellynch-by-the-Sea."

"Of course. I will be downstairs in a moment." She pulled papers from her portfolio. "These are the details about each of the houses. Examine them, and I will be back as soon as I can to discuss them with you further."

"You are going to leave us to make sense of this, ... this pile of papers?" Father pushed the pile away. "Surely, there cannot be a crisis at Kellynch of greater magnitude than our own."

"I am sure you and Elizabeth are up to the task. I will return soon." She hurried out.

"Balen has arrived with a message for you, Lady Wentworth," Bragg whispered as they descended the stairs.

If it came from Balen, it had to be serious. Anne barely nodded to the innkeeper on the way out.

Balen waited inside the carriage. Her feathers were ruffled, just a bit, just enough to suggest distress. "I hope you were able to conclude your business with your father."

"He and Elizabeth can manage, or at least if they apply themselves they can. What is so urgent at Kellynch?"

"The cluster has arrived at Kellynch, and are desperately in need of direction."

NOT ONLY HAD THE cluster arrived, but they had gathered inside the cellar under the manor house, or at least that was what Corn and Wall seemed like they were telling her when they met her outside the coach, twining around each other in a rapidly shifting knot like the garden wyrms did.

"Stop talking over one another and tell me again, one at a time, what has happened. Wall, you go first." Anne crouched near them, restraining the urge to separate them.

Corn harrumphed and curled into an angry little knot, face tucked under his black tail, only the tips of his white ears showing.

To his credit, Wall did not gloat, though he seemed immensely proud of himself as he launched into a detailed account of how Gravel and Pebble led the cluster onto Kellynch's territory, first asking directions to his lair. Since Kellynch was in the sea cave, Corn and Wall took it upon themselves to lead them there. Apparently, their meeting with Kellynch was amiable, if lacking in necessary details, which was the crux of the matter now.

It was never a good day when the tatzelwurmlings took matters into their own paws. One day they would have Laconia's good sense. One day.

Kellynch had not told them where they could establish their new lair, so naturally the wyrms had fixed on the most desirable location.

"...and that is why they are in the cellar right now. We have been able to keep them from digging new burrows there, but I do not know for how long we will be able to keep that up." A touch of desperation tinged Wall's voice.

"Did you see that several had already left the cellar?" Corn peeked up from his knot, blue eyes darting to and fro. "They did not say where they were going or what their errand was."

Balen paced behind the wyrmlings, like an irritated schoolmistress. "What was their mood when they left?"

"They seemed altogether pleased, I think. Not hostile, or even hungry, which is a very good thing, I should think." Corn unfurled and rose on his tail. "I cannot fathom what it will take to feed them. Have you and Kellynch given any thought as to what they will eat?"

"I am sure we do not have to worry about having sufficient food." Wall snapped. "Kellynch would not allow us to go hungry. I am certain he would not allow them to."

"I did not say he would, but I worry about those wyrms. You know how hungry they can be." Corn ran his paws over his ears, over and over again.

"I am more worried about their digging. Their tunnels—" Wall looked toward the house.

"Kellynch has taken all those issues into consideration and will be managing those issues with them." Balen tucked her head under her wing and shook it sharply. Sometimes the wyrmlings could be a bit much, even for her.

"But then, why are they in the cellar?" Corn asked.

It was a good question. "I suppose the only way to find out is to go talk to them, yes?" Anne picked up her skirts and hurried inside.

The housekeeper tried to say something as Anne walked in, but one glance at Anne and her dragon entourage and she stepped back out of the way, silent and sober. Sometimes knowing when to get out of the way was a crucial quality in household staff, especially when dragons were involved.

Candle in hand, Anne made her way down the creaky cellar steps, the noise of slithering and scraping and chattering growing louder with each step. The smell of the wyrms' musk combined with the damp, cool must of the cellar to create something not entirely unpleasant, oddly homey in a way. The sort of smell that belonged in a low-ceilinged space, lined with storage crates and barrels, with only a sliver of wan sunlight peeking in through high narrow frosted windows along the nearest wall, opposite to the tunnel entrance.

From behind her, Balen announced, "Lady Wentworth comes."

It seemed a bit of an overkill, but then again, the wyrms, unaccustomed to much warm-blood interaction, might do better with more formality.

The slithering sounds stilled as the candle's light touched the cellar floor. Maybe a dozen shaggy wryms, with rough-scaled bodies and leonine heads, gathered in pairs at the edge of the candlelight. There may have been more in the shadows beyond. Perhaps a letter to Lady Elizabeth was in order to help sort out exactly what sort of wryms they were.

Gravel and Pebble, twining together, moved forward as a unit, closer to Anne. "Lady Wentworth, Lady Wentworth. You are come to see us. Kellynch has welcomed us, now, he says, you must as well."

That made a great deal of sense, though it would have been nice to know that was the plan. That was probably Kellynch's not-so-subtle way of telling her she had not been sufficiently attentive to this matter.

One problem at a time.

"What do you require of a welcome?" Perhaps it was in poor form to ask, but unprepared, what else could she do? Offering them tea and biscuits was probably not appropriate.

"Kellynch said you would assign us a place." Gravel, mottled grey and brown and covered in dust, stretched out and laid his shaggy chin on the ground before her.

"Yes, a place like the old rock shed. A place where we are welcome to nest and sleep safe in the cold times." Pebble, darker brown and more slender than her mate, mimicked his posture.

How surprising. The wryms were entirely polite and proper. Not what one normally expected in a cluster of common wryms. Still, it would have been nice to have had time to prepare an answer.

"Would you like to make a request of the Lady?" Balen asked.

Bless her!

"Would the Lady hear our request?" Gravel peeked up toward Balen.

"Present your request, and she will hear you." Balen caught Anne's eye for a moment and Anne nodded.

Gravel and Pebble twined around each other, whispering nervously, their anxiety almost palpable. "We are asking a very large favor, we know. It is more than we have a right to. We know. There is a pile of stone at the far side of the barns."

"The pile of stones dug out when Kellynch's official lair was prepared." Balen said softly, her beak near Anne's shoulder.

"It is a very fine pile, a large one. It is a great deal to ask. That is why Kellynch said you should be consulted."

"I see." Kellynch was right. The site was a mite inconvenient with its proximity to the barns. Horses did not like wyrms.

Gravel rose high on his tail and glanced back at the cluster in the shadows. "But we know it is a great thing to ask, so we bring, we have brought, a gift to you that you might look favorably on our request."

"I am intrigued. What do you bring?" Unprecedented. Lady Elizabeth needed to know about this. To think wyrms—

Pebble slithered into the darkness and returned, dragging a leather-wrapped object. A suspiciously rectangular object. Was that...

"We offer you this, now. And, if you are well pleased, we promise more."

Balen strode past Anne, stepping over the wyrms with her long legs. She picked up the object by the leather wrapping and brought it to Anne.

Great heavens, it was a book! Balen took the candle from her and she unwrapped it, hands trembling.

"When the office burned, we were able to preserve some records. We can bring them all to you. If that will influence your favor about the lair." Gravel inched closer.

Balen twitched her head. Anne swallowed her first response. Too much enthusiasm in a negotiation was not a good thing. Anne opened the book midway through. "Let me examine the book."

Pendragon's Bones!

A detailed illustration of a serpent-whale, with a comprehensive description of an encounter with them in tiny script below.

Anne closed the book and took several slow, deep breaths. "These may be of some interest. Bring me all the books you possess. Then I will introduce you to Jonty Bragg, who handles all matters of the stable. You will come to an agreement with him as to how to share the land with the horses, then you may have the rockpile you have described."

"For how long?" Pebble asked.

"As long as you maintain your agreement, you may stay as long as Kellynch's charter is in force."

"We have many books. You will not be sorry!" Gravel's entire body quivered. "They will go now and bring them to this place. You take me and Pebble to this horse-man to talk now?"

"I will oversee the delivery of the items, if you wish." Balen said.

"Pray do so." Anne clutched the book to her chest. There would be many late nights ahead.

Chapter 13

November 14, 1815

Wentworth and Gillingham trudged down the inn stairs. Hopefully, no new guests had arrived and they would have the breakfast room to themselves. Perhaps it was selfish, but there were times when selfishness could be justified. Like when an unprovoked dragon attack ruined your week.

That would not be to say a provoked attack would be much of an improvement, but it would have been foreseeable, which definitely would have rendered the situation tolerable. At least somewhat.

The cold, narrow breakfast room, with its whitewashed walls and meager fire in the equally meager fireplace, was indeed empty of company. Whether that was from lack of visitors or the meanness of the space, it was difficult, and perhaps utterly moot, to tell.

A tray of toast, cheese, and cold meat occupied the center of an otherwise bare round wooden table, battered and scarred with wear. A handwritten note, written in scrawling penciled letters in awkward, childish handwriting, balanced atop the toast rack.

Hot water on the hob through the doors behind ye. Cook returns before supper. Call for the maid if you have need.

Well, that was unsettlingly convenient.

Wentworth tossed the paper aside and fell into the nearest chair. It wobbled and creaked under his weight. But it did not collapse, which was a material point in its favor. He let his head fall back and closed his eyes. Where to even begin today?

"I suppose this means I am left to make the coffee." Gillingham dragged his feet toward the kitchen.

"I've had men flogged for less complaining than that." Wentworth called over his shoulder. Actually, he had not, but Gillingham was getting on his nerves and whatever it took to put a bit of propriety in him would be worth it.

Given the look Gillingham just gave him, he might have at least a few hours of relief.

He raked his hair back with his hands. Really, Gillingham was not such a bad chap, but he lacked the natural discipline Wentworth expected in a junior officer. Perhaps that was not the correct way to view the young man. He was not precisely under Wentworth's command, but then again, he was not exactly his own man either.

Bah, this was not what Wentworth needed to be worried about right now.

"Mrrow." Laconia landed with a soft thud on the chair next to him. "If it is of any consolation, I agree."

"Agree with what?" Wentworth opened his eyes and slowly focused on the black tatzelwurm.

Laconia hunched low, whispering, "That man is just barely not an idiot."

Wentworth slapped a hand to his mouth to contain the laugh he should not express. "You are too kind."

"I know. We have served with worse, though. And you managed to shape them up."

"The ones that survived." No, that was definitely not what he wanted to think about—how many they had lost...

Gillingham dropped into the chair across from him in a haphazard sprawl. Everything about him seemed not quite finished, not quite polished, leaving Wentworth with the perpetual urge to straighten his coat and properly tie his cravat. "It will take a bit to brew up. Should be able to smell it when it's done."

Which was to say, it would be a bitter, unpleasant brew. But it was hardly as though the cook would do a better job with it. So, there was that.

"Good morning, Laconia. We missed you last night." Gillingham raked the hair back from his eyes. "Were you—"

Gillingham was about to say something stupid.

Laconia's upper lip pulled back to reveal the edge of his fangs. "Do not dare ask me if I slept well."

Gillingham raised open hands and leaned away from Laconia.

"I have been talking to every intelligent cold-blooded creature in a five-mile radius."

"Dragon's bones! Do you need a cup of coffee, too?" Was Gillingham being serious or flippant?

"What do you think?" Laconia snarled.

Gillingham sprang up and headed toward the kitchen.

"Tell me he found himself something useful to do yesterday after we located the trunks." Laconia licked his paw and ran it over his face.

"After he got over his amazement that the donkey should have the sense to run back to the docks," Wentworth did in fact roll his eyes, "he got the trunks back here and put his medical supplies to good use. It seemed the fairy dragon's tail injuries were more extensive than expected."

"Of course they were. Do you think a prey species like fairy dragons would be forthcoming with the extent of their dominant's injuries?" Laconia flicked his tail.

"Gillingham seemed surprised. There are moments when I wonder what he has been learning from Sir Edward. No criticism of the good physician, to be sure, but one would think the simple dynamics of dominance would be basic information in an apprenticeship such as his."

"There is nothing simple about the dynamics of dominance, and you know that." Such a glower Laconia offered.

"I suppose that is wishful thinking. At least he has established good relations with the local harem, and he's going to learn never to underestimate fairy dragons."

"If you can teach him that, I would say you have had great success. Too few understand that truth."

Gillingham sauntered in with a coffeepot in one hand and three—thank goodness he had that much sense—cups in the other. He filled them, handed them around, and fell back into his seat.

Laconia curled his serpentine tail around the cup twice, all but melting into the warmth. The chill of being out and about all night was probably difficult to break. Balancing both paws on the edge of the cup, he lapped at the dark, too-bitter brew. He wrinkled his nose, but continued to drink, little droplets of coffee spattering off his forked tongue.

"Not the worst you've had?" Gillingham asked, peering over the rim of his cup.

Wentworth sipped carefully. "Not the worst." Close, but not the worst.

"What is to be done about the dreadful to-do yesterday?" Gillingham started and stared at the window.

What? Wentworth looked over his shoulder.

A small drake peeked in the window, poked its head inside, and glanced around the open room.

"Mrrow. You may come." Laconia unfurled from the coffee cup to reveal his full length. It was only courteous to allow the visiting dragon to assess the size of the other dragon in the room.

"It is safe to enter." Wentworth stood and beckoned the dragon in.

The dirt brown dragon with darker brown spots scurried in, looking to and fro, far more like prey than predator for Wentworth's tastes. It was always a bad sign when a dragon acted like prey.

"I ... I have been sent from Cornwall Keep." The dragon stood on hind legs and did his best to look big. It was hardly an impressive sight.

"What message have you?" Wentworth flared his elbows and stared down at the messenger.

"The dug, Dug Cornwall requires your presence for an audience when the sun is at its highest." The dragon bobbed his head and looked around, twitching like a mouse before a cat.

"Has he indicated the reason for this audience?"

The drake's eyes widened, and a small hood behind his head lifted. "Not to me. I am not one to know such things. Only that you are required to come." He worried front paws together as though about to beg not to be required to deliver bad news.

"I understand. Are you to take a message from us in return?"

"I was not instructed to."

"Then you may go, your duty is done." Wentworth pointed at the window.

The drake scurried toward the window, then stopped and turned back to them, head cocked. "Are you going to attend the dug?"

"What business is it of yours?"

The drake's tattered hood flared, and he hissed—more reflex than threat, though. "I ... if ... the Dug will be displeased if his orders are not carried out."

"He takes that out on the messenger, then, I suppose?" Wentworth caught Laconia's eyes.

The tatzelwurm's long whiskers twitched, and he wrinkled his nose in a profound expression of disdain.

The messenger gulped and skittered back, talons leaving little scrapes on the worn wooden floor. "I have said nothing."

"Of course not. Gillingham, what do you say? Since meeting with Dug Cornwall is on our agenda, will noon do for you?"

Gillingham's eyes seemed ready to fall out of his head. "It seems a sound enough idea."

"I suppose we will work it into our plans, then." Wentworth turned his back on the messenger, who skittered on his toes and twitched.

Laconia growled. "What are you still doing here? Have you no other business to attend?"

The drake yipped, leapt through the window and away.

"Was that really necessary? To frighten the little creature so?" Gillingham raised his mug, though it did nothing to hide his disapproval.

Laconia's tail lashed, sliding his coffee cup halfway across the table. "It was a kindness to tell the creature that he did not have to worry for his life. And better that there would be no evidence to suggest there was any sympathy between us to cause Cornwall to become suspicious of his messenger and thus endanger his life another way."

"I had not thought of that." Gillingham fell back against his chair.

Poor sot was one of those unfortunate young men who did not know how much he did not know, nor how dangerous his ignorance could be. "Nothing is ever as simple and straightforward as you might hope with dragons. Always, always remember that, Gillingham.Which is why you must keep your mouth shut and leave all of the talking to me, with Cornwall. All of it. Do you understand?"

"But Kellynch—"

"Damnit!" Wentworth pounded his fist on the table. "Kellynch, for all his foibles, is a civilized dragon who, though he has been ill-used and offended, has avoided violating the tenets of the Accords at level the level Cornwall is treading upon. Kellynch is not a creature of privilege and power. He knows his place in England and in the Order. That makes him entirely different to Cornwall."

Laconia step-slithered across the table and pulled himself up tall in front of Gillingham. "What is the worst thing that has ever happened to you?"

"The worst thing? I don't know. I suppose it was when my father died, and I had to help my mother sort out how we would then live."

"That is a terrible thing, no doubt. I do not mean to belittle that." Perhaps he ought to tone down his ire a bit. "But as bad as that was, it did not leave you with an experience of the evil that one creature might inflict upon another. To be sure, I wish that on no one, but I fear it leaves you at a disadvantage to grasp the situation we are in now."

Gillingham averted his gaze and set his cup aside, shoulders slumping. "You do not think I should come with you to speak to Cornwall?"

"No, I do not. Kellynch displays his ill temper in words, and a great deal of splashing about. Cornwall, as evidenced by his messenger, will not hesitate to dispatch whomever displeases him."

Gillingham rubbed his hand over his mouth. "And yet you will go?"

"It is my duty. One for which I am slightly more prepared than you. You may follow me at a distance, but do not show yourself to Cornwall."

***

This was not the time for the Dragon Slayer, so it remained behind, locked in the false bottom of Wentworth's trunk at the inn. Walking into the situation better armed would have been Wentworth's preference, but it would have only escalated tensions unnecessarily. He would rather have had Laconia to walk with on the way to Cornwall, but it was better that Laconia make his own way there, to observe from some hidden vantage that Wentworth could not accidentally reveal. If things went badly, there was no one he trusted more to bring the truth back to the Order. To Anne.

At least Gillingham kept to himself as they walked. Perhaps he had been too harsh with him. But if it kept him alive, it would be worth it.

In the winter-denuded dragon woods, halfway to the Keep, Wentworth stopped. "Do you smell that, Gillingham?" A skeletal canopy of bare branches knit together over them, casting strange, lifeless shadows on the carpet of crunchy deadfall below.

"Dragon musk?" Gillingham sniffed the air. "Yes, now that you mention it."

Bloody hell and damnation! "Where is it coming from?" Wentworth closed ranks and turned back-to-back with Gillingham. Not that they had much with which to fight off another ambush.

"Grand Dug Matlock has sent us." A large, deep green drake emerged from the shadows, wearing a harness with the Blue Order's seal. He signaled into the underbrush and five more sizeable minor drakes, all wearing Order seals, came forth. Bulging muscles flexed beneath their oiled hides. Their eyes shone and fangs, which might have been artificially sharpened, glittered. These were not common minor dragons, but ones prepared as an elite team in the service of the Grand Dug Matlock.

Far better than the weapon Wentworth might have carried.

"You have been sent as witnesses, in the hopes that Cornwall will observe the dictates of the Accords?" Gillingham asked, sufficient awe in his voice to temper Wentworth's initial ire. Gillingham probably had never seen such impressive minor dragons.

"We have been sent to affirm that all proceeds as it should. If our presence facilitates that, then that is a positive outcome as well." The leading drake thumped his tail against the ground.

That was a dragon also trained as a diplomat.

"You will be taking word back to Matlock or to the Order as a whole?" Wentworth asked.

"Both."

"Then there is more news that you must bring them." Wentworth quickly related the news of the ambush.

A red-brown striped drake approached. Her bearing suggested she was the second most dominant dragon of the squadron. "Several fairy dragons approached us bearing that news."

"Did you believe them?" Wentworth asked.

"In these days, it does not behoove us to ignore their messages." The red-brown drake winced as though the admission hurt.

"Then I trust you will not mind that the local harem has been welcomed to discreetly observe all aspects of our stay at Land's End should they be so inclined."

The leading drake growled softly, his tail sweeping broad strokes through the dead leaves. "Understood, Sir Frederick."

That was to say, the drake did not approve, but he was a dragon who understood dominance and authority. Good enough.

"Cornwall expects me on the beach, just beyond his Keep, at noon. Whether or not he will be there at that time is another matter entirely." Wentworth glanced up through the canopy, searching for the sun that hid behind thin clouds.

"Our orders had been to make you aware of our presence, then be waiting there for you to stand witness over the proceedings. Given what you told me, we will accompany you to your audience," the leading drake said.

"As you will." Actually, it was a relief to know that Gillingham would not be left to himself to await the outcome or have to figure out what to do on his own if things went poorly.

Thankfully, the security team was no more talkative than Gillingham, allowing Wentworth to rehearse those items that needed to be communicated. Not that any of them would come out in the way he rehearsed them. They had a better chance at being muttered out, though, with his practice.

The woods ended at a rocky slope with a narrow path down toward the smell of salt water and the sounds of lapping waves. A sound he knew like the beating of his own heart, one that usually soothed and comforted him, but since the Battle of Lyme Bay, that had changed. Ominous now. Hinting at something with large teeth lurking in the dark unknown.

Blast it all. He had not realized that. Damn it all. He would think on that more. Later.

He waved Gillingham off where the trees stopped and the rocky hills leading down to the shore began. He might be able to listen from there, depending upon how loud Cornwall chose to be. He probably would not be able to see, which would disappoint him, to be sure. But that also meant he would not be seen, which was utterly necessary.

The Blue Order guard accompanied Wentworth all the way to the sandy shore, with waves licking up the beach with the rising tide. Probably what they had been commanded to do. At what risk, though? At least it was a risk they surely understood.

Finally, the rocks trailed off, and he was left on the sandy shore, staring into the ocean, a reasonably familiar situation. He was accustomed to watching for ships on the horizon.

Not dragons.

A knot tightened in the pit of his stomach. Like it had before the cannons fired and the air filled with smoke. He did his duty then, and he would do it now.

Dear God, somehow, he would do it now.

"He comes, he comes!" A yellow and black fairy dragon warbled from overhead, circling twice, then disappearing somewhere behind him.

At least he would not have to worry about reports of this encounter not reaching the Order.

Wentworth pulled his shoulders straight and drew a deep breath, glancing at the sturdy Blue Order guards to his right and left, who also made themselves as big as they could. In any other circumstance, he would be confident of the outcome flanked by such company.

A dark shape gathered beneath the water. Ripples fanned out from the center, deepening, growing until the tips of a series of spinal ridges cut through the water. A broad back followed, then the tips of horns.

Strange.

The sliver of fear sloughed away, like the water from the back of a breaching serpent-whale.

The approaching creature was so much smaller than Chesil. Yes, Cornwall was terrible, with fang and claws and fire, but compared to Chesil? A children's pony compared to a mighty draft horse. Wentworth chuckled under his breath.

The nearest Blue Order drake looked up at him, brow knotted. Surely, he thought Wentworth was going daft.

Maybe he was. A deep breath, and another. No more fear—he was angry! Bloody furious!

Yes, that was exactly what he needed. Damn it all! Now, he was ready to meet Cornwall. He tugged his jacket straighter and pulled back his shoulders.

And the miserable, arrogant lizard was going to take his sweet time in making an appearance. It should be intimidating, no doubt, but it was more irritating than anything else. Such a show of dominance he was putting on—it made him seem more insecure than indomitable.

Great Scott, he had definitely been around dragons too much. If he survived this, Anne would find this incredibly amusing.

If.

A huge, but still far-smaller-than-Chesil, head finally emerged, dripping. Cornwall rose from the waters, sea water sloughing off in streams from his outstretched wings. Was that meant to look mighty? A firedrake was all the wrong shape to be wet. He just looked silly.

"You came," Cornwall thundered, flapping his wings in long, powerful strokes that dragged the ocean's surface.

"As an emissary of the Blue Order and of Chesil." Wentworth stepped forward.

Cornwall roared, then laughed. "And that is supposed to impress me?"

"That is not my business. Chesil requires that you stop interfering in his territory. You are trespassing in his domain, and he insists that you stop. Grand Dug Matlock echoes the sentiment and insists that you—"

"What do I care for either of them?" Cornwall lumbered—lumbered!—toward the beach, like some farm animal caught at the edge of a muddy pond.

"Excuse me?"

"You heard me. What do I care for either of them? I am master of this territory. Me. It is mine, the land and whatever I can reach in the sea. It is my domain." Wings spread, Cornwall threw his head back and bugled.

"No. I am instructed to say, it is not."

"I do not care what your instructions are. As long as dragons have been, our territory is defined by what we can claim and defend. I claim the land and the sea. I can and will defend it against any who would try to take it from me."

"I am instructed to say that the Blue Order—"

"I am the next brenin, I am the Blue Order." Cornwall threw his head back and roared. Crescendos of dragon thunder rang off the rock faces and stirred the waves.

Could he possibly believe such a thing? "Chesil—"

"Who is Chesil to me?"

"The rightful dominant in the territory you are trying to claim."

Cornwall stopped mid-roar. "How dare you, little man." He clambered further up the sand and leaned into Wentworth's face, hot, stinking breath stinging Wentworth's cheeks. "How dare you. You think that because that blood-and-fire-damned Council ruled in favor of your mangy marine wyrm that you are anything, anything to me?" Green ichor dripped from his fang onto Wentworth's cravat.

Was that poison?

"I do not come on my own authority, but on that of those I have been called to represent."

The air filled with smoke. Bad, bad. very bad. The security team closed ranks around him. Lesser dragons would have fled.

"Who is this Chesil, and who does he think he is? What manner of creature is he?" Cornwall stirred the waters behind him with his tail.

"A sea drake. An exceedingly large and excessively angry sea drake."

"Has he legs that walk the land?" Cornwall slapped the ocean into a mighty splash.

"No." Technically, Chesil's feet were not well suited for walking.

"Has he wings to dominate the skies?" Cornwall's wings beat the air into a great wind.

"No, he does not."

"Has he fire to decimate his enemies?" Cornwall spewed a jet of flame into the air above him.

The blistering heat slapped Wentworth's face. His eyes watered. Dragon fire was as impressive as the texts said it could be.

And highly illegal under the circumstances.

To their credit, Matlock's team barely flinched, but ears flicked and tails twitched.

"No, he does not."

Cornwall roared again. "Then what is he to me?"

"Chesil is the dominant dragon of the territory you are trespassing upon. He will defend his territory—"

"Let. Him. Try." Cornwall huffed acrid breath in Wentworth's face.

Wentworth blinked rapidly against the eye-watering acid. "Is that the message which you would have me take to him?"

"And this." Cornwall crouched down, pulling his head back.

No, he didn't dare!

But this was not a time to bet on a dragon's restraint. Wentworth whirled on his heel and fled, sand flying at his pounding steps. The Blue Order team kept pace with him.

Nearly at the rocks. Behind them—cover against…

Cornwall roared—was it possible to feel the sound buffeting his back? A choking cloud of gas, sulfur, rotten eggs, enveloped him, burning his face, his eyes, his lungs.

The security team leapt as only dragons could, behind the rocks.

Still too far to take shelter.

Another roar. Blistering heat against his back. No air.

Need to breathe.

The sand slipped from beneath his feet. Darkness closed over him.

Chapter 14

November 15, 1815

Anne closed her eyes and pressed them with her thumb and forefinger. At this pace, she would need glasses by year's end. Father would no doubt criticize her for it—dreadfully common for a woman to wear glasses, he would say. And Elizabeth—shudder to think what inane words would drop from her mouth. Pray they were not still lurking about Lyme by year's end.

Yes, it was uncharitable to think that way, maybe even unkind. But it was true and pretending that it was not only magnified the frustration.

She would have to return to them today and inevitably listen to why every house that Mr. Harville presented to them was insufficient. No, that was not fair. They had not said that, not yet. But they would, and she would have to argue with them over each complaint, many times, to get them to condescend to accept something.

Dragon's bones! The game had gotten old!

She leaned back in her chair and stared at her office ceiling. The ornate plaster ceiling rose, a symbol of a place to speak plainly, without repercussion. Her thoughts were certainly doing that today. Closing her eyes, she pressed into the soft upholstery. Balen had been right. She did need a comfortable chair in this space. It made these thoughts slightly less awful.

Perhaps Wentworth had a point. It was time to be done with them. It seemed so wrong, though, to abandon her family, but, on the other hand, all things considered, what did she really owe them?

She opened her eyes again and blinked the blurriness back. Mr. Harville's draft of the new charter, neatly arranged on her desk, slowly came into focus. Yes, all the new provisions seemed correct, it only needed to be signed. And for that, she needed Mr. Wynn. Such another joyful soul in her life that—if she had her way right now—she could do without.

Heavens, it felt like far too many people in her world were finding a place on that list right now. She really should not permit Kellynch's grumpiness to so influence her own mood.

A face tapped at Anne's window—Jasper. How did such a lovely, even-tempered dragon become friends with such a curmudgeon as Wynn? Perhaps that was a question better not asked. Anne opened the window and leaned out into the crisp morning air. "Is Mr. Wynn available?"

"It was a good idea to give him a day to recover from his travels. He is in a much better humor this morning. I told him of your need, and he will receive you," Jasper said.

Oh, how very good of him to deign to do his job. Anne bit her tongue. Jasper probably had little understanding of exactly how condescending that all sounded. "Tell him I will be at the cottage soon."

"Yes, Lady Wentworth." Jasper bobbed her head and scurried off. She might have stayed to chat a bit. She so often did. But minor dragons tended to be perceptive and made themselves scarce when dominant creatures were cranky.

Heavens, was she becoming like Kellynch?

Anne glanced back at the imposing stack of books and writings on her desk. The wyrms were anxious to curry her favor and brought far more volumes than she ever imagined they would have had. The Order owed them a debt for simply acting to save the documents, whether or not they were valuable. Once she got through the stack, the debt would probably be far greater. Some of those texts looked important. The challenge would be convincing the Order to show gratitude to such 'lowly dragons' who 'should be grateful for any notice at all' as Mr. Wynn put it.

One thing at a time. She slid the charter into a portfolio and resigned herself to a conversation with Mr. Wynn.

It was probably a good thing that the walk to the cottage was brief. Less opportunity to become distracted by the fine crisp weather and other errands she could be managing instead of this one—the Widow Martin was due a visit, after all. Less time in which to change her mind and find something else productive to do.

Mrs. Frankel's warm welcome helped, as it always did. A plate of clear cakes and a cup of fresh tea in the front room, and conversation with a sensible woman, always improved one's mood.

After a quarter of an hour, Mr. Wynn strode in, a vague look of annoyance in his eyes. Sunlight glinted off his bald pate, highlighting the scar on the left side of his head in stark relief.

How dare he!

"Lady Wentworth, I understand you wish to see me." He looked as though he was picking a chair to sit in the front room with her.

"Yes, a great deal has come to light while you have been away in Bath. However, these are serious Order matters which should be discussed in your office." Anne stood and headed for his office.

Mrs. Frankel pressed her hand to her mouth and turned her face aside.

He sputtered and stammered, but followed. Sometimes he was too much like her father. Too comfortable looking down his nose at others and treating them as secondary to his own concerns. She had played that game with him for too long and today, it was simply too much to ask.

Mr. Wynn closed the door behind her and stalked toward his desk. "I understand that the matter with your father must be vexing to you, but—"

Anne made herself tall and pulled her shoulders back as she turned ever so slowly to face him. "Do not presume to understand the business which I bring today and do not presume to devalue the importance of my concerns."

"Do calm down, Lady Wentworth." He sat, wearing that affected, placating look that declared anything she said would be summarily ignored.

"Do not tell me to calm down, Mr. Wynn. I am in good regulation of myself and I do not need you to intervene in such personal matters." She slapped her hands on his desk and leaned toward him, over him. "I would suggest, for just a moment, sir, that you forget you are dealing with a mere woman, and consider me as you would a dragon. An impatient, annoyed dragon." She did not bare her teeth, but it might have been a good idea.

He pulled back, startled, and skidded his chair back from the desk. The scars along the left side of his head pulsed. "If you wish. Keeper."

Keeper. That was better, much better.

"Should I expect that the presence of Sir Walter and his daughter in Lyme is not an issue, then?" There was that bloody smug look creeping across his face again.

"It is not my primary concern at the moment." She sat down and slapped the portfolio on the desk. "When were you going to tell me about the boxes of books appearing at your doorstep?"

"Books? Doorstep?" His brow wrinkled, and he looked up at the ceiling. "Ah, yes, that. I recall now—"

"You only recall now? When they had been appearing for days before you left for Bath?" She jumped to her feet and slapped the desk again; there was no point in sitting.

"I really do not understand why this is a matter for your concern." Superior, condescending, shallow-pated little man.

"Sir, it seems you have forgotten. I am Special Liaison to the Order for the Dorset-Somerset region. What does that mean to you?"

His gaping jaw and lack of response suggested he barely stopped himself from saying 'not very much at all.' His eyes still conveyed the message.

"You appear in need of a reminder. I am tasked with identifying anything unusual in this region. Anything unusual. Does it not occur to you that mysteriously appearing boxes of documents are a mite unusual?"

He sputtered and flushed, his face well on its way to a pronounced shade of puce.

"I will save you the bother of answering. Yes, it is unusual. Yes, I should have been made aware. And yes, those items are important." Oh, if only she could kick the desk to punctuate her point.

"You have reviewed all the documents?" The emphasis he placed on 'all' ... he was well aware of the volume of material that had been delivered to the office and still had not mentioned it?

"Not yet. And certainly, there are a great number of items that are mundane. But that is not the point. You are actively hindering me in accomplishing my duty to the Order. How can you justify such behavior?"

"I understand you are worried about your husband and your nerves—"

"Do not presume to talk to me about my nerves!" Hands on hips, she flared elbows. "My nerves are my business and mine alone. Your concern is the business of the Order, which you are actively hampering." And she growled.

Definitely too much time in Kellynch's company.

Or not.

"What ... what do you want?"

"I need to be kept informed of such unusual occurrences. I need full access to the newly discovered documents. And I need you to approve and file this." She pulled the charter from the portfolio and slammed it on the desk.

He gawked at her, then glanced at the paper on the desk, then back to her, as though afraid to take his eyes off the predator in the room.

An improvement.

Oh, so gingerly, Mr. Wynn picked up the paper with thumb and forefinger, and read it. Twice. He swallowed hard. "I would like to help you, Lady Wentworth—"

"But what? Is there a problem with the charter?"

"Not the document *per se*." He laid it on the desk and smoothed it with his fingertips.

"Then what?"

"The charter, it clearly states that Kellynch has two Keepers. Consequently, for there to be any change in the charter, the Order legally requires that both Keepers must sign the document."

"And considering that is impossible?"

"Then I am sorry, I cannot help you."

Cypher popped up from between the bookcases. "There is something you can do."

Mr. Wynn had definitely made a mistake not checking for minor dragons before they began. Oh, the talk that was going to fly! Anne's cheeks prickled and burned. Nothing to be done for it now.

Mr. Wynn's eyes narrowed, and he glowered at Cypher. One hand flexed into a tight knot.

"Pray explain, Cypher." Anne beckoned the dusky red drake toward the desk, the script-looking markings on her hide rippling as she scurried.

"Do tell me." Mr. Wynn folded his arms across his desk and leaned toward Cypher. The scar on the side of his head pulsed, just enough to be noticed.

Bully. Anne rose on her toes and looked down her nose at him.

Cypher glanced from him to Anne, her posture gaining confidence as Anne nodded. "As Regional Undersecretary you have the authority to sign as a Keeper's proxy when the Keeper is unavailable."

"And how am I to know that these changes are agreeable to the other Keeper? They are significant and will require fundamental shifts in the management of the Keep." Mr. Wynn drummed his fingers along the edge of the charter.

Anne drew a deep, chest-filling breath. "Of what are you accusing me?" Her deep, booming question reverberated off the walls.

Officer voice. That she had learned from Wentworth.

"Nothing, to be sure, Lady Wentworth. But proper protocol and procedure demands—"

"There is nothing proper, normal, or expected about the situation we are in. You will sign the proxy or you will go personally to Kellynch's sea cave and explain to him why you have not."

Mr. Wynn started and blanched. "I cannot get to that sea cave."

"You do not want Kellynch visiting you here, sir. I assure you, you do not. But I cannot stop him if you refuse to handle this matter appropriately—"

Balen swooped into the window, landing on the desk, spreading her wings wide. Interesting technique, one Anne would have to remember for the future. "Forgive my interruption, but I have urgent news, for both of you."

"It seems to be a day for all things urgent and unusual." The edge of Mr. Wynn's lips curled back.

"Kellynch requires your presence immediately, Undersecretary." Balen glowered at him. "In the sea cave. He has asked me to offer you my assistance in getting there."

Anne held her breath and pressed her lips hard. Had Balen been eavesdropping, or was that really a well-timed demand from Kellynch? Or both.

"Tell him I can meet him in the official lair provided by the Order." Mr. Wynn had the audacity to roll his eyes.

"I told him you would say that. But, with all due respect, I would strongly recommend you do not push that demand. He is in a disagreeable mood as it is and has been talking about filing official complaints—"

Mr. Wynn pinched the bridge of his nose. "Will you ask Kellynch's favor to meet in the lair as a concession to my warm-blood frailties." That admission cost him dearly.

"Under those circumstances, I think he may be amenable." Balen turned to Anne, careful not to step on the charter document. "There is an immediate issue demanding your attention at the house, Lady Wentworth."

How entirely convenient. It could hardly be an issue she less wanted to deal with than Mr. Wynn, though. "I shall leave you to sign and approve the charter, then. Yes?"

Mr. Wynn growled under his breath.

Good enough.

Anne marched from the office and waved at Mrs. Frankel on the way to the door. A cold wind slapped her face. Refreshing, bracing. Precisely what she needed to reorder her thoughts. She paused and turned to Balen. "Dare I ask?"

"What is the worst thing you can imagine—not involving Sir Frederick?" Balen scratched at the bare ground.

"My father at the manor house."

Balen resettled her wings across her back and bobbed her head. "It is not that."

Anne swallowed hard.

"It is your sister."

Bloody dragon bones!

***

Anne all but ran to the house and entered through the kitchen door, listening carefully for Elizabeth's shrill voice. There was no shouting, at least for the moment. That was positive.

The housekeeper approached, looking far more harried than the cluster of wyrms in the cellar had left her. "In the front parlor, Lady Wentworth. She came to the door. I could not keep her out. I have never seen such a thing."

That described Elizabeth.

"I well understand. I will deal with it." It could hardly be worse than dealing with Wynn, now, could it?

She stormed to the parlor, Balen at her side. "What can I do?" Balen asked.

"I suppose it would be ill-mannered to ask you to pretend to be a pet bird and to bite her." Anne gasped and pressed her hand to her mouth. "I am sorry, pray forgive me. I do not know what came over me."

Balen hiccupped a soft, squawky laugh. "If I thought it would help, I would be willing. Perhaps I should stand outside, in case the opportunity arises."

Bless her! A dragon with a sense of humor.

"I would be happy for that." Anne gulped in a deep breath. Now was the time to remember that she, not Elizabeth, was mistress of this house and had the right to declare how things were to be. She smoothed her skirt and strode in.

Elizabeth stood at the window overlooking the sad little winter garden. "Your housekeeper said you were not at home." She sniffed and did not turn to face Anne.

"I was not. Someone was sent to fetch me. You have disrupted my business." Anne stopped three steps into the room.

Elizabeth turned slowly, as though the action cost her dearly. "What could you possibly be doing of such importance that you cannot receive callers?"

"Why are you here? Do you not understand that the terms of your stipend mean you cannot be here?"

Fire flashed in Elizabeth's eyes. "What sort of requirement is that? It makes no sense. You are making things up." She stepped forward, not quite stomping. "I do not comprehend how you have convinced Father to believe such a thing, but I know better. Why are you so spiteful?"

Oh, the temptation to answer that honestly. It would be impossible to honestly claim she felt no spite. She fought it regularly, and strenuously. Not always winning the effort, but often enough that she had not lost her courage to continue. "Why have you come, Elizabeth?"

"Can you not guess? Every one of those houses you tried to foist on us is utterly unacceptable. I cannot believe you would even consider condemning us to live in such places." Such hand-waving and expressions of offense and oppression.

"You expect me to ask what is wrong with them? Well, I am not going to do that. I am tired of hearing you complain, tired of your endless entitlement and ignorance of your own faults. You are not a stupid person, or at least I have not considered you so." Maybe not entirely true, but still… "Stubborn and willfully ignorant, yes, but not stupid. Why must you carry on so and try to convince me otherwise?"

Elizabeth pressed the back of her hand to her forehead, as though she might swoon. Best she did not continue along that path, as Anne would not be there to catch her. "How dare you speak to me in such a fashion. I am the one who has been injured. Injured by you and Mary being allowed to marry before me. Injured by our loss of Kellynch. Injured by your selfish unwillingness to take us in at Kellynch-by-the-Sea as you should. How can you not see that?"

"And how can you not see the connections between your selfish demands and your current state? Even you can do simple maths. You spend too much and are in debt. That is the core of your problems. If you were to practice economy—"

"A baronet—"

"Do not dare say 'must be seen to live as a baronet.' That is exactly the notion that got you to this place."

"I have half a mind to give you a good shake for speaking to me that way!" Elizabeth stepped closer. This was not the first time she had said such a thing, and she clearly did not mean it more now that she did the last time.

"Mrrrow!" Wall leapt from the shadows, green eyes shining.

"Rrrrow!" Corn followed closely, white eats twitching.

"Gracious merciful heavens, what is ...are those?" Elizabeth staggered back, grabbing for something to support her, but found nothing. She flailed as she struggled to regain her balance.

"Kittens, two large, playful kittens." Anne said through gritted teeth.

Yes, we are kittens, Wall insisted, his persuasive voice rasping Anne's ears.

Everyone loves adorable kittens, Corn added.

Elizabeth screamed and covered her ears, collapsing into a quivering puddle on the floor. "They are not kittens! Horrible monsters! Snakes! Get them away from me!"

Chapter 15

NOVEMBER 16, 1815

Dear God in heaven, it hurt to breathe! Wentworth rolled to his side and gasped for breath, only dragging in enough air to cough.

Spasms seized him, rocked him, fit to turn him inside out, shaking him so hard not a single breath stayed long enough to nourish his lungs. Not a single thought stayed in his mind. Thick, viscous clods came up. Bitter, sour slime coated his tongue.

He spat and spat and spat, wet splotches that he could not have controlled if he tried.

Another breath dragged over lungs as rough as the rocky shore, but lingered in his chest without protest.

Gulping air like a drowning man now, he pushed back. One breath. Another. He really could breathe again. Even if it felt like his chest was being torn open with each gasp.

A hand on his shoulder. "Can you drink this?"

He forced his eyes open. Gillingham stood at his shoulder, worse for the wear, a pewter cup in his hand.

Quiet, so quiet? Where were the waves, the wind? Where was the beach?

Wentworth blinked the fuzz from his eyes. Grit raked across his eyeballs, scouring tears to the surface that leaked down his face. He dragged them away with his sleeve. The shabby inn's room wobbled into focus. "How? What?" he croaked, reaching for the cup.

Water sloshed down his arm, splashing against his chest. Damn, that was his hand shaking.

Gillingham wrapped Wentworth's fingers around the cup, covering them with his own, and lifted it to Wentworth's lips.

Water.

Cool and liquid. Had there ever been such a glorious substance? He hunched over the cup and poured it into his mouth, spilling over his face and neck.

"Slow down, there is more, plenty more. Don't drown yourself in it." Gillingham eased the cup out of his hands.

The shaking moved up his arms, to his shoulders, then his entire body quaked so hard he nearly fell off the ... bed. Yes, he was sitting in bed.

"Lie down now, before you do yourself another injury. The fit will pass. They have been growing shorter each time. This one should be barely noticeable."

Perhaps not noticeable to Gillingham.

But he was right. The uncontrolled tremors faded, and the room finally settled into proper focus. Candles lit the meager chamber against the darkness outside the window. Shadows that made Wentworth twitch and his heart race danced along the walls, reaching for the ceiling and halfway across the floor.

"How long?" Was that really Wentworth's own voice?

Gillingham pulled something from his pocket and squinted. "It's been a while. It's a bit before dawn now, so maybe sixteen hours?"

"How ... how did I get here?"

"That is a story for another time, but the Blue Order security team is largely to thank for it."

Wentworth pushed himself up to sit. His shoulders burned underneath a dressing he only now noticed. "What happened?"

"It is difficult to say, precisely. My vantage point did not give me the best view." Gillingham slicked back his hair. "Not that I am unthankful for your precautions. The situation would have been far more ... challenging... if we had both been caught in Cornwall's demonstration."

Laconia hopped to the bed and pressed against Wentworth's leg. "Challenging is not the word I would use for that disgraceful scene."

Laconia's purrs rumbled through Wentworth's chest. Was it his imagination that it was easier to breathe now? "It was Cornwall then, yes? The last thing I remember was running and the smell of rotten eggs."

"You are quite the runner, you know. I have never seen a man of your size achieve that much speed in so short a distance. And it is a bloody good thing you are." Gillingham pulled a lopsided chair near and sat down backward, bracing his arms over the back of the chair. He raked his hands through his hair. "Bloody hell, I have never seen anything like it, and I hope I never do again."

"What happened?"

Laconia growled deep in his furry chest, his entire body vibrating with the sound.

"Cornwall—I can't believe ... he violated every statute of the Order. You were no threat to him, completely unarmed. Not even your words could have been considered a threat."

"If you think that, you are a fool!" Laconia hissed and spat. "Anything which challenges a major dragon will be construed as a threat."

Wentworth scratched behind Laconia's ears. "It would not be the first time a messenger bore the brunt of the message delivered."

"Cornwall had just spewed fire into the air. The Blue Order team started running, and you followed. They reached the rocks before you did—I suppose four legs give them an advantage in speed. Cornwall belched gas of some sort, then flame at all of you. I still cannot believe it." Gillingham covered his face with his hands and shook his head. "We have so little record of firedrakes using their flame. I have seen nothing about the gas that came first. I am certain it was more than a by-product of the flames. There was poison in it, for which I have been treating you, and several dragons of the team who were similarly overcome—"

Wentworth ground the heels of his hands into his temples. "Where? The dragons, where?"

"The innkeeper has given us the use of a shed behind the inn. I have good hope for their recovery. But they are to a man, rather to a dragon, badly shaken."

"They are not the only ones." Laconia's tail lashed.

"I think you were overcome by the poison, that is why you fell. The bump on your head was a fair price for being out of the line of fire. The flame that followed might have killed you if you had been upright. As it was, you were on the ground and the barest edge of it caught the top of your shoulders."

"If that was what the edge of it did," Wentworth shuddered. "You're right, I would not have survived. Water?"

Gillingham filled the cup from a dented pewter pitcher and pressed it into Wentworth's unsteady hands.

This time, Wentworth managed to drink alone. "I hate fire." God, he hated fire. The greatest danger at sea came from the very force they could not do without. He handed the cup back to Gillingham and covered his face with his hands.

Laconia curled into his lap and pressed against his chest, purring again. He had lived those nightmares, too.

"I have heard tales." Gillingham filled the cup again and set it aside. "But I know I can never truly understand."

No, he could not and there was no point in trying to make him. Wentworth closed his eyes and drew several deep breaths. "The poison?"

"Similar to several other dragon poisons. You can thank Kellynch's foresight in insisting that the kit we packed contain remedies for those."

"He was involved in that?" Had Anne asked for his help?

"As a matter of fact, he insisted that his input was necessary, and he was right. He is going to be enraged at the injustice done here."

"We do not need more angry dragons. Cownt Matlock's ire is going to be enough." Ire was putting it mildly, for certain. Hopefully, he would not take it out on the messenger, too. He was supposed to be above such things. Supposed to be.

"When is he supposed to arrive?" Gillingham stroked his jaw and scratched the back of his neck.

"Soon. I do not know. But I'm sure it will be soon."

"Then finish this water and lie down. Sleep if you can. You will need it to face the Cownt."

Gillingham was not wrong, and even if he was, Wentworth was too worn to argue.

*** November 17, 1815

Wentworth slept all day and into the next morning, only to be awakened by Matlock's messenger.

The look on the cockatrice's face suggested that the tale of Cornwall's temper had already reached Matlock. No doubt by fairy dragon. That was one conversation Wentworth was glad to have missed. But such a courageous fairy dragon to bear such news to a cownt. Sounded a bit like a fairy story for children. *The very brave fairy dragon.*

"The cownt requires your presence, Sir Frederick." The cockatrice shifted his weight from right to left and back. "He is waiting in a cliffside cave, technically outside the boundaries of Cornwall's Keep. You are to attend him, as soon as you are able."

That time proved to be mid-afternoon. It might have been an hour sooner had Wentworth been able to drive the images of Cornwall and his fire from his mind a bit more effectively.

Those of the Blue Order security team who were still able accompanied him to the cave, all humbled and flying at half-staff from the ignominy of their defeat before Cornwall. Yes, it was ridiculous to be ashamed of their fall before Cornwall's greatest weapon, but even small dragons had their pride.

The cave Matlock had chosen was tucked into the hillside, well-shielded by a thick dragon wood, at least a mile from the shore. Old hardwoods arched overhead, winter-bare branches intertwining into a sparse canopy around the cavern. Thick overgrowth tumbled over the hill, obscuring the entrance, which seemed too small to accommodate a dragon of Matlock's grandeur. Like a king forced into sheltering in discreet accommodations in preparation for battle.

The leader of the security team took it upon himself to announce their arrival to Matlock. He scurried to the mouth of the cave, prostrated himself on the dirt, and called out.

The ground beneath Wentworth's feet quaked. The cownt approached, and he was none too happy. He was capable of walking without thundering when it suited him.

Wentworth willed his own feet in place. Matlock might be cranky, but he would adhere to the tenets of the Order no matter how vexed he might be.

He would.

Wentworth would believe that. He had to. If Matlock failed him, then all would be lost.

Matlock lumbered out from the clearly too-small cave, ducking and pulling in his magnificent wings as he came into the dappled afternoon light. His blue-green hide bore a coating of dust, no doubt from the long journey through the dragon tunnels. With his brow drawn low, and his neck drawn back, none could mistake his temper. Even his breath was low and throaty, just short of growling.

Wentworth offered the proper bow, slowly, painfully, accepting the aid of a security dragon's shoulder to finally get to his feet.

"So, it is true." Matlock's voice rumbled through Wentworth's bones.

"A fairy dragon brought you the news?" Wentworth glanced up. Though he could not see them, the fairy dragons were probably there.

"They can be useful little flutterbits at times." High praise coming from Matlock. "Useful, but stupid. I would hear the full account from you."

"Cownt Matlock," the security team leader prostrated himself before the cownt. "Sir Frederick has been injured in your service and would be better able to carry out your direction if permitted to sit."

Unfortunately, he was right.

Matlock grumbled and slapped the ground with his tail. "So be it."

Two drakes hurried to bring a fallen log to Wentworth. He trembled as he lowered himself onto it. How correct the little dragons were. He had not even realized how ill-prepared he was to simply stand.

Damn it all, that was not a condition in which a wise man presented himself to a major dragon. But it was the only condition he could offer at the moment. Good thing the minor dragons with him were on the alert—probably felt as though they had failed him as much as their cownt.

Would have to deal with that later.

"When we arrived at Land's End, we were informed that we were not welcome at the Keep, and so have taken residence in a local inn." Wentworth then detailed the ambush in the thicket.

As he spoke, tendrils of smoke drifted from Matlock's nostrils. Two of the security team edged in close, shoulder to shoulder with him as if they could hear his thundering heart. They were not running, even though he could feel the tremor in their hard, muscular shoulders.

But they were not running. They had run from Cornwall, but not now. He trusted their reactions then. He should do so now.

"Minor dragons accosted you?" Matlock stomped, rattling the trees.

The cownt did not need to shout. Wentworth forced his eyes out of their squint. "The fairy dragons can bear witness to the event, if you wish. Though I suspect they already told you of that as well."

"A warm-blood, a member of the Order, one of the Pendragon Knights, was threatened by a band of minor dragon? I will have their hides."

No doubt he meant that quite literally.

Matlock's tail slammed against the cave opening, sending down a shower of dirt and rocks. "This is Cornwall's doing. What of your meeting with him?"

Wentworth hesitated. With Matlock already angry, the thought of increasing his ire was, at best, unpalatable.

"Speak, warm-blood. Your injuries are obvious, your silence does not hide them."

No, there was no hiding them, even though they marked him as vulnerable. Still, he needed to decrease his appearance as prey. He forced himself to his feet. "Cornwall refused the behest of the Order, and that of Chesil. As the future brenin, he declared himself above the rule of the Order. And he used his flame to make his point."

Matlock pawed the ground, leaving great gouges with his glistening black talons. "You brought no weapon?"

"None. And spoke nothing that I had not been directed to speak."

Matlock pressed his mouth tightly shut and paced a circle around Wentworth and the security team, smoke pouring from his nostrils.

Wentworth choked and coughed on the smoke.

Matlock whirled on him, red rims surrounding his dark, wild eyes.

The security dragons pressed Wentworth tightly, preventing him from moving. No, not holding him for Matlock's wrath, but keeping him from running and triggering a prey instinct that a raging dragon might not be able to control.

Matlock stalked three steps away and turned his back on Wentworth. He sneezed seven times, each one forceful enough to rattle the surrounding branches and shower them with dead leaves as smoke billowed around him. He beat his wings and cleared the residual smoke from the air, then turned back to Wentworth. "Cornwall has crossed the line." He spoke each word as a decree.

Of course, Cornwall had, attacking a warm-blood … Pendragon's bones! That was not what Matlock meant.

"Cornwall has issued a challenge that he will regret."

Chapter 16

NOVEMBER 17, 1815

Anne closed the guest room door. It had taken a cup of very strong poppy tea, but finally Elizabeth was resting quietly once again. Perhaps this time when she awakened, she would not be hysterical, like the last several times.

Anne leaned heavily against the wall outside the door, resisting the urge to slide down into a quivering little heap on the floor. How could this have happened? No one in the history of the Order had come into their hearing after thirty. Anne herself had been considered an oddity, hearing so late, but this? Unprecedented.

Unprecedented and inconvenient.

Anne slid down the wall to the floor.

Corn and Wall had strict orders to stay out of view, which, at first, they had been reluctant to obey, but finally Elizabeth's screams became unamusing and they slinked off to find other entertainment.

Balen needed no such instruction. She was off asking Mrs. Frankel if she had any more dried poppy or knew where they might obtain some, in case Elizabeth's histrionics did not abate. In which case, Balen offered to push her off a cliff into Lyme Bay and let Chesil deal with her. Balen had only slightly less patience for these tantrums than Anne did.

But the unseemly displays were really not the problem. No, not at all. If that were all it was, Anne might be tempted to give up and join Elizabeth's outburst herself. Who knew? It might be cathartic. That would do nothing to address the crux of the matter, though. What was she to do now that Elizabeth heard dragons?

Lady Russell had been there to ease Anne's transition and help her learn the new world around her. Incomplete and biased though it was, it helped. Elizabeth had no such assistant. Father was certainly incapable of being useful in such a case, and Anne could no. Would not. So many reasons why she dare not.

And chances were that Mr. Wynn would hardly be more helpful, but he was the only resource Anne had, so she would do her best with what was available. She climbed back up the wall, shook out her skirts, and headed downstairs and out to the Blue Order office.

This time Mrs. Frankel led her back to the compact office, where Mr. Wynn waited behind his imposing, cluttered desk. He rose politely as she entered. Whatever had gotten into him?

"Welcome, Lady Wentworth. Pray forgive me if I am too forward, but is what Jasper has told me true?" His voice was level, but the scar on the side of his head seemed flushed and ready to pulse.

"If she has brought you news of my sister, I am afraid so. It was most unexpected. I can usually tell when one is about to come into their hearing, but Elizabeth gave me no such signs."

"She is, after all, quite old for this to happen." He spoke 'old' as though it were some curse.

"I know of no records of such a thing occurring. But here we are. We can pursue the academic aspects of the matter later. It is the practical issues that concern me." Anne pulled a plain wooden chair closer to the desk and sat down.

"Indeed. This is something that should come under the Dragon Sage's jurisdiction." Mr. Wynn's forehead knotted and his scar pulsed.

"It seems you think that more complex than sending a courier to Pemberley with a message for her."

"I sent such a message almost as soon as Jasper brought me her report on the matter." Mr. Wynn pressed his lips together and looked away.

"You did?" How surprising—and how exactly did she feel about that? Was he overstepping his authority or was that what he was supposed to do? Hard to know.

"It seemed the sort of thing we needed to get ahead of as much as possible. Unfortunately—"

Anne cringed, a chill snaking down her spine.

"The Dragon Sage is indisposed and will not be able to consider the matter for some time." He refused to meet her gaze.

"She is in her confinement?" That made sense, but that alone did not seem enough to keep Lady Elizabeth from attending to correspondence. The opposite, in fact. She was such an active person, she would turn to correspondence and study to keep from running mad from the boredom of it all.

"Yes." He bit his lip and sighed. "As I understand, it has been rather complicated."

'Complicated' was not the word one wanted in the discussion of a confinement. "That does not sound positive."

"The message did not go into detail. It was not even written, only a verbal report relayed by the courier that her lying-in had not a favorable outcome. The Sage lives, or at least was living at the time of the courier's encounter, but we have no further detail than that." Color faded from Mr. Wynn's scar.

Dragon's fire! What could have happened? Not a favorable outcome seemed mild, ordinary words for something that must surely be heart-breaking, devastating, whatever it might be. Anne struggled to breathe. This, on top of Wentworth—no, all her resources had been focused on holding on through that. Now this for her friend?

"Lady Wentworth?" Mr. Wynn leaned forward, as though genuinely concerned.

"Forgive me. This was ... unexpected."

"Unexpected on top of the unexpected, indeed. We are facing very uncertain times. There could hardly be a worse time for something to befall the Dragon Sage." Had he truly just said that? He had never seemed sympathetic toward Lady Elizabeth.

"I suppose," she drew in a deep breath that should have been calming, but hardly achieved that goal, "until we know more, all we can do is manage as best we can without her wisdom. The current situation will not improve on its own."

"You are quite correct, Lady Wentworth. Quite correct. We must focus on the situation at hand." He tapped his desk and shuffled a few papers as though sorting the ideas in his mind. "As I understand, your sister still has not come to terms with her new perspective on the world."

"That would be a polite way of describing it. But I am hopeful that will change within a few days."

"That would be the normal expectation, but we must be prepared for a different trajectory. Even the possibility that her hearing was a momentary affliction and can be passed off as the reaction to bad fish or some such. Worse, she may never make peace with the new world she is a part of and it may be necessary to consign her to—"

"Bedlam?"

"It is an unpleasant and extreme possibility, and probably one we should not expect, but it still is possible."

"It is a wholly shocking experience." To put it in the politest possible terms.

"One which you weathered effectively, as I recall." Was that a compliment? From Wynn's lips? "Are you able to serve as a sponsor for Miss Elliot?"

"No. Kellynch has made it quite clear he will tolerate neither of them on the estate."

"But she is here, now."

"And after we are finished here, I will be on my way to Kellynch to discuss the matter with him. I expect a spectacular show of temper. I imagine that the circumstances of her coming into her hearing might be a mitigating factor in canceling their stipend because of her trespass. It is not difficult to argue that she was not in a right state of mind at that point."

"It is a compelling argument, to be sure. And the question of her hearing complicates that whole matter significantly. If she can now hear, she will have to be presented to the Order and offered the opportunity to become a proper member, regardless of her father's crimes against the Order. For that a family sponsorship is preferable."

"I hope you are not trying to change my mind. For I certainly do not wish to be involved in sponsoring her. I have my hands full with other Order business, and quite frankly, I think the Order has demanded enough of my husband and me that I feel no compunction at refusing this latest responsibility. My brother, Charles Musgrove is Keeper to Uppercross. Perhaps, he and my sister Mary might be given the task." She schooled her features into a glare learned from Kellynch.

"We will explore that possibility. In the meantime, someone must tend to her. I heard there was a vicar's widow in one of your cottages who might be suitable? Is that possible?"

"Widow Martin is a kind and gracious woman and member of the Order, but of small means. I cannot in good conscience ask her to keep my sister without remuneration, and I am certain Kellynch will forbid the use of any estate resources for her upkeep. And it does nothing to address her being on Kellynch's territory."

"Given the dearth of options we are faced with at the moment, you need to—that is, are you willing to seek Kellynch's opinion on the matter? Perhaps ask his temporary indulgence as we sort out the best course?"

"There seems to be little choice." Anne pushed off the desktop to stand. "I will go to Kellynch and let you know his response. And in the meantime, I expect you will be looking for additional alternatives, no?"

Mr. Wynn grunted something vaguely affirmative.

***

Corn and Wall met her outside the Order office. They had probably been trying to overhear what she and Mr. Wynn were talking about. And given that they immediately asked if she wanted them to take a message to Kellynch, they were probably successful. Laconia would have to train them out of that, somehow.

Once they returned and life settled into something normal.

If ...not when... it would be when ... that happened.

They spring-hopped off, happy for the excuse to be with the Laird and away from the house at the moment. It was difficult to blame them. Between Elizabeth and Kellynch, she would rather be with Kellynch, too. She pulled her shawl more tightly around her shoulders and turned for the narrow path that led to the dragon woods and the hillside cavern that housed Kellynch's official lair.

Had he heard any news from Little Pemberley? Should Anne share what she knew of the Dragon Sage, even if it was little better than rumor?

Wall appeared from the shadows and caught up to her. "Corn has stayed with Kellynch. I thought you would want to know, Kellynch is very pleased you will visit."

"Very pleased? It has been some time since Kellynch has been very pleased about anything. I hate to say this, but what is wrong?" Anne squeezed her eyes shut, trying to drive disagreeable possibilities away.

"Balen has been discussing matters with him." Wall spring-hopped alongside her as she walked.

"What matters?"

"Those that Sir Frederick is attending to. With Cornwall and Chesil so involved, he had many questions. Some of which Balen has been able to answer."

"I would have thought Balen would have at least let me know about such discussions."

"Kellynch asked her not to trouble you."

Anne covered her mouth with her hand. "That does not sound like Kellynch at all."

"You have not asked me," Wall peered up at her, green eyes wide and thoughtful. "But I believe the addition of the wyrms to the estate has made him think a great deal and given him a different perspective on matters."

"Well, that is something, is it not?" Anne took a candle from the box hidden behind a rock at the cavern entrance, lit it with the fire kit kept with it, and followed Wall down to the lair.

As ever, where the narrow path widened into the cavern, a convenient box held torches. She lit several from her candle and fit them into wall niches to provide a warm, useful glow in the lair.

Larger than the old lair near Kellynch Hall, it held a spring -ed a pool in the far corner where Kellynch's lower half was curled, as he waited for her. Corn paced near the water's edge beside the stone Anne usually used as a seat. The quiet in the cavernous space rang profound. Just their breathing, the soft lapping of the pool, and the odd crackle from the torch. Sounds which one normally ignored, demanded one take notice today. Kellynch's musky-fishy-barnyard dragon scent hung lightly in the cool, damp air, a vivid reminder that this would never be an ordinary cavern in the woods.

"You are come." Kellynch's deep voice rumbled off the walls, not threatening, but definitely dominant.

"Indeed, I am." Anne sat on the stone beside him.

"It has been a long time since you have come."

"I can count the days on one hand. Not so long at all." Pray he was not building up to a temper.

"I have heard there are many things happening."

"Balen has kept you abreast of the news from Land's End?" Anne swallowed hard.

"I do not like having nothing to do. He is my Keeper. I should—"

"I appreciate the sentiment more than I can say. Truly I do, but Cornwall is a Dug and is a far bigger dragon and has a deep and unyielding grudge against you. Your presence would only complicate a difficult situation even further."

"I do not like it." He hunched in a sulk. "But I understand. I do not want anything to happen to Wentworth. I am fond of my Keepers." He stretched his neck toward Anne.

"That is good to hear." She reached toward him and soon found his huge head pressing into her shoulder, nearly enough to knock her off balance. "It is a privilege to be your Keeper."

Kellynch leaned in more firmly. "Things are dangerous now. I do not know how the situation with Cornwall can resolve without fracturing the Order. I could be caught between the Blue Order and Chesil."

"I had not realized that you may be called upon to make such a difficult decision." Sadly, she had never given that a thought, so caught up in her own turmoil. "I will support whatever you must do."

Kellynch snorted and snuffled. His mustache whiskers tickled her face.

She pulled back to look into his eyes. "I am afraid I have more bad news, though not nearly of the magnitude you have mentioned, so there is that."

"Your sister?"

"The wyrmlings have mentioned the situation? My sister arrived at the manor unbidden and has most inconveniently begun to hear dragons. Corn and Wall were the first she has recognized for being what they are."

"At least she had fine specimens for her introduction." Kellynch flicked water with the tip of his tail.

"I can hardly argue with that. But even so, I am still left with a difficult situation. I will not ask you for permission for her to live here or to provide for her. Those possibilities are as disagreeable to me as they are to you. But we need time to make arrangements for her, for the Blue Order to decide how to handle her."

"What do you want?" Kellynch pulled back and settled into his coils.

"Most of all I would like for her to meet you. For her to understand what a major dragon is and how Father harmed you and other minor dragons, too. Second to that, I would beg your indulgence, to allow her to be kept on the estate, perhaps with Widow Martin, or failing that, with Mrs. Frankel, until a permanent sponsorship might be obtained for her."

Kellynch grumbled deep in his throat. "It will be a great difficulty for you if this cannot be done?"

"I don't mean to sound manipulative, but yes, it would be difficult."

"Then I will tolerate it. Temporarily. For your sake. She may stay under the care of a responsible party, who is not you, on my territory. I will consider meeting with her. At some point convenient to me."

"That is gracious of you and I appreciate you putting yourself out in such a way."

Kellynch looked up, away from Anne. "I ... I appreciate the addition of the wyrm cluster to my territory. They have expanded my vision, and while difficult, it is a good thing."

"I hope this is the beginning of a long and amiable relationship for all of us."

"They think highly of you and have brought you another gift."

"So many? I am not complaining, but I fear they may consider me ungrateful as I have hardly begun to work through the generous piles they have already brought." The ones threatening to overwhelm her small office and spill into the house's main library.

"It is rare that wyrms have such an opportunity to be useful. They relish the status that brings."

"I suppose that makes sense."

Kellynch stretched his neck up to reach a high rock shelf and picked up a small, stained wooden crate the size of a large book in his teeth. "This seems to be very old. Pebble and Gravel say it was kept in a special part of the old offices."

"Is that to say they think this might be of particular value?"

"Yes. And I agree."

Chapter 17

November 17, 1815

Wentworth made it back to the inn unscathed, at least insofar as there were no further injuries that Gillingham would fuss over. To be fair, the man was not a fussy sort, but he was as thorough with his warm-blooded patients as his cold-blooded ones. And when one wanted nothing more than to be left alone, it could be annoying.

Forced to share quarters, Gillingham surely heard Wentworth's nightmares that night but was good enough not to mention them. It was a problem for which he had no solution, not even any suggestions to assist, though he offered to find a bottle of something very strong if Wentworth wanted it. Which he did not, but the offer was appreciated.

All told, having a new monster to add to his nighttime trials was hardly one of his goals for this trip to Land's End, but it certainly was one of the most memorable achievements.

The first rays of dawn finally came and offered Wentworth sufficient excuse to rise and escape the torments of the night before.

He sat up—carefully with the damned burned shoulders—and scrubbed his hands over his face.

"Was it Cornwall or Chesil you have been fighting?" Laconia step-slithered up from the foot of the bed. "Gillingham retreated to the common room downstairs hours ago, you were so animated."

It must have been a tumultuous night for him to have slept there. "I stared at the ceiling for a great deal of it. And it was Cornwall."

"Not without good reason. I do not suppose you will be honored to know there is probably no other man alive today who can say they saw a firedrake breathe his flame." Laconia sat back on his coiled tail and licked his paw.

"Oh, yes, that does make me feel remarkably better. I had never considered such an advantage to my situation. Thank you for bringing it to my attention."

"Sarcasm is not going to get you very far. You do realize that?"

"It is one of the few tools I have at my disposal." Wentworth stood, bare feet hitting the cold floor. At least that was bracing, good for shaking away the last of the nightmare's muzziness. "At least in the Navy I had the luxury of discussing my experience with my comrades, which you have so conveniently reminded me is not a possibility in this case."

"You are lucky to be alive."

"While I agree with you without hesitation, I am ..." Wentworth paced along the edge of the narrow bed, hands laced behind his head, looking up into the cobwebby ceiling. "I am ... I am weary. Weary of such situations, weary of the threats and the coercions and the close calls. There is no end to this battle in sight. Nothing that marks a victory to strive for. Merely one more crisis after another with little hope of them ever being resolved."

"I suppose you are not looking for advice."

"Not in the least."

"The Dragon Sage must avoid venomous wyverns since her exposure to Longbourn's venom."

Wentworth stopped and stared at Laconia. "Why is that significant?"

"You should discuss with Gillingham, or perhaps Sir Edward is the better choice, if you might have that same manner of sensitivity now, that you need to avoid contact with firedrakes."

"That seems entirely too convenient."

"Be that as it may, it is a worthwhile question and concern. And it could be a real limitation to your future service to the Order."

"You think I need to retire from my service to the Order as I did from the Navy?"

"You should have a furlough, at least. Consider, your encounters with angry dragons now outnumber the Sage's. It is worth noting." Laconia licked his shoulder as though he had merely commented on the weather.

"I ... I will keep that in mind."

Laconia slithered closer to the edge of the bed, an odd, unsettling motion whereby he held the front of his body high and relied only on his tail to move. "I hesitated to mention it, but Kellynch is going to be displeased with Cornwall over this. Possibly with the entire Blue Order."

"And how will he find—never mind, the bloody fairy dragons." Wentworth threw his hands in the air and immediately regretted the impulse. "Anne does not need to be further alarmed about what is going on here. She has enough on her plate now."

"I expect Balen will arrive soon. The fairy dragons will likely have contacted her first and no doubt she will take it upon herself to find out exactly what has happened. Anne deserves the courtesy of knowing you have survived the most recent encounter."

"So bloody unfair to her."

"Do you think dragons care about fairness? No, it is strength and dominance that we care about." Laconia stretched up to meet him nearly nose to nose. "And you, my Friend, are establishing that in droves. You do not realize it, but the respect of having stood up to Cornwall and lived is enormous and will do much for your family."

"Assuming that I do not have to carry the damned Dragon Slayer." Wentworth turned away—how could he face any dragon if such a thing came to pass?

"Even then. You would be surprised at how much offense Cornwall's actions will cause—have already caused, to be more accurate. Yes, there is great animosity about the Dragon Slayer, but when one is bodily threatened, then things change. The self-defense provisions in the Accords are taken seriously, and they allow you to respond to a threat not only in the moment, but afterward in actions to prevent it happening again."

It was difficult to believe that, but Laconia seemed sure.

Wentworth dressed and trudged downstairs for coffee—horrid, bitter, nearly burnt stuff that the cook prepared. Gillingham's was better, but he was sprawled on the settee in the common room, snoring, and he deserved what sleep he could find.

A caw from the morning room window—Balen.

Leaving his coffee cup on the table, he hurried out the back door, toward the shed where the injured members of the security team were recuperating.

Balen touched down momentarily, signaled with her beak, then took off in a leisurely flight that ended in a small clump of trees not far from the inn. Naturally, she would have already figured out where to meet before finding him. Her thoughtfulness rivaled Laconia's.

So did her good sense.

"Would it be wrong to note that you look much the worse for the wear, Sir Frederick?" She studied him up and down with the same critical eye that Anne had. Were they already alike that way when they met, or had Balen adopted that attitude from Anne? It fit her so well, it was difficult to guess.

"It is time to stop calling me 'sir.' I still wonder who people are speaking of when they call me that." Wentworth chuckled. "Please, it is Wentworth, or I suppose Captain, if you must."

"I like Captain, yes, that feels right. Captain. Thank you." Bird-type dragons, especially those with bills as large as Balen's, had a difficult time smiling, and yet, somehow, she communicated the sentiment. "I still maintain that you do seem rather hard ridden and put up wet." She scratched the dry, leafy ground with long taloned toes that crunched and crackled through the deadfall.

"Laconia said the same thing this morning. Do you mind if I sit?"

She gestured with her wing to a convenient spot.

He dropped down, tailor style. "I do not wish to worry Anne, but you must already know from the fairy dragons—"

"One is always cautious in accepting tales told by such messengers, but from the look of you, it seems their tale of Cornwall's ill-temper..."

"—is probably not exaggerated. But the key point for Anne to know is that I am well enough and doing everything possible to remain so."

"I will see she gets that message." Something about the turn of her head suggested that would not be the only message she gave Anne, but there was no force in the world that would stop Balen from giving Anne her honest opinions.

"You will not be surprised to hear that I would much prefer to talk about the news of Kellynch. How is ... everything?" God, the thought of Kellynch-by-the-Sea made his chest burn and his soul ache.

Balen patted his arm with her wing. A totally awkward, wonderfully comforting gesture that only made his heartache worse. "Anne does as well as can be expected under the circumstances. All goes well with her increase, or so the midwife tells us. She is happy for the busyness of the estate to keep her distracted from ... well, this ..." She spread her wings.

"I am grateful for anything that makes this easier for her. I imagine it is not all calm waters, though?"

"Hardly. The most pressing issue is the charter document for the estate."

"What of it?"

"The charter, as it was originally drafted, contained no provision for minor dragons on the estate. I imagine there was no thought of that possibility when it was written. It is an unusual charter, as it expresses specific permission for him to consider part of the bay his territory, which of course Chesil has taken exception to, but he and Kellynch seem to have resolved that, at least for now. In any case, that part was not altered. It will be dealt with at a later time, I assume. But it has been redrafted, by Mr. Harville, to reflect the tenancy of minor wyrms on the estate and to give Kellynch, and his Keepers, the right to establish those terms within the parameters of the Pendragon Accords. Unfortunately, it requires signatures from both Keepers."

"Did you bring it for me to sign, then?"

"No, for legal reasons which I do not care to sort out, Mr. Harville says that I cannot render that service." Balen clapped her beak and snorted.

"So, it will wait until I have returned?"

"Kellynch was impatient for the wyrms to take residence. And the situation required arrangements for them to be made quickly. Kellynch is already fond of them, and quite sympathetic to the plight of wyrms in general. But violations of the charter are serious matters that can require extensive penalties. So, it was deemed most expedient for Undersecretary Wynn to sign the documents as your proxy."

"I do not like that man and do not relish the idea of him touching anything related to Kellynch-by-the-Sea." Wentworth's lips curled back into the sour expression that came on him whenever Wynn came to mind.

"Anne was concerned about that. But the charter will need another adjustment soon regarding the ocean as part of his territory, so this version of the charter is likely to be short-lived. She did not say as much, but I think she hopes that this will make you feel better about the situation. And I think your forbearance will win you some favor with the cranky laird as well. Having things his own way does so soothe his temper. In truth, something about having the wyrms there and the sense of taking the role of a proper laird has done wonders for his disposition. Who would have thought?"

Wentworth snickered under his breath. Balen delivered sarcasm like no other.

"He might lose his good humor, though, when he learns of the ambush you recently suffered."

"I would like to believe he is not so short-sighted as to judge all minor dragons by the foolish act of some, and it could motivate him to be diligent in the way he manages the cluster. I am hopeful that things will be far better with us than they were with Sir Walter. Speaking of him, has Harville found a house, yet?"

Balen turned her head aside and clacked her beak. "That has become more complicated."

Wentworth ground his teeth. Balen did not deserve the string of epithets threatening to roll off his tongue—then again, she might find them interesting. She was broad-minded that way. "Complicated is never a good thing where Sir Walter is concerned. What do you mean?"

"Anne's sister forced her way past the housekeeper, into the manor. She saw Corn and Wall for what they are."

"Good Lord and Pendragon's bones! So late? Is it possible?"

Balen snorted. "Most assuredly it is."

Wentworth scratched his head. "That changes things. Drastically. Miss Elliot was not a knowing part of Sir Walter's crimes against Kellynch. And, if she becomes a member of the Order, she should not be punished for her father's wrongdoing."

"Precisely. Assuming the experience does not drive her utterly mad and permit us to consign her to Bedlam—"

Wentworth snickered.

"—there is little precedent regarding what to do with such a creature. It would be helpful if you could offer an opinion regarding your openness to sponsoring her in the Order."

"Sponsoring Miss Elliot?" That got him to his feet. "Her? You don't mean to say Anne wishes that?"

"Anne has said nothing on the matter insofar as I know. It is an inevitable question that will arise, though. It would be helpful for her to know where you stand on the matter."

Damn, damn, and bloody damnation. He kicked a pile of leaves. "This is the sort of thing I would talk out with her, not make a decree."

"I am not recommending a decree, only an opinion. A well-thought-out one. One that I expect will mirror her own and strengthen her resolve in maintaining it." She cocked her head and peered deeply into his eyes. "Forgive me for mentioning it, but the way things are going, it might be the only chance you have to offer it."

Wentworth indulged in a string of epithets that would have singed a fairy dragon's feathers.

Balen stood unblinking. "Shall I wait for your response?"

"Please do."

BALEN WAITED ON THE roof of the shed while Wentworth trudged back inside. His letter to Anne was confused and rambling and hardly a credit to his schoolmasters, who had taught him better. But it was placed in Balen's care an hour later, and would be in Anne's hands soon. That was all he could do, not as much as he wanted, but all he could.

Pray it would be enough. Balen seemed satisfied, which was not nearly as good as hearing the same from Anne. But it would do for now.

"How are you feeling?" Gillingham sauntered into their shared room, cup of—by the smell of it, burnt—coffee in his hand.

"Are you asking as a friend or as a clinician?"

Gillingham guffawed, and he pulled the other chair close, spun it backward, and straddled it. "Is both an allowable answer?"

"No." Wentworth pushed back from the desk and raked his hands through his hair.

"Then I will confess, it behooves us both to gather clinical data regarding the effects of exposure to firedrake venom." Gillingham sipped his coffee without a grimace. Either he had no sense of taste or a strong constitution.

"Enough! You do not need to stare at me like a specimen in a jar. My lungs still burn when I cough. I still taste his bloody breath in the back of my mouth at random times and my joints feel as though I have aged twenty years in the time we have been here. Is that sufficient?"

"It will do. That is better than you said you felt yesterday, so I hope that indicates you will make a good recovery." Gillingham raised his mug in salute.

"And what of the injured dragons?" Wentworth jerked his head toward the window from which they could see the shed.

"They are no worse today, but their progress is not as good as yours, I am afraid. It is possible the poison is more efficacious against dragons than warm-bloods." Gillingham squinted at the window. "It looks like a messenger comes."

A small red drake sprang through the window. She must have run up the side of the inn at full speed. "You, you," she pointed at Gillingham. "The cownt requires you right away. You are to come as well."

Gillingham was required first? Dragon's blood and fire! They pelted down the stairs and followed the drake to the cave Matlock occupied.

"There! There!" The red drake pointed to a knot of several security team members surrounding a prostrate drake.

Matlock stomped out of the cavern.

"What happened?" Wentworth dodged Gillingham's dash past him.

Matlock growled and huffed, tail lashing. "That was the final straw."

The words rumbled through Wentworth's chest, "Forgive me, cownt. I do not understand."

"That was his response to my summons. He is a dug and does not answer to a mere cownt."

"You are Grand Dug." In hindsight, that was probably not something Wentworth needed to say.

Matlock stomped, rattling the trees. "He is out of order and no longer to be tolerated."

"What does that mean?" What he really wanted to ask was 'what does that require from me?' but that did not seem a safe question just now.

"There is no longer a choice. I must confront Cornwall. Only one of us can walk away from that encounter. And you—" he leaned down into Wentworth's face, "— must ensure it is not him."

Must not run, must hold position. Now was not the time to trigger a prey response. Matlock was so far gone now, he would not be able to restrain it.

Matlock pulled back. "The Blue Order may not survive this."

"What do you mean?"

"When the heir to the throne is executed, there will be division. There will be vying for that seat. There will be dragons seeking their own gain. There may be war."

"And if he is not executed?"

"Then Chesil will kill him, and the Blue Order will go to war with him."

Chapter 18

November 19, 1815

Balen stood near the fireplace in Anne's office, wings spread in the soft glow. The overnight flight from Land's End had chilled her to the bone. She liked the warmth of a fire more than she admitted, so Anne took pains to keep a large basket with a soft pillow next to the fireplace for her to settle upon and be comfortable. Beaky dragons' expressions could be hard to read, but somehow the first time Balen saw it, she seemed to smile. Maybe it was the expression in her dark, expressive eyes. Incredible how much she spoke with them.

"I am not exaggerating when I tell you, he was well," Balen stared into the flames, blinking as though to break through the sluggishness her chill brought on.

"Cornwall breathed fire at him." Anne barely forced the bitter-tasting words out as she stalked along the center of the room.

"Yes, he did. And yes, it was traumatic, and horrible, and in the Blue Order's eyes, unforgivable." Balen looked over her shoulder to follow Anne's frantic movement. "But he has survived and his injuries were minimal, considering the attack. He wanted very much to assure you of that fact."

"I am sure he does. Even if that is as true as you insist, that does not mean that today something worse has not already happened. Considering he has been ambushed by minor dragons, and then ... this ..." Anne covered her face with her hands. "It feels like the fabric of the Order is breaking down."

"I wish I could argue with that sentiment, but I fear you are right. If Cornwall is permitted to continue as he has been—" Balen shook her head and the movement continued down her body, leaving her feathers like windblown hair.

"And there is absolutely bloody nothing I can do from here." Anne stomped and returned to pacing.

"Except to continue to do your work for the Order."

"But it seems so irrelevant! Nothing I am doing is making any difference at all."

Balen walked to Anne's side, her peculiar long-legged gait gave her the somber air of a judge considering a verdict. "That is patently untrue, and I will not hear you say such things."

Anne's jaw dropped and she stared at Balen.

"Because of you, Kellynch has found justice and now resides in a Keep befitting his nature. Cornwall has faced scrutiny for his crimes against the Order, which had been summarily ignored before you stepped up to be Kellynch's Keeper. You were instrumental in the rescue of the Dragon Sage—I know it does not seem that way, but you were. There is a cluster of wyrms settling into that rock pile, that a week ago was homeless and wondering where the gravid females would lay their eggs—"

"There were females ready to clutch in the cluster? They did not tell me."

"Wyrms would not mention such a thing—it does not do to draw attention to vulnerability that way."

"I had no idea. I will have to visit and inquire after their needs—"

"And you have given me—" Balen's voice broke, and she turned aside.

Anne knelt beside Balen and placed her arm over Balen's shoulders. "I had long been jealous of Wentworth and Laconia. I never thought I might be privileged to have such a Friend."

Balen clacked her beak softly and leaned into Anne.

At last, Anne sat beside Balen's basket and encouraged Balen to take her ease there. "So, what do you think about the situation with my sister?"

"I agree with what Wentworth said. Entirely. I am glad we are all aligned on the matter. His suggestion that you contact the Crofts seems sound."

"I hate the thought of doing that to someone whom I like as well as Mrs. Croft."

"One cannot argue with that sentiment, to be sure, but she seems to be the caliber of woman who would be up to managing your sister. And possessing enough backbone to tell you 'no' if she did not want to be involved with the matter."

Anne chuckled. It was a good assessment of Wentworth's sister. "Then, I will write to her and ask. And no, there is no need for you to take that letter. Mr. Wynn has Blue Order couriers assigned to the office who can manage that task. I hope I am not too selfish, but I would very much like to know I will have your company after I go explain this turn of events to my father."

"Shall I go to Lyme with you and wait in the carriage while you talk with him?"

"I would consider it a great favor."

***

The innkeeper greeted her two steps inside the door, in the middle of the empty front room. He wrung his worn apron in his meaty hands, glancing over his shoulder at the maid and the cook poking their heads out from behind the kitchen door. "Pray, Lady Wentworth, may I speak with you a moment?"

This could not be good. "Of course."

He drew a deep breath and seemed to be arranging his thoughts. His face worked through a number of expressions: annoyed, frustrated, and finally settled on determined. "The rooms your father and sister are letting, I am expecting a large party to come in next week, and I will need those rooms to accommodate that party."

Anne winced. Of course. Of course. It was probably a party of well-heeled, well-paying customers who would be far less bother, and greater income than Father. One could hardly blame him. "I see. How much longer can you accommodate him?"

"Three days—" He broke eye contact.

She glowered and only barely avoided snorting. The danger of consorting with so many dragons.

"Perhaps five." He edged back half a step. "But no more."

"I will make arrangements. Prepare for me their bill, in detail, and I will see it is paid before he takes his leave. My sister will not be returning, though, so you may reclaim her room immediately, and remove it from our account."

He blinked several times, clearly unhappy with the reality of losing that income. "Of course, Lady Wentworth. I mean no—"

She lifted her hand. He meant things exactly as they sounded. He only prolonged the disagreeable encounter to protest it, and she only had so much patience to bring to bear right now. "The matter will be handled. Excuse me, I need to see my father."

The innkeeper looked like he might say something more, but she shook her head. Any chance he had of preserving her good opinion relied on him keeping his words to himself.

Whether he was astute or intimidated, he did just that.

Surely, the staircase had become longer by half since the last time she dragged herself upstairs. She would not be sorry to be done with this place.

She knocked on the door, only to hear a grunt beyond. How gracious. It was below him to come to the door himself. "Good day, Father." She let herself in.

He jumped up from his chair at the far side of the sitting room and cast his newspaper aside. "Is your sister with you?"

"No, she is not."

He crossed the room toward her in brisk steps. "I assume she is staying with you at Kellynch-by-the-Sea, then? Good, I shall have my things—"

She raised an open hand. "No sir, you will not."

"Excuse me?" His face wrinkled into an offended raisin of an expression that she had seen far too much of. "You will watch your tone with me. If Elizabeth is staying with you, then there is no reason I should not as well."

"I imagine you sent her to force her way into being a guest in my home." Anne folded her arms over her chest, pulling her elbows out a bit.

"Do not insult me." He dropped his gaze.

"I will take that as a confession, then." Distance, she needed distance. Three steps was all the room afforded her. "You should know that what you have done has complicated issues far more than you can imagine."

"Whatever do you mean?"

Anne dropped onto the largest, most ornate chair in the room, the one Father gravitated toward for most conversations. "As of yesterday afternoon, it appears that Elizabeth can now hear dragons."

"How dreadful!" His eyes bulged, and he worked his tongue across the roof of his mouth as though trying to dispel a bad taste. "I had thought to keep her safe from such a fate."

Anne dragged her hand down her face. While tempting, sorting out exactly what he meant by that was not what she needed to do right now. "She is currently staying with Widow Martin in a quaint little cottage on Kellynch-by-the-Sea—"

"Ah, you see! She is on the estate, exactly what you told me was impossible." His train of thought read so clearly in his eyes.

"She is there only while we sort out where to send her. You realize she needs a sponsor to make an entrance into Blue Order society, yes? I will not be sponsoring her. You cannot sponsor her."

"So, then we are to be admitted again—"

"No. Categorically and absolutely not." Anne slammed her hands on the arms of the chair.

Father jumped back and started.

She had raised her voice, not intentionally, but what did he expect at this point? "Elizabeth is to be admitted because, by virtue of being unaware of dragons at the time, she is not party to your guilt. She will join the Order—assuming she overcomes the shock of suddenly learning the true nature of the world—with a clean slate. Sadly, your reputation as an enemy of the Order will cling to her and be difficult to overcome, but there is little to be done for that, save finding you a quiet abode, far away from the attention of Order society."

"I will not tolerate hearing such insults from my own daughter." He turned his back and stomped toward his room.

"Father, I have not the time nor the patience for this discussion. We have been over this far too many times. I will neither cajole you nor sugarcoat the alternatives. The hard truth of the matter is that the innkeeper gives you no more than five days to be out."

"What?"

"You have worn your welcome far too thin here, it would seem. And I would be surprised if any establishment in Lyme will accept you, now. I know you work hard to disprove it, but it is true, your behavior has consequences. Like the fact that Kellynch will not have you on his territory and my husband wants nothing to do with you."

He turned to face her, face dangerously red. "You will not speak to me in such a way, daughter."

"And I am tired. Very, very tired. You have been given more choices than you deserve in housing options and have found faults with every one. You are out of alternatives, and I am out of patience. Either you select a house to take right now, right this minute, or I will walk out of here, pay off the innkeeper, and tell him to remove you from his property tomorrow. I will answer no letters from you and if you come anywhere near my home again, you will find yourself set on by a pack of—"

Father hurried to the window behind Anne. "Dogs? Dogs?"

"What of them?" Anne stood and peered over his shoulder.

"There has been a pack of curs wandering the streets at night, standing below this window, yapping and growling as though they would climb the walls to get in and attack us in our beds."

Anne gulped. Later, she would deal with that later. It could be exactly as he said, a pack of loose dogs. He knew he could call them dragons in her presence, and he did not. They might well just be dogs. "All the more reason for you to leave immediately. So will you choose, or shall I leave now?"

He locked eyes with her as she pulled back her shoulders and lifted her chin. One, two, three breaths and he broke eye contact and shuffled to the writing desk near the fireplace. Grumbling bitterly, he opened a drawer and withdrew a sheet of paper. "There, if you must, that one." He shoved it at her as he walked past to peer out the window.

"Exeter?"

"It is the farthest from the sea. The shoreline disagrees with me."

"I shall make it so then. I will go to Mr. Harville directly." She tucked the paper into her reticule, pretended to curtsey, and left.

She hurried downstairs, ignoring the innkeeper's curious look. He would not have any delectable bits of gossip from her.

Jonty Bragg—bless the man!—waited with the carriage near the front door and handed her in. Best not ask how he managed to be so timely. "Where to, Lady Wentworth?"

"Mr. Harville's office." She fell into the squabs beside Balen.

"Immediately, madam." He vaulted to the box and set the horses into motion.

Anne pulled the paper from her reticule and showed it to Balen.

"That is an interesting choice." She bobbed her head from side to side as she often did whilst thinking.

"He said it was farther from the sea, that was why he chose it. It makes sense that he might find the ocean disagreeable."

"I suppose. What do you know of Exeter?"

"I suppose the ordinary things one learns. Nothing that strikes me with immediate concern. Is there something of which you are aware?" Anne asked.

"Not specifically, but it seems notable that there are no dragon estates within a day's ride of Exeter."

Interesting. "I suppose it is not difficult to imagine he wants to stay away from Blue Order territories as much as possible."

"While that makes a great deal of sense, I do have some concerns." Balen preened her wing. A tiny feather fell loose and floated to the carriage floor. "Of course, I know nothing for certain—"

"You know I always welcome you to speak freely." Even if, at times, Anne wished Balen required less encouragement to do so.

"All things considered, I am concerned about any place where there are not sufficient major dragons around to keep the minor dragon populations under good regulation."

A cold knot settled in Anne's gut. "But he is unknown in Exeter."

"That may not be as true as we would like to believe. Apparently, the harem of fairy dragons they disturbed suffered the loss of a nest and the death of several females at the business end of a cat procured by your father. Word has gotten around. It would be one thing if he were dragon-deaf and could claim ignorance. But..."

"Oh, merciful heaven. But would it be any better to have him in proximity to major dragons who would be offended by his presence? I hope Mr. Harville can offer some useful advice in this matter." Anne rubbed her temples hard.

"I almost forgot!" Balen hopped down from the seat and pulled a leather-wrapped package from under the facing seat. "I do not know if this will make you feel better, or add to your workload. But the wyrms left this with me while you were at the inn. They were quite happy not to have to drag it all the way back to Kellynch-by-the-Sea."

Anne picked up what could only be yet another set of Blue Order documents rescued from the fire. She peeled away the leather wrappings. In gold lettering on the front cover: *Survey, specifications, and charter documentation. Cornwall County.* The date was blurred, but it was definitely over a hundred years old. Was it possible this could contain something related to Cornwall?

Chapter 19

November 19, 1815

Wentworth lay on the narrow, hard bed, hands laced behind his head, and stared up at the ceiling. Not that he could see it. The room was pitch-black, moonless. The kind of night when firedrakes and wyverns stretch their wings and fly, away from the notice of men. Would Cornwall and Matlock be flying tonight? Or would they be in their lairs, preparing for the coming day?

Did it matter? Nothing would change what loomed on the dawn's horizon.

War. The Blue Order would be going to war. After all these generations of peace, dragon war would erupt, and the world would never be the same. Tomorrow.

Tomorrow, he would be in the middle of the field that would decide the course of the war. Would the Order turn against itself or against the forces of the surrounding seas?

Neither was a good option. Neither would lead to safety or prosperity. All he knew and loved would be thrown into chaos. The world as he knew it would end.

Tomorrow.

This would not be the first time he went into battle, far from it. But it was the first with so much on the line, with a wife and child-to-be, an estate and a dragon to Keep. So much potential loss sat on his chest, slowly suffocating him.

No, it was not Kellynch's fault. None of this was his fault, despite being caught up in the middle of it all. He was a pawn, used by one more powerful than himself, one that would meet his fate, one way or another. If Matlock or Wentworth did not kill Cornwall, Chesil would.

Did Cornwall know this would be his last night? That there would be no more tomorrow? Was he even capable of believing it was possible? That a creature like Chesil was possible?

Wentworth shuddered. Despite Chesil having saved his life, he could never meet that dragon without deep, visceral dread. One might think the intimacy of seeing a dragon from the inside would create some kind of a bond, some lasting regard, given that it had been the vehicle by which his life was saved.

Wentworth snorted, softly so as not to wake Gillingham—that man could sleep through anything.

No prey regarded his predator with romantic fondness, only caution and respect. They might be able to live together under a truce of some sort, but the underlying truth would always be there.

Predator would always be predator, and prey would always be prey.

The Blue Order liked to obscure that fact with fancy words and promises in treaties signed by those long dead and now upheld by those who had never known the primeval reality of the situation.

Predator. Prey. Always.

He should write one more letter to Anne. He rolled up to sit, elbows on knees, face in his hands.

But what was there left to say? He had told her everything before he had left. Written it all down in a letter locked in his desk with all the important papers she knew to look for when—if—the need arose. So many words, many pages, the pouring out of his soul then, far more agony than hope. Line upon line, until there was no more to add.

Even if he could write, with whom could he send it and be assured it would arrive? Laconia, Gillingham, the Blue Order security team, all were imperiled as much as he. The local fairy dragons, though helpful, were quite occupied with keeping out of reach of Cornwall and his minions. And it was not the sort of thing one trusted to a fairy dragon, no matter how much respect he had for them in general.

That was why he had written as he did, when he did. So, he could be assured she would know everything he needed her to, and the worry that she might not know would not add to his already crushing burdens.

He forced himself to lie down, ignore Gillingham's snores, and accept Laconia's comforting weight next to him. Sleep was the most useful thing he could do now.

Dawn on such a day should have been spectacular, a trumpeting riot of color and splendor announcing the magnitude of what lay before them.

It was not. Muted colors, tired clouds, vaguely grey and dreary. A greeting that made one want to roll over and stay in bed.

If only he could.

He dressed and opened the false bottom of his trunk. He had already cleaned and checked the dread article yesterday. There was nothing left to do but carry it.

Laconia laid his thumbed paw on his arm, purring encouragement and sympathy far more eloquent than men's words could ever be.

A crossbow. A bloody crossbow. He was proficient with a sword. Facing Cornwall with that in hand would have been natural. But this?

Heavy, ungainly, awkward. He held it up in the faint rays of morning. At least the lines of a sword were refined, elegant, graceful. But this?

Ignoble, somehow, to face a dragon this way. At a distance, where Cornwall might not even know he was lying in wait.

He laid the crossbow across his knees. That was the real issue. To be forced to lie in the shadows and hunt a dragon, as he would game. Ungentlemanly.

But this was war. And he had had to do many things in war that he would erase from his mind if he could.

This would be another one of those.

Across the room, stirring and footsteps.

"It is time," Gillingham's tone was not far from the one physicians used to announce a death.

Laconia, silent as a shadow, led the way down the stairs, maybe for the last time.

Matlock and the Blue Order security team waited near the path to the beach. Overhead, cockatrice screamed persuasive warnings to keep the warm-blooded away.

It was hard to appreciate the point of the effort. When war came, all the warm-blooded would know of dragons.

What would happen to the world then?

Matlock, standing erect, regal in his teal majesty, the color of the deep sea, looked down to Wentworth. "My plans are unchanged."

"I understand, Grand Dug. Has a messenger been sent to the Order?"

"No. I want no interference." Matlock raised his chin, silhouetted against the somber sky, the portrait of a monarch on the eve of battle.

"What of Cornwall's minions?"

Matlock waved a wing at the security team, and they dispersed into the woods. "They will handle the matter. If the cowards would even dare interfere."

"Where do you want Gillingham?" Wentworth looked back over his shoulder. How very young Gillingham had become on the journey here.

Matlock pointed to an arrangement of boulders on the clifftop that had not been there before. "Conceal there and do not reveal yourself until Cornwall is dead."

Gillingham clutched his leather bag to his chest, nodded, and scrambled to his position.

"You," Matlock pointed at Wentworth. "There. The highest of the three."

On the other side of the path, three haphazard arrangements of boulders, like the other, new to the landscape. Wentworth, crossbow at his side, nodded and headed toward them.

"Remember, hold your fire until I fall. The Dragon Slayer must only be used as the final resort." The words were loud, meant to be heard by the circling cockatrice.

No one would accuse the Grand Dug of reluctance or cowardice.

"I understand." Wentworth took his position as Matlock made himself big and marched down the rocky slope to the beach.

Chapter 20

NOVEMBER 19, 1815

"Do you think—" Anne ran her fingers along the worn book cover. It may have once been gilded, but now the leather cracked and flaked, threatening to come apart in her hands.

"It might be nothing, but..." Balen paused and rocked her head back and forth. "... given what we have learned while trying to revise the Kellynch-by-the-Sea charter ... to me it makes it more likely that this is a document that could prove directly useful."

"In that case," Anne rapped on the ceiling, opened the side glass and called, "We have had a change in plans. Take us home."

"Right away." Jonty Bragg made quick work of changing course and brought them to the steps of Kellynch-by-the-Sea.

Anne and Balen re-wrapped the book and rushed inside. It was so fragile. They dare not risk it coming apart before they could discover the treasures it might contain. Still, the possibility of being of some actual use in the current crisis renewed her hope and energy.

Balen flew ahead and opened the curtains of Anne's office. Anne dragged her favorite chair close to the window while Balen pulled a small table close.

Anne unwrapped the musty tome. Smoke and water and fire had all left their marks—no wonder the wyrms had waited so long to bring her this volume. To one who could not read its title, it seemed a meager offering.

The cover creaked—it literally squealed under her hand as she pried it open. Bits of leather flaked off, dusting the table top. Grand, monk-worthy illustrated script graced the title page, confirming it was indeed *Survey, specifications, and charter documentation. Cornwall County*. Below the title, a blurry line seemed to suggest that these were original documents!

Her hands trembled and blood pounded in her ears. Pray, let there be something of use here!

The pages—dusty, sneezy, and stiff with age—threatened to break apart as she turned them.

Blast and botheration! No list of contents where one should be. That must be a more modern convention for Blue Order documents. And the blessed pages were stuck together in great clumps from some long-ago water damage, now sealing the leaves together with waves and warps.

"Here," Balen appeared at her elbow, a paper knife in her beak.

"Brilliant, exactly the thing." Anne took the carved paper knife, the wooden blade a handspan long and blunt on both sides, and slipped it between the first two pages to free.

Lovely. Not only were the pages warped, but they must have been written with iron gall ink that was eating through the paper. Such a moth-eaten, decrepit tome. At least it was written in human script, not dragon. Or so the first pages implied.

Balen laid her beak on Anne's shoulder and peered at the open page. "If I am not mistaken, that looks like a county survey map."

"I think so. Hmm—" Anne chewed her knuckle. "On my desk, in the left-hand bottom drawer, I have a map of all the Blue Order Keeps—"

"I know the one!" Balen flew to the desk. Usually, she walked in the house. She returned and laid out the document on the table, letting the upper part hang off the table's edge to make Cornwall County front and center.

"Yes, yes, they do match." Anne traced lines on the map. "The boundaries of the Land's End Keep are the same in both maps."

Balen tapped the page. "It looks like the book has all the Keeps and Blue Order-related properties numbered—"

"With Land's End being the last one. So—"

"If you start at the end of the book—"

Anne flipped the book over and worked her paper knife between the cover and the final page. Dragon's bones! How long could this take?

Finally, the cover fell aside and revealed the last page was blank.

Bloody damnation!

But there was iron gall damage that suggested the pages inside were not. Her hands shook, and she tore the leaf. Her fingers itched to tear it out entirely, but no, that was exactly the kind of impulse she would regret.

Separate the next page. Focus on that, not the simmering tension threatening to boil over.

The page was not stuck near the spine. She slipped the paper knife in and worked it along the top edge. "Land's End Keep" became visible at the top margin. "Yes!"

She set the knife aside and rifled through the pages that were loose at the top. If there were more top margin markings, perhaps she could find the start of the Land's End document.

There! A blank margin, with the edges of fancy lettering barely visible below! That was the form that the first page of the current charters took!

Somehow, it was easier to separate the larger sections, and the book fell open to the title page of the original Land's End charter documents.

Oh, merciful heavens! The next several pages were loose. The document form had not changed much in all that time. Not surprising really, all things considered.

She skimmed the flowery, illuminated bits—beautiful artistry she would study later—that discussed how the charter was granted and all the related genealogy and inheritance documentation. Provisions, provisions—she needed to know the provisions of the grant. If there was something helpful to be had, that was where it would be.

There! She let her eyes race on ahead.

Gasping, she pointed to a paragraph.

Balen clapped her beak in Anne's ear. "Yes! Yes! That makes all the difference!"

"Can you get this to Wentworth in time enough to be useful?"

"Kellynch can get there faster than I, and his word will carry more weight."

"Yes, I hate that you are right. This needs to be heard in a major dragon's voice." Anne jumped up, tucked the book under her arm, and ran for the cellar with the tunnel to Kellynch's lair. Was it too much to hope that he would be there?

Ladies did not, should not run, particularly ladies in her delicate condition. But Special Liaisons with life and death information in their hand did. The house staff dodged and pressed up against walls to give her and Balen right of way.

By the time they reached the lair, she had no breath to speak. Anne braced against the nearest wall and gulped the cool, dank air. A single, dim torch lit the lair. He was waiting for her to arrive for her promised visit to him.

"Kellynch! Kellynch!" Balen shrieked. "There is vital news!"

"Of what sort?" Kellynch asked, slithering close to Anne.

"The wyrms brought it this morning. Here, here, look!" She opened the book and pointed to a block of text.

Kellynch leaned down and squinted. It was difficult for him to read in the dim light.

"Does that mean what I—we, Balen and I—think it does?" Anne held her breath.

Kellynch threw his head back and bugled. Apparently, it did. "Wentworth and Matlock must know immediately."

"I can take the message—" Balen flapped.

"No, it is best coming from me, and not only because I am a major dragon. I know what must be done."

What did he mean by that? "Are you strong enough? You are only now recovering—"

"I must be, I will be. Balen, you fly as well, that way if I do not make it, they will still know."

Balen followed Kellynch out. He would need her persuasive help to get to the shore. How fast could he get there? Would it be enough?

Anne dragged herself back upstairs, feet, heart, growing heavier with each step. If only she could have gone with them. Been more actively useful to them.

She had much practice waiting, too much. She and Wentworth had waited so long, it could not all be taken from them now, could it?

And now Kellynch and Balen were at risk as well. Everyone but Corn and Wall were away to try to save the world, while she waited and watched and hoped.

She would scream, but that would frighten the staff. They looked uneasy enough as she trudged past them. No point in making things worse.

At least she was not the only one, lonely and frightened. Corn and Wall came to her room and curled in unhappy little balls beside her on the bed while they all pretended to sleep.

Chapter 21

Sunrise, November 20, 1815

Matlock's footfalls thundered and shook the ground as he paraded toward the beach. On the surface, it might have seemed a show merely for the sake of dominance. And it was, but Matlock was not one to indulge in such demonstrations without serving a greater purpose. With everyone's attention focused on him, Wentworth had a greater chance of reaching his position undetected.

Ducking behind the cleverly arranged boulders, Wentworth found the prepared vantage point, where the rough stones formed an arrowslit, like in a castle of old. Behind them, he might be able to remain hidden while preparing to shoot. After the first bolt, his location would be revealed and the advantage lost. If favor was with him, he would only need the one shot.

No, if favor were with him, none would be necessary.

More than once he had been laughed at for his determination to become a marksman, some romantic harkening back to the days of the longbowmen. Or accused of seeking entrance to the toxophilite society merely as a means of meeting eligible society maidens.

But nothing so refined as either of those motives swayed him. He was a soldier and proficiency in another weapon could not be a waste of his time. More than once, it had served him well. Pray today would be one of those days.

Laconia spring-hopped to a small ledge near the arrowslit. He had stood with Wentworth in battle before. It was right that he should be here now.

Wentworth set the crossbow on a conveniently placed rock and laid out several bolts. If the first one missed, it would take time to reload and every second he could save might be crucial. He closed his eyes and mentally rehearsed each step of loading and firing the weapon. Once, twice, thrice.

He needed to be able to do it without thinking, without hesitating, with an angry dragon breathing fire. The smoothed and varnished burn marks on the stock suggested it would not be the first time this Dragon Slayer had met a fire-breathing dragon.

That it had done so and been dubbed a Dragon Slayer felt oddly reassuring.

Matlock slapped his tail on the beach sand, at the edge of the rising tide. The damp sand squelched, rasping and sploshing, hardly the impressive sound his tail made on solid ground. "Cornwall, you are summoned." His voice echoed like a gunshot off the cliffs.

Wentworth latched the bowstring into position and set the razor-tipped bolt in the rail. The four-bladed arrowhead forged from specially-formulated steel glistened in the morning sun. It could penetrate a dragon skull.

Wentworth had seen the skull to prove it.

But not until—unless—Matlock fell.

He sidled behind the arrowslit. The security team had done a good job giving him the widest line of sight possible. Hopefully, it would be enough. He raised the stock to his shoulder and laid his cheek against the polished wood, fingers laid along the cool metal of the trigger guard. Ready, but not at risk of anticipating his moment.

Flush away all thoughts, save one: the dragons below. Breathe, slow, controlled. Nothing but the dragons before him.

"I order you to present yourself." Matlock stomped a step into the lapping waves and swung his tail, churning up a mighty wave. "Now!"

Dragon thunder echoed off the cliffside, piercing Wentworth's ears, rattling his skull.

A dark form gathered in the water twenty yards from Matlock. Definitely in range of his bow. But closer would be better. Far better.

Sharp spinal ridges appeared first, then horns and wingtips, slowly revealing the gleaming, deep gold dragon from the dark waves. Cornwall spread his wings and shook water from them, showering Matlock with a saltwater spray.

In dragon parlance, he might as well have spat upon Matlock, then slapped his face. If Cornwall's fate had not already been sealed, it would have been now.

"You dare order me to appear?" Cornwall thundered, spreading his wings and broadening his chest, head held as high as possible.

Matlock matched his stance. Of the two dragons, he was slightly taller and made certain Cornwall noticed. "You dare hold yourself above the Blue Order Council?"

"I am the next brenin. What is the Council to me?"

"You know our laws."

"I know you ruled against me in favor of that wyrm who was not even a proper member of the Order. Or have you forgotten that insult?" Cornwall's eyes narrowed, his pupils constricting to serpentine slits.

"Had we wished to insult you, we would have done so unequivocally."

Cornwall bugled. "You mock the injury done me! You mock my rank, my dominance!"

How much Cornwall seemed to have in common with Sir Walter. Wentworth set his sight on Cornwall and followed him as he slowly stomped toward Matlock.

The resistance of the water and the awkward splashing around his feet hardly reinforced his attempt at a regal bearing. He looked like a child playing in puddles.

A deadly fire-breathing child with fangs and talons.

"As Grand Dug, I outrank you."

"A made-up rank for a dragon pretending dominance."

"You question my legal dominance?" Matlock leaned closer, close enough that Cornwall should feel Matlock's breath on his face.

"I recognize no such warm-blood concept. We are dragons. We do not make up laws or follow laws, we are law." Cornwall reared on his back legs and flapped hard enough for the wing-wind to cast waves upon the beach sand.

"You challenge my dominance?"

"I am Dug and Heir to the brenin. I am dominant!" Cornwall roared into Matlock's face.

Matlock growled, an unholy, feral rumbling that sent the cockatrice above diving for cover and drove all the warmth from Wentworth's blood. All emotion flowed away with it.

Now he was as cold-blooded as they. He could, he would, do what needed to be done.

Matlock leapt into the air, wings spread, shrieking as tendrils of fire stretched out on echoes of his scream.

"Fool! None can best me in the air!" Cornwall launched.

Good, good, he was taking the bait. Matlock's spies had advised an aerial approach. Cornwall was not accustomed to staying aloft for long periods. Fat and self-indulgent, the spies said. Lean into that weakness.

Wentworth shifted to follow their flight. So far overhead, the arrowslit would not contain it. He shifted back, crossbow now aimed high, waiting until the obstreperous dragons flew into range.

Matlock pierced the sky, climbing higher and higher with Cornwall in pursuit. With a sudden burst of speed, Cornwall lunged and caught Matlock's tail with his teeth. Matlock's flight halted with a jerk, but he ducked and twisted and came up under Cornwall's belly, ripping away a great chunk from Cornwall's side. Dragon blood rained down on the waves below.

Cornwall's scream freed Matlock's tail. Powerful wing strokes propelled Matlock higher to exhale a plume of fire at Cornwall's wings.

Cornwall pulled back at the last moment, his fragile wing membranes safe from the flames. Backlit in the sunrise, the dragons hovered, studying each other.

Wentworth's lungs froze, tension building in every sinew.

Matlock dove and spun. Cornwall followed, a ball of roiling, screeching gold and teal, impossible to tell where one ended and the other began. They plunged down, uncontrolled, necks suddenly entwined in a deadly embrace.

They broke apart just before reaching the waves below, soaring once again.

Out of range.

Bollocks! Wentworth permitted himself several ragged breaths, a roll of his shoulders and a shake of his head, and resettled himself into position.

Cornwall pulled ahead, but Matlock bit his tail and tore away the tip. Cornwall whirled on him, rage and fire pouring from every inch of his being. But his flight was unsteady, suddenly uncontrolled.

The tail must be like a ship's rudder!

Cornwall back-winged and scrabbled at the air with talons widespread, wobbling right, left, and right, losing altitude with each swipe of his wings.

Matlock snarled and dove for Cornwall's throat. Another moment and—

Cornwall spewed a cloud of flame and smoke and poison into Matlock's face. Matlock pulled up short. Cornwall clamped his jaws around Matlock's throat. They plummeted, screaming, into the sea.

Chapter 22

November 20, 1815

Fitful sleep made the night last twice as long as it should. By silent mutual agreement, the three rose and stared out into the cloudy dawn, the ocean just visible through the corner of the window. The wyrmlings licked themselves. They still left little tufts of fur standing up along their shoulders when they did that, like rumpled little children who had tried to dress themselves without their nurserymaid's help.

Anne forced herself to dress and pin up her hair. The presence of a maid was too much intrusion for today. The housekeeper, who somehow always knew everything going on in the house, appeared with a tray of tea and toast, disappearing as quickly as she appeared.

Wise and sensible woman.

Anne buttered a slice of toast and broke it in half for the wyrmlings. No, it might not be their favorite meal, but it would be rude not to share. They dove on it, licking the creamy spread from the surface. When they stopped and looked up at her with huge, sad eyes, she slathered butter on the once-licked toast again. They set upon it again, mewing gratitude.

Tea. Hot and sweet, that helped. She wrapped her hands around the cup and held it close to her chest. Something normal, and dependable, perhaps a sign of things—

A fairy dragon, one of the local harem, hovered at her window pecking the glass furiously.

Anne nearly dropped her teacup. She hurried to open it.

The fairy dragon darted in, shrieking, "Your sister! Your sister!"

"What has Elizabeth done?"

"She is frantic! Widow Martin, so afraid!" The fairy dragon zipped circles around the room.

Corn and Wall sat back on their tails, heads twitching as they followed the fairy dragon's frantic movement.

"Afraid of Elizabeth?" Anne grabbed her pelisse.

"Not her, no, not her. She is afraid of them."

"Them? Who is 'them?' Is someone unwelcome at the cottage?"

"Yes! Yes! You must hurry and send them away!" The fairy dragon dove out the window, disappearing into the morning.

If only the flutterbit could have told them more!

Who could be at the cottage? Lyme was a port, and it was not unusual for occasional ruffians to be about. But what would they be doing here?

"Vicar Martin often helped those in need." Wall wove side to side, whiskers twitching. "Sometimes they return to visit."

"Yes, yes, that makes a great deal of sense." Anne jumped to her feet. "Corn, rally the footman. Wall go find Jonty Bragg.

Have them meet me at the fork in the path to Widow Martin's cottage."

The wyrmlings chirruped and spring-hopped away.

Anne's heart thundered. Perhaps she should not go. She was in a delicate condition—no, someone had to handle Elizabeth and she was the properest person to do so, especially in Elizabeth's hysterical state.

Anne grabbed her sturdiest bonnet on the way out and tied it as she rushed downstairs.

She ran out into the cold morning. Clouds billowed above as the wind gusted about her, dark, threatening. The smell of an incoming storm. But no rain yet, so the path would not be slick.

She ran.

A burly footman and Jonty Bragg were waiting for her at the fork in the path. Thank heavens they had learned Corn and Wall were worth attending to.

Anne did not stop as she reached them. "There is some to-do at Widow Martin's. I fear someone her husband helped in the past may be troubling her. My sister is with her."

The men acknowledged with grunts, keeping pace beside her. Quickly, quickly. They must hurry!

Female voices cried out in the distance. Anne forced herself faster. The fear! The fear in those voices! No matter what Elizabeth had done in the past, she did not deserve whatever was making her cry out so.

The cottage came into view, squat, dark—no light coming from the windows, only voices. Dark shadowy trees gathered behind—were they protective or ominous? Hard to say.

"I will go to the right." Jonty Bragg broke away from them.

"Lady Wentworth, stay behind me." The footman waved her back. "You must not endanger yourself. There—" he pointed, "the well, stay behind that. If we tell you, run, do not hesitate. It is not right that you are here at all."

"Go, go. I will stay by the well, go!" Anne dashed to the old stone well, with its lopsided wooden awning and bucket that danced in the wind tied above.

Anne ducked behind the well, bracing her hands on the cold stone as the footman burst inside the house. Bragg shouted. He was inside, too, now.

But where were the screams, the noises that should have been there?

Anne turned slowly. Something was not right. Mewling cries of fear, terror.

Wyrmlings? Corn and Wall?

She closed her eyes, listening, searching. The sound was coming from the cover of the trees. Louder, more desperate, now.

Cautious, it would pay to be cautious. She crept toward the trees, listening, watching. The ground, yes, there were tracks from the wyrmlings there. But why? Why would they have gone into the woods? They could be silly, even foolish, but not at such a time as this.

Were they looking for someone?

Or...

Had they been taken?

Anne's skin prickled, and she hesitated.

More mewling and a scream—no, those were screams.

A dark blur ran from the woods and knocked her to the ground.

Chapter 23

NOVEMBER 20, 1815

They hit the water with a thunderous splash. Torrents of water obscured Wentworth's sight, parting like a theater curtain to reveal Cornwall dragging Matlock under.

In the sea, Cornwall had the advantage.

How long could firedrakes endure underwater?

Damn arrowslit once again did not give him enough view. Wentworth stood and scanned the ocean, crossbow ready. Laconia leapt up beside him, keeping watch, too.

Silence, but for the lapping waves. The ocean breezes. Languid, heavy clouds drifting, floating. Nothing. Waiting, the land itself held its breath, watching and waiting.

There!

Darkness gathering in the water, rising, swelling.

Color—what color?

Barely breathing, Wentworth sighted the crossbow.

Larger, larger, closer to the surface. Rising still, but only dark beneath the waves.

Something else, floating on the water now. Dark too, but liquid.

Blood.

Spinal ridges penetrated the surface. Dark, too dark to tell which. Tips of horns could be either.

Come on, damn it. Matlock, show yourself!

Roaring, bugling, a head broke through the waves.

Bloody damnation!

Wentworth's finger hovered over the trigger.

Cornwall's wings freed, he leapt into the air, screaming triumph.

Cold calm, smooth as ice over stone, flooded over Wentworth's every fiber. Awareness narrowed to a single point within the sight of his weapon.

Time and movement slowed. Close, close, feel the dragon's movement, lead the target ... there.

He pulled the trigger and his bolt disappeared into the morning. With one hand he grabbed the next bolt, with the other, he dropped the bow and fit his foot into the stirrup reload.

Cornwall screamed—but was it a mortal wound? Can't wait to find out.

Pull back the bowstring, firm, steady, do not yank. Knock the bolt—

A shadow enveloped Wentworth's vantage point.

In a single motion, he shouldered the crossbow and fired a bolt straight into Cornwall's belly.

Screaming, swooping, enormous paws scooped him up off his feet. Talons locked around him, more robust than any iron chain.

Wentworth's feet came off the ground and he dangled from Cornwall's grasp, the Dragon Slayer falling useless below him.

No match for the dragon's force, no weapon at hand, no words would matter. A child's doll, dangling.

Helpless.

Utterly helpless.

Cornwall, unstable with his injuries, careened drunkenly through the air, upward, ever upwards. "Do you know what happens when a warm-blood falls into the water from great height?"

As a matter of fact, he did. Wentworth writhed and squirmed. One arm free.

"He dies. He dies. Squashed like an insect against a rock, he dies!" Cornwall flapped upward. "You have defied me! I will see you die!"

Another arm free. Not much, but better. Don't look down. Don't look. Nothing to be gained. Up, look up. Yes, there, a back-facing spur, on the wrist, above the digits, thick, bony, streaked with blood, probably Matlock's.

Could be venomous.

Doesn't matter.

The tension surrounding Wentworth shifted. He kicked and lunged for the spur. Only one chance.

Cornwall released his grip.

Wentworth grabbed the spur with both hands and wrenched himself up and over Cornwall's front paw, clutching the outside of the dragon's leg. He wound arms and legs around Cornwall's wrist.

Dangerously off balance, Cornwall listed left, overcorrected, swerved right, then dove. Straight for the water.

Wentworth looked down. Cornwall was not going to drag him under.

Closer, closer, the waves raced toward him.

Now!

Wentworth released his hold and kicked off Cornwall's leg, sending him into a frenzied, flapping spin. Wentworth hit the water in a painful flop, but whole and breathing and in command of his arms and legs. That was something.

Treading water, he scanned for the nearest shore. There, too damn far, but the only choice. Too much like Lyme ...

Cornwall hovered, screaming. "I will kill you, Dragon Slayer!" He dove at Wentworth.

Two dozen yards off, the waters roiled and a toothy head burst forth. "You will have to go through me to do it."

Kellynch?

Kellynch!

Dragon's bones and fire! What was he doing here?

"You trespass in my territory, wyrm! I have had enough of you!" Cornwall plunged like a raptor after a fish, straight and deadly as an arrow into the water.

Wentworth should swim for shore, but that would be to abandon Kellynch.

A round, hard form nudged his side. A serpent-whale?

Familiar. Very familiar. "Siren?"

"Kellynch sent me. I will take you ashore."

The matriarch of the Lyme Bay pod? Rescuing wayward warm-bloods was not the work of a matriarch. "How is Kellynch here? I do not understand."

"Now is not the time. Take hold of my dorsal fin." Siren chirped and clicked what must have been the sea dragon equivalent of a growl, the tips of her many sharp teeth visible.

Wentworth grabbed hold with both hands, and Siren sped toward the shore. "Wait, wait, there! Look!"

Siren paused and turned toward Wentworth's frantic gesture. "Is that—"

"Matlock? Yes, it is!" But was he alive?

"I must, we must... if he lives, we must..."

"I understand." Wentworth barely kept his grip as Siren raced toward Matlock, who floated, wings spread, nose barely above the water level.

Maybe, just maybe. "Cownt Matlock!" Wentworth's call would never reach the dragon over the waves at this distance, but he had to do something.

An eyelid fluttered, revealing a glassy eye.

He lived! "The cownt needs to get back to shore."

"Go to him. I will find assistance." Siren disappeared

Wentworth swam for Matlock's side. Cold, bone-chilling cold. He could not hold out for long. But Matlock was more important to the Order. Stroke, kick, stroke, kick.

Face to face with a huge, teal snout.

Matlock snorted softly. "We have not stopped him."

"Not yet." Wentworth's teeth chattered.

"You must. He cannot be allowed—" Matlock gasped for breath.

"He will not. You have my word." Every promise he had made to a dying man, he had fulfilled. Matlock knew that. "But the Order still needs you."

"I cannot swim. It is only a matter of time— very little time."

"Kellynch is here, with help. I know not why, but he is here. There are serpent-whales, they will get you to shore, to Gillingham." With broad strokes of his hands, Wentworth treaded water, searching for some sign of Siren.

"You know it is death to show weakness." Stubborn, prideful creature!

"Or an acceptance of your dominance that Kellynch and the others would help you. Recall Pemberley and Bolsover."

Siren whistled. "I have help, but we will not approach without permission." She bobbed in the waves, surrounded by four large young males.

"It is in the interest of the Order that you survive, Grand Dug." Wentworth said.

"Clearly he will." Siren called. "It is better for us that he is out of the water sooner, rather than later. We are serving ourselves, not him." Her entourage chirped and clicked. "It is a favor to us to allow us to speed him from Chesil's territory."

Siren was a canny, wise dragon in her own right.

"Very well," Matlock grunted and snorted. "I will permit your aid."

Siren returned to Wentworth, and her company stationed themselves around Matlock, pushing him to shore as Siren gathered Wentworth on her back and swam ahead.

Ten yards from Matlock, the sea shattered and Cornwall surfaced. "You will not take my prize!"

Cornwall snarled, teeth bared, but stopped mid-growl, eyes wide. Surprised. Alarmed. Something struck him from below, throwing him back.

"You will deal with me first!" Kellynch rose, like the sea monster he was, rendering flapping, floundering Cornwall weak and ridiculous in his shadow.

Chapter 24

NOVEMBER 20, 1815

Anne caught herself on her hands, just before her face hit the ground. She shook her head and tried to stand.

"Stay where you are, warm-blood." That was a dragon's voice, but not a familiar one.

She shook her head again and found a drake, larger than most minor drakes, standing over her, staring into her face. Two forward-pointing horns framed its face while especially large fangs protruded from its top and bottom jaws. It seemed the sort of creature that would be called Fang, built for intimidation and violence.

"Who are you and what are you doing trespassing on Kellynch's territory?" It was difficult to sound dominant while lying on the ground with a dragon dripping spittle on one's face, but she tried.

"I am who I am, it does not matter to you. Kellynch is not here, so why should I be bothered about him?"

Anne sat up, though the dragon growled and bared a full complement of teeth. Two more came out of the shadows to surround her, the wyrmlings dangling from their mouths by the scruff of their necks. They reached for her with scrabbling paws. "Let the wyrmlings go! What do you want?"

"To make a point." Fang hissed.

"What point? And how can you make it here?"

"Your father is a criminal against dragonkind."

"I am well aware of the situation. He has been duly punished by the Order. What more do you want?"

"His crimes continue."

No! What else had he done? "What do you mean?"

"You have heard of what he did to the fairy dragons? Even knowing their nature, you heard what he did."

The drakes holding Corn and Wall growled.

Anne winced, her stomach dropping. "Unfortunately, I have."

"Yet, he goes unpunished."

"What would you have me to do?"

"Nothing, save to stay out of the way."

"Out of the way of what?" Anne cast about, not sure from where the next danger would spring.

"Bar the door!" Fang cried.

The other two drakes dropped the wyrmlings in Anne's lap and bounded to the cottage.

Corn and Wall mewed and huddled into her lap, trembling.

"Are you hurt?" she whispered, pressing them close.

"Not yet." Fang snarled. "Not yet. Stay out of our way and you may remain so."

"They are wyrmlings and no threat to you. If you harm them, how are you any better than ... than my father?"

That seemed to give Fang pause. "Go then, wyrmlings, but you, lady, you will stay and watch the fate of those who hold our kind in too little esteem."

"Go now, to the house! Stay and do not move until I come for you." She pushed Corn and Wall off her lap.

Corn and Wall mewled, hesitating, but she gave each another little push, and they spring-hopped away. Pray they had the good sense to do as they had been told.

"For that favor," Fang jerked his head toward the departing wyrmlings, "you will be our voice to the Order, Special Liaison. Tell them of our demands. Tell them of our power. Tell them we cannot be stopped."

We? How many were there? "What do you want?"

"We want rights, protection, representation in the Order. We outnumber the major dragons hundreds to one. Our voices must be heard."

"This is not the way to make that happen."

"This is the only way to make it happen. We have the ear of the next brenin. He will give us our due."

Pendragon's bones, no! "Cornwall? You are allied with Cornwall?"

"Alliance is a strong word."

"Then what would you call it?"

"An exchange, an even exchange."

"Terror for recognition?" She forced her voice into something clear and strong and dominant.

"Cornwall has been wronged by the Order. It is his right to assert himself."

"Do you realize the judgement rendered against him resulted from lies and broken promises to another dragon? He abused Kellynch, that is why he was punished."

"Kellynch was a fool. He is responsible for his own suffering."

"Do you think Cornwall is going to keep promises to you? He was willing to deceive a major dragon. How much less will he give you the respect you are due?" Anne braced for Fang's response.

"You think I am so stupid? You think us all so foolish? We know with whom we are dealing. And we will protect our interests." He bared his teeth and stared into her eyes.

Chills raced down her limbs, leaving everything numb and thick in their wake. Was this how it felt to be cold-blooded?

The dragon looked away, head cocked, his eyes widening. "Do not move. Do not even think of moving, Special Liaison. For now, you are of greater value to me alive than dead. Do nothing to change that." He galloped down the path toward an odd, dark form.

Had Matlock or Wentworth any idea of the breadth of Cornwall's influence?

What was it the drake wanted her to witness to the Order?

From inside the cottage, pounding. Fists and boots. And screams, women's voices. Elizabeth. Widow Martin. Odd, muffled sounds rolled up from the path. Familiar somehow, but not clear.

She squinted into the early dawn light at the dark, writhing bundle dragged by three substantial drakes. Fang led them toward her.

A man! That was a man!

Fang stopped at Anne's side. "Take off the hood."

Father! Bound and gagged.

"This is what you are to tell the Order. This is the fate of those who would trespass against minor dragons." Fang's tail slashed the air.

Father's eyes, wide with terror, pleaded, begged.

"You do not have to do this. You have made your point very clear. I will take this to the Order, to the Council, to Londinium himself, if you want. Just stop!" Hopefully, that sounded like an order, not begging, which would only seal Father's fate.

"Begging does not become you, warm-blood. He chose this fate. In every possible way, he chose this fate. He wronged

Kellynch, he wronged Lady Russell, he wronged those fairy dragons. We are done with him. Put him in the house."

The dragons dragged him toward the house, opened the door, and shoved him inside.

"What are you going to do to them?"

"Fire."

"But Widow Martin. Jonty Bragg, the footman, they are innocent! You cannot—"

Fang leaned into her face, huffing his fetid breath in her eyes. "Do not presume to tell me what to do!"

"You will gain no sympathy from harming those who have been Friends to minor dragons!"

Fang twitched, brow creasing, and growled.

"Think about it! Think! You are not stupid. Will harming those in the Order who have been supporters of minor dragons make your case? Or will it brand you as simple thugs, criminals, who need to be silenced?"

Fang snapped his jaw in her face.

"Killing an old woman does not make you sympathetic. It does not make you worthy of notice. It makes you ruffians, murderers! Your cause will fall on deaf ears."

The dragon panted, hard. Bitter, acrid spittle sprayed Anne's face. "Mercy comes at a price."

"I told you. I will plead your case to the highest—"

"To the Dragon Sage? Will you take it to the Sage?" Fang drew himself up tall, puffing his chest out.

"She is my friend." Pray he believed her. "I will go to her personally, and make your case face to face with her."

"Pemberley has been impenetrable." He thumped his tail hard and clapped his jaws. "Release the men and the old woman when you put that one inside."

Dare she—"My sister's crimes were committed when she could not hear—"

"No. I will hear no more." He turned and slapped her shoulder with his tail.

Two dragons opened the door while another dragged out Widow Martin, bound and gagged. The footman and Jonty Bragg stumbled out as the dragon pulled them. Two others shoved Elizabeth back inside, then they barred the doors.

"Do not do this!"

"Another word, and I will return them to the cottage. Be thankful I have granted this much." The dragon did not bother to look at her. "Fire, I want fire!"

Chapter 25

November 20, 1815

"Out of my way, wyrm. I will kill you for this one way or another. If you leave now, you might have a few more months to live." Cornwall snarled, though the effect was somewhat dampened by his flapping about.

"I come on behalf of the Blue Order. You will be answerable to them one way or another." Kellynch rose higher in the water and trumpeted screaming, aching notes.

"Unless it is with an apology and offer of what is rightfully due me, I do not care."

"You are in violation of your charter."

Charter? Wentworth shivered so hard, the thought nearly shook from his mind. How would Kellynch know about Cornwall's charter?

"What charter? This land is mine. This sea is mine by rule of dominance." Cornwall tried to match Kellynch's height, but failed. "I have taken it, I hold it, it is mine."

"You were assigned your territory like every other dragon in the Order. Like Matlock and Dunbrook and Chudleigh. All assigned a territory, suited to rank and dominance. The Order gave you the territory."

"It was no gift. It is my right!"

Kellynch swam closer. "And you are bound by the strictures of the charter."

Did Cornwall realize he was backing away? "Nothing binds me! My will is law! I will be brenin!"

"Not even Matlock is—"

"Was! Matlock was but is no more!"

Siren continued her swim for shore. Matlock's assistants did the same.

"Not even he is exempt from the binding agreement of the Charter. You are in violation of yours!" Kellynch threw his head back and bugled.

"You cannot speak to me that way."

"The Land's End Charter specifies your territory is the land and only the land. You have never had rights to the sea."

"I do not care. I have taken what I can hold."

Kellynch stared directly at Cornwall, puffing his body. "The penalty for violation of this clause in the charter—"

"You cannot penalize me!"

"The penalty is not only the loss of territory, but the loss of membership in the Order."

"What do I care? I am the most dominant dragon in the kingdom. There is nothing you can do about that!"

"In the name of the sovereign brenin and the Blue Order, it is my right and responsibility to challenge you." Kellynch roared.

"You cannot stand against me."

"And yet I will try!" Kellynch swam into deeper water. "If you are master of the sea as you say, come out here to me!"

"Coward! I will face you anywhere and I will prevail." Cornwall dove in Kellynch's direction.

Siren reached the shallows where Wentworth could once again stand. He slogged his way onto the beach, where Gillingham met him, a fire already built, medical supplies in hand. "Tend Matlock, if you can." If they had any sense, they would both run. But Wentworth had not the strength, not yet. And Gillingham, for all his faults, would not leave a wounded dragon.

Wentworth staggered to the fire and sank to his knees, panting, shivering. How was it that Kellynch was even here?

Cornwall surfaced a wingspan from Kellynch.

"You have threatened the Order. You have threatened my Keeper and my Keep. I have had enough." Kellynch snarled and lunged at Cornwall's throat.

Around them, the sea ruptured and—good Lord, how many were there?—small sea dragons broke the surface. Wyrms, serpent-whales, hippocampi, small drakes, and a few Wentworth could not place. Dozens, maybe more, surrounded Cornwall.

"You brought an audience to watch your demise! How enchanting!" Cornwall bellowed. "Get back, you miserable sea lizards. Get out of my way or I will do to you what I will do to him!"

A sea drake, almost a miniature of Chesil, jumped to the back of a nearby serpent-whale, balancing on four feet, and he made himself big. "You will regret underestimating us. Chesil's vassals—"

"What do I care for Chesil? This territory is mine!"

A wave easily twice, maybe thrice the size of Cornwall, fountained up and broke over him. "I. Am. Chesil." If a voice could have had physical presence, his would have smothered them all.

Kellynch and the smaller dragons backed away from the deep green, frigate-sized sea-drake. Chesil's long, flattened crocodilian snout cast an ominous shadow over Cornwall. Backwards-pointing yellow horns ringed his face ahead of four deeper-yellow finlike frills behind his skull, increasing his apparent size even further as did the emerald-green fin running down the length of his spine. Neither firedrake was anything to him.

Cornwall sputtered and flapped, clearly trying to take to the air once again. "You are nothing to me!" He belched a cloud of flame at Chesil, who splashed it away with a single sweep of his front foot.

"I have no more patience for you, land-lizard. You have trespassed long enough."

"You challenge me? You would make war upon the Blue Order?"

"Your membership in the Blue Order is at an end, Cornwall," Kellynch said. "You violated your charter, unrepentant. You have nothing to do with us."

"I am the next brenin!"

"The brenin must be a member of the Order. You are nothing to us."

Chesil shook his head and looked toward Matlock. "Nevertheless, I will not act against the Order. I respect their efforts on land and would keep civil relations with them."

Cornwall drew back, as though to produce another flame.

"But I expect my vassals will not be so tolerant. Do your duty to your lord." Chesil dropped back underwater and, as far as Wentworth could tell, swam away.

"Our duty is to protect his territory. And we will do that the way Pemberley has led." Kellynch roared and the surrounding sea dragons disappeared.

Cornwall's eyes bulged as he frantically pulled one foot, then another, from the water. He flapped, but tiny sea dragons leapt from the water and attached themselves to the edges of his wings. He sank, lower and lower, shrieking and screaming and flailing, until nothing remained but blood on the sea foam.

Wentworth trudged to where Gillingham treated Matlock. Covered in wounds, the Grand Dug looked worse off than Kellynch after the Battle of Lyme Bay. Gillingham feverishly applied salve and dressings to the gaping throat wound as though it might make a difference.

How that attack had not opened up Matlock's jugular—unfathomable. Perhaps dragon anatomy was different.

Wentworth knelt beside Matlock's head.

"Did Kellynch—" Matlock croaked.

"I cannot tell how yet, but I am convinced Cornwall is gone. It might have been by Kellynch's fang, but more likely, his was the death of a thousand cuts, with no single dragon responsible."

"Excellent." Matlock sighed and closed his eyes, his breath slow and regular. "Then I will rest now."

Chapter 26

November 20, 1815

Common drakes could not breathe fire. Surely, they had a plan. It would have to be brought. There was still time.

Two drakes herded Widow Martin and the men to Anne, and forced them to sit. After several bared-tooth growls, they returned to guard the house.

Anne untied Widow Martin, who calmly adjusted her bodice and sleeves.

"What is to be done?" she asked softly. "There are two still inside."

"I do not know. He will hear no further pleas." Anne wanted to cover her face and huddle into a little ball, but that was a prey response.

"There are too many of them for us to overwhelm." Jonty Bragg crouched beside them and stared at the cottage. "I count no less than six, possibly eight, and we are unarmed."

A bright spot appeared overhead, growing larger, closer. A cockatrice? Anne shaded her eyes with her hand and squinted. It looked like a cockatrice ...with fire?

Fang rose on hind legs. The cockatrice swooped low and dropped a burning stick into his paws. "Now there will be justice for the oppressed." He transferred the stick to his mouth and climbed the cottage wall to the thatched roof.

"No!" Anne pressed her fist to her mouth.

The roof glowed, then burst into flames. Whipped into frenzy by the winds, the fire grew and spread and soon encompassed the entire roof.

The rogue drakes gathered around Fang.

"Go, go now," he ordered. "We will meet as agreed."

The dragons dispersed into the trees.

Smoke billowed from the structure and the screams from within faded.

With a final growl, Fang bounded away.

Anne jumped up, but Jonty Bragg and the footman caught her.

"It is too dangerous. Stay, we will try." The men ran toward the cottage, fighting suffocating clouds of smoke.

Rain, rain! Why would it not rain?

"I tried," Anne murmured into her hands. "I tried..."

"Of course you did, Lady," Widow Martin slipped her arm across Anne's shoulder. "We owe you our lives. That was no small thing you did, negotiating with angry dragons."

Rustling, scraping sounds, from the trees—had they returned? Anne stood, smoke burning her eyes, tickling her throat. Shadows slinked across the ground. They were returning? The dragons were returning? Had Fang changed his mind? Had he lost control of the group?

The shadows split apart and surrounded the cottage, circling it. But the smoke made it hard to see more.

Jonty Bragg and the footman staggered back, driven by one of the shadows. But it was too small to be a drake.

Not shadows!

Wyrms?

Wyrms!

"Stay away." That was Pebble with Jonty Bragg! "We know how to do." She slithered back to the blazing cottage.

Smoke engulfed the cottage. The footman dragged Anne back, Widow Martin close beside her.

Something, someone, someones furry wound around her ankles.

"Corn! Wall!" She crouched to gather them into her arms. "You brought them ... the wyrms, here?"

The wyrmlings purred and rubbed their cheeks against hers.

"We thought—they saved documents, maybe?" Wall looked over his shoulder at the blazing cottage.

"Clever, clever dragons. Whatever ...whatever happens...you are brave and wise beyond your years." She held them close and kissed their furry heads. "Laconia will be proud of you. I am proud of you."

They purred and wrapped their tails around her ribs in a wyrmling hug. Had they any idea how much she needed that, needed them right now?

A fairy dragon she did not immediately recognize zipped around them once, twice, thrice and flew off.

"Lady Wentworth, look..." Widow Martin touched her arm and pointed.

At the far right of the cottage, four, no, six wyrms dragged something from the cloud of smoke.

Widow Martin held her back. "Stay here, away from the smoke. Do not forget your delicate state."

She was right. For the sake of the baby, she needed to breathe.

And perhaps she did not want to look.

"Another one!" Jonty Bragg and the footman ran toward the wyrms and their burdens.

Anne clutched the wyrmlings tightly. They had done everything they could, more than any could have expected. There was hope now and that alone should be celebrated.

The men took the wyrms' burdens and dragged them toward the well. Father and Elizabeth, both still bound and gagged.

"Pendragon's bones!" A male voice behind her.

Anne spun toward the path.

Wynn ran full out, Cypher and Jasper at his side. "A fairy dragon alerted us to the fire..."

"Is there anyone else inside?" Jasper asked.

"No." Anne dragged her sleeve across her eyes.

"And the dragons?" Cypher panted hard.

"That accusation must have been an error." Wynn stood transfixed, staring at the flames.

"It was no error. A pack of drakes deliberately attacked and held my sister, Widow Martin, my driver and groom, kidnapped my father, and with the help of a cockatrice, set fire to the cottage."

"She convinced them to let us three out." Widow Martin squared her shoulders, daring Mr. Wynn to challenge her.

"They deliberately targeted your father and sister?" Mr. Wynn's eyes bulged and the scar on the side of his head throbbed.

"For crimes against minor dragons. They want me to take their statement to the Order, to the Dragon Sage, specifically."

"You will do no such thing! Think of the damage, the chaos—"

"Mr. Wynn, I do not even know if my sister and father live or have died. Now is certainly not the time to have such a conversation with you. Cypher, can you bring Mrs. Frankel, and Jasper, would you bring my housekeeper? I will need help tending my family."

The dragons chirruped and scurried off.

Mr. Wynn edged back. "Of course. Forgive my thoughtlessness."

Horrid man.

Soon, soon, Father and Elizabeth would be in good hands. If there was anything to be done. She should go to them, check and see—

"I will tend to them. You should go back to the house. You have no color in your face and even I can see you are trembling." Widow Martin looked her up and down. "There is nothing you can do for them that I cannot. For the sake of the wyrmlings and the baby you carry, go back to the house. I will bring you news myself when there is any to be had."

"But your home. You must stay with me—"

"You are most gracious, thank you. Go now. I will bring you news as soon as I can." She turned Anne toward the path and gave a little push.

But she should stay, she should take care of them. That was what she did, her role in life. She managed things. She took care of things. She made things right.

But some things were beyond her ability to make right. And there was little she could do about it.

Anne managed a few steps toward the house, then the world went grey, then black.

Chapter 27

November 21, 1815

Wentworth drew his knees up to his chest and repositioned himself nearer to the fire. Thank heavens Gillingham had thought to light that fire, otherwise the cold might have overcome him. His outer clothes were not quite dry yet, laid out across the rocks near the fire. He could not go far right now, in naught but his small clothes, but, at least for now, the damp garments would not kill him.

He focused one eye on Matlock, the other on the now quiet sea. To say Matlock looked the worse for wear would be like saying Chesil was a largish sort of dragon.

The somber grey dawn had given way to clear, bright skies lit by a winter sun that was all light but no warmth. Fitting, all told, very fitting.

The gaping wound Gillingham tended in Matlock's throat was only the first among many. Tears from talons and teeth—no limb was untouched. His wings might have been burned, it was difficult to tell with them folded, but his ribs and the side of his face certainly were. Gillingham had not indicated they were on deathwatch, so until he did, Wentworth would choose to believe the Order would not lose the most sensible voice it had.

Among the dragons, in any case.

The world as he knew it had not ended today.

It would go on. The Order would go on. The dragons would go on. Not as if nothing had happened. But they would go on.

How few would understand how close they had been to cataclysm, how much they owed Matlock. How much they owed Kellynch.

Kellynch had said something about Pemberley. About following the way Pemberley had led. That young dragon was making some mighty waves in the Order. So many implications…

A chill snaked across his shoulders. Surely, Pemberley could not understand the repercussions of what she had done, when the minor dragons of her estate came to her aid defending her territory against Bolsover. But Kellynch had, and if he did, others would as well.

What would that mean for the future?

The Blue Order security team swarmed over the beach, most heading toward Matlock, but a pair came to him.

"What should be done?" The leading drake, a dark brown male with a flaring head crest, bowed to Wentworth.

What should be done? That was a good question. "Send for Sir Edward in London. Matlock will need the most skilled dragon physician we have. Is there a cockatrice you can call upon for that? Beyond that, though, wait until we know something more. At least until we have seen Kellynch and know exactly what has happened to Cornwall."

The brown drake turned to his smaller, brindled companion. "Go, make that summons to the Lord Physician happen."

The brindled drake scurried off, kicking up sand in its haste.

"I expect the Dragon Slayer has been lost?" Wentworth's eyes were still on the sea.

"No, it is still on the cliff, where it fell." The brown drake shuffled his feet.

"See that it is retrieved, then. Yates will want it back."

"Understood." The drake scurried off, probably to avoid being asked to do something even more disagreeable.

It probably was not terribly decorous to ask a dragon to retrieve a Dragon Slayer, but sometimes duty was disagreeable. He rubbed his arms over his shoulders and edged a little closer to the fire. The shivering had finally stopped, but every muscle was still knotted as though it would begin again.

Where was Kellynch? The nagging little knot in his stomach that had started as a simple overhand knot was rapidly working its way up to a monkey's fist knot as big as a melon. Granted, Kellynch could stay underwater for extensive periods. He was a marine wyrm, after all. But surely, they should see something from him soon.

A fuzzy head bumped his elbow, then leaned in close. "Mrrrow."

"Did you see it all?" He stroked Laconia's furry shoulders.

"Yes, and I hope never to see such a thing again." Laconia pressed against his chest, purring hard enough to loosen the knots around his ribs. "There were many witnesses among the winged dragons. This will not be kept quiet."

"No, I do not suppose there is any way for that to happen. Once we know about Kellynch, do you think you can find a fairy dragon who could let Anne know we have survived? It isn't much, but I would want her to know that much as soon as possible."

Laconia's tail lashed the sand. "That is interesting. A fairy dragon from Lyme just flew by saying Anne is well. I did not know what to make of it..."

"Pendragon's bones! What has happened in Lyme?"

"The fairy dragon did not say, but Anne is well. I am sure Balen will be here soon to tell us more."

Wentworth ground the heels of his hands into his temples. Anne was well. Anne was well. That was all he needed to know. "Pray, find a messenger to take a similar message to Anne. And ask if any have seen signs of Kellynch."

"I will." Laconia spring-hopped away.

Wentworth pushed to his feet. Perhaps not the best of ideas. Being carried in a dragon's paw was not an ideal way to travel, even if it provided an interesting view of the world. Not one he ever wanted to see again, but it was interesting.

He wrapped arms around his chest, bracing for a deep breath. Standing seemed to require a great deal of breath right now. Oh, if the dizziness would settle, maybe he could venture a step or three.

Maybe one. That worked, more or less. Another. His clothes, he needed those. Yes. Finally dry enough, he could move about decently now.

Gillingham. He would be worth talking to right now. He forced one step, then another, limbs as heavy as if he were slogging through waist deep water.

The sea of security drakes parted, offering him a narrow aisle between them to walk.

Must not step on tails. Dragons often forgot to get them out of the way of clumsy, warm-blooded feet. So clumsy right now.

"How is he?" Wentworth croaked, panting, hands braced on his thighs. He sounded like an octogenarian, but it was getting better as his limbs warmed under the wool clothing.

Gillingham grunted, then looked up. "He is worse than Kellynch. The neck wound—so close to major vessels. I do not know what to tell you. I need Sir Edward."

"A messenger is already being dispatched. I am sure he will be here as fast as possible."

"I hope that is enough. Matlock should not be removed from this beach until—Lord above! I don't know when." Gillingham raked both hands through his disheveled hair. Blood spatter started on his forehead and stopped at his boots. The other gore and gobbets were more difficult to identify, but no less disagreeable for it.

Wentworth pointed to the largest drake in the security team, a ruddy female with a spiked ball at the end of her tail. "The Grand Dug needs a team to protect this beach from any warm-blooded incursion."

She rose on hind legs, spiky tail thumping on the sand. "I will organize that, sir. Air and ground persuasive teams?"

"Yes, double what you might ordinarily need, if you have the dragon power. And be on watch for those marauding drakes. They were attached to Cornwall in some form or fashion and could show up here."

"Understood." She dropped and moved among the team, calling them away from Matlock and into action.

Was it his imagination, or did their tension seemed to ease once given something useful to do? It made sense that it would. Dragons were not so different to men.

He hunkered down beside Gillingham and laid a hand on the young man's shoulder. "Do you need help?"

Gillingham dragged his sleeve across his forehead, leaving a dark stain on the sleeve of his brown coat. "Not yet. I'll have a list of things I need from the inn soon, though."

"I will see to that. Going to walk the beach for a bit and look..."

"Good luck. I hope you find him."

Wentworth pushed off the sand and forced his knees to drive him upright. Brushing sand from his hands, he scanned the sea—which direction? West and south, that was how the currents ran. He set off to the left, sand squelching under his boots.

A sharp gust of wind caught his face. Cold. He was still cold. But not dangerously so. Just miserable. For now, he could live with miserable.

Step. Step. Step. Search. It would have been nice if he had thought to bring his spyglass.

Step. Step. Step. Search.

Oh, bloody hell, why was there nothing there?

Step. Search.

A quarter of a mile down the beach, cliffs at his back, edging him into the lapping waves, he cupped his hands around his mouth. "Kellynch! Kellynch!"

Seabirds and perhaps a cockatrice circled overhead, cawing, screeching.

"Kellynch!" Pointless. Pointless. How would he even hear—if he even still could?

"There, that shadow! He comes." A cockatrice voice squawked.

Was it possible? Wentworth scanned again. Was that a shadow there, or was it something more? That nearby swell... Yes, it was a dragon.

A blessedly familiar dragon.

The right dragon!

It would be stupid to run out to meet it. It would be stupid. But commanding his feet to remain still was difficult.

The steady growth of the dark figure made it easier.

"I am grateful to see you are well and that Siren fulfilled her promise." Kellynch slithered from the waves to his side. He remained stretched long so his face could be near Wentworth. "She insisted on having the honor of your care."

"Honor? I am grateful, no doubt, but an honor?"

"You have earned their respect, in Lyme Bay, and by standing against Cornwall now. It means a great deal to them. You have made me proud, Keeper." Kellynch allowed one side of his mustache whiskers to drape over Wentworth's shoulder.

What did one do with such a statement? Greater than any medal that might have been pinned upon his chest. "And you have honored me with your courage. How did you come to be here, to take on Cornwall?"

"You have forgotten to ask, but yes, he is dead. He might have been a huge, dominant dragon, but with fairy dragons flying to her defense, baby Pemberley was able to best Bolsover, many times her size. So, it was here."

"Which again begs the question, how did you come to be here?"

"My wyrms gave Anne documents which included the original Land's End charter. Cornwall was strictly and categorically prohibited from ever entering the sea, much less claiming it as territory. On pain of forfeiture of his membership in the Order."

"So that is what you meant! It was not a bluff. He really had left the bounds of the Order?" Wentworth's jaw gaped.

"And as such declared himself both an independent dragon and an enemy to the Order. Upon learning that, I saw—" Kellynch hesitated a moment. "I saw that such information drastically changed the situation. And since he was trespassing upon Chesil's territory, it was my duty as Chesil's vassal to defend his territory. With Cornwall no longer a member of the Order, my duty and loyalty were no longer divided. I gathered Chesil's vassals as I came. It seems there were many who relished the opportunity to serve their liege, and vent their spleen on Cornwall."

"To say I am impressed would be to damn you with faint praise. Matlock owes you a great deal. For Cornwall to have met his demise at Matlock's fang—"

"He could not have done it. On land or in the air, our Grand Dug would have been dominant over Cornwall. But by drawing Matlock into the water, Cornwall had a decided advantage."

"Evidence suggests you are correct."

"It is hard for the sane to take on the insane and win." Kellynch looked over his shoulder, raining small drops of salt water on Wentworth. "It was not satisfying."

"I should be worried about you if you found it so."

"I suppose I would as well." Did dragons sigh? "There was also evidence, that Anne is continuing to explore, of a treaty, unknown to us, between Londinium and Chesil. That was why Cornwall's charter so explicitly forbade him from the sea while mine did not."

"A secret treaty?"

"One that Chesil was trying to honor by not going after Cornwall himself."

"Why did he not tell us?"

Kellynch snorted. "Secret treaty."

"But why a secret treaty?" Wentworth rolled his eyes and dragged his hand over his mouth.

"I cannot say for certain, but I think it served them both. Chesil did not wish to be known among the warm-bloods and Londinium hoped to use the terms to secure his reign or his power in some fashion."

"Have I ever mentioned how much I hate these machinations?"

"No, but I am not sure that you needed to." Kellynch settled into a coil beside Wentworth.

"We have sent for Sir Edward. Gillingham tends Matlock now. He cannot predict the outcome."

"If he is lost, it will have been in defense of the Order against a rogue dragon. It is a noble death."

"Is that to say you think the Order can survive this?" Wentworth sat beside Kellynch and scrubbed his face with his hands.

"Much better than other alternatives."

"I suppose it should make me feel better."

"It will be difficult, regardless."

"Is it ever not difficult?" Wentworth leaned against Kellynch's side. "It seems like everything dragons touch is complicated."

"We say the same of warm-bloods." Kellynch chuckled, the rumbles rippling through his coils.

"A fairy dragon flew by not so long ago to tell us that Anne is well. Have you news of what she meant?'

Kellynch tensed, his eyes wide. "Anne is well? That was the entirety of the message, that Anne was well?"

"You do not know what that means?" Every muscle tensed as a new chill suffused Wentworth's limbs.

"No. When I left, her sister's situation was managed, the wyrms were well, things were quiet. I know of no reason why we should need to hear that message now. But I am going to find out."

Chapter 28

November 21, 1815

"Anne! Anne!"

Balen's voice.

Anne willed her eyes to open against the crusty grit that glued them shut. She coughed, rolled to her side, and coughed until she curled into a tight little ball under the counterpane. "Balen?"

Heavy wings embraced her as a thick beak rested cool on her shoulder, near her face. "He is well, he is well. They all are."

The tension that bound her together shattered and every feeling she had under tight rein exploded out. Crying, babbling, no words made themselves available as gasping sobs rattled every joint, every sinew of her being.

Whatever had happened, Wentworth was well. Balen would never be mistaken about such a thing. And if he was well, especially if they all were, then it did not matter what had happened. At Land's End, or here. They were well.

Corn and Wall, who had been curled against her legs, mewed and slithered into her arms, purring so hard it seemed the bed itself shook.

Balen helped her to sit. "Be careful, be careful. You took a nasty fall yesterday."

"I did?" That explained why her head hurt so. She touched her head. Yes, definitely bruised. How did that... oh, walking home after—Anne gasped.

Corn and Wall wrapped their tails around her waist and leaned hard into her chest, purring and mewling.

"You frightened us," Corn whispered, barely audible over his purrs.

"Laconia and Kellynch insisted we should take care of you." Wall rubbed his cheek against hers.

"And you were brilliant, both of you." She hugged them hard. "That my fall should have been the thing to frighten you, after all that happened. You precious, silly, dears." She kissed their furry heads.

"I have been told that the local surgeon was sent for, and he is quite confident that you will make a full recovery. But you must not overexert yourself." Balen clapped her beak and resettled her wings over her back in a return to her usual composed demeanor. That, even more than her message, assured Anne that things would be well.

Dear, reliable, solid, Friend.

"The fire?" A better constructed question would have been nice, but totally impossible.

A soft knock at the door, and Widow Martin peeked in. "We heard your voice and thought you might like a cup of tea."

Balen waved her in to sit at the edge of Anne's bed. Still smelling of smoke, and wearing one of the housekeeper's gowns, Widow Martin handed Anne the teacup and sat.

The teacup rattled against its saucer in Anne's shaky hands. The hot, slightly too strong liquid soothed her raw throat. "What happened? My head is so muzzy right now."

"The three of us you saved, we are all well. And grateful, so very grateful. The way you stood up to them! We could hear you talking with them, like hearing Abraham negotiating for Sodom. It is still hard to believe you got them to listen to you." Widow Martin dabbed her eyes on her sleeve. "And the wyrms! I can hardly believe it. Even after they pulled your sister and father from the cottage, they continued to salvage a few things for me. Not much, to be sure, but far more than they had any call to do." She paused again, pressing her fist to her mouth. "The dear, dear creatures. They had no real reason to do such a thing and yet, they did."

"We will find a way to thank them properly."

"Do you think I might call upon them? I ...I have not had a Friend in a long time, and I would like to know them better."

"We can certainly ask if they are receiving callers. I think they would be pleased for your company." Anne sighed and leaned back against her pillow, sipping the tea slowly. Yes, she was avoiding the next stage in the conversation as she chewed her lip and looked for courage somewhere in the mess of anxious thoughts.

"You have not asked after your father and sister." Though her words could have been a condemnation, Widow Martin's eyes were compassionate.

Anne held the teacup tighter. "Yes. I find it difficult to want to know news that I might not care to hear."

Balen edged closer, and the wyrmlings tightened their tails around her waist.

"Mrs. Frankel has taken them in at the Blue Order office."

"Have you heard anything about their condition?"

"They are neither well nor at death's door, but hovering somewhere between. It is not the worst news in some ways, but hanging in limbo is hardly good news either." Widow Martin shrugged.

Anne exhaled in a rush. Widow Martin caught the teacup before Anne dropped it.

"For now, I am pleased it is not worse. I suppose I should go to them. Unless Kellynch is here?" Anne glanced at Balen.

"No, he tried to return, but was called back. A fairy dragon came to Land's End with news that you were all right, but without further details. A thing a young fairy dragon anxious to be useful might do. So Kellynch immediately headed for Lyme. I crossed paths with him after a serpent-whale was sent to call him back. He is now waiting on Cownt Matlock. After all that has transpired, there is much to discuss," Balen said.

Anne bit her lip. There were more details she wanted, but in Widow Martin's presence, it was hardly appropriate.

"If you will excuse me," Widow Martin stood and curtsied, wise enough to discern the awkward situation and too polite to make note of it. "I will see if the wyrms are accepting callers, and try to offer them my thanks." She closed the door behind her as she left.

"What then of Cornwall?" Anne drew her knees up to her chest and wrapped her arms around them. Corn and Wall sat back on their tails, breathlessly waiting for Balen's answer.

Balen clapped her beak under her wing. "It ended as it had to."

"How? Who was responsible?"

Balen quickly related her account of the Battle of Land's End and Cornwall's grim fate.

"Oh, merciful heavens!" Anne pressed the back of her hand to her mouth and rocked against the headboard, then wrapped her arms around the trembling wyrmlings. "I can hardly conceive. I suppose it is a good thing, yes? But so many implications. So many complications! And what of Matlock?"

"Gillingham will remain with him. Sir Edward has been sent for. They will attend him until Matlock cannot stand their presence any longer." Balen chuckled, though it came out as more of a 'caw' than a laugh. "To be sure, his injuries are serious and more extensive than Kellynch's were, but all expect that he will survive."

Anne leaned her head against the headboard. "That is a relief. With all that is going on, the Order needs its Grand Dug. Chesil? What of him?"

"I do not know." Balen blinked several times, as though annoyed she did not have the answer. "I left before he appeared. I thought you needed—"

"Yes, yes, absolutely. And I meant to imply no criticism."

"For what it is worth, I think Chesil will be entirely satisfied with the outcome. Cornwall was removed, in no small part thanks to your efforts. If you had not recognized the importance of that document, Kellynch would never have become involved. Kellynch-by-the-Sea has served both the Order and the sea dragon well."

"Is Kellynch well? Mr. Gillingham had not considered him well enough for travel."

"He is a bit worse for the wear, but not nearly so poorly as he would have been sitting by doing nothing."

"I suppose he is like me in that way. We all seem to be cut of that cloth, do we not? You, me, Wentworth, Kellynch, even Laconia, Corn and Wall. We are designed for activity and usefulness." Anne stared at the ceiling and sighed. "I suppose I should call upon the Order office now."

"I can go for you if you wish. You do not have to see them." Balen spread her wings enough to be bigger—just a bit. She often did that when she offered a suggestion that might not be well received.

"Would that not make me a horrid person, a horrid daughter?"

"No doubt some would say it. But that does not make it true."

"How do I know what is true in this circumstance?"

"I suppose you must decide that for yourself." Balen clacked her beak as she settled her wings. "But you have been kind and gracious and accommodating in all things. That they did not appreciate it does not negate that fact. It only underscores their foolishness."

Balen was right. Nothing she could do would ever please them, ever be enough. A reasonable person would recognize that and let it be. But it was also exactly the kind of decision she was likely to look back upon and regret.

"You mean to go to the office, then?" Balen said softly.

"Yes, but not just for them. There is an unfinished conversation with Mr. Wynn that I cannot ignore."

***

Balen accompanied her to the office. Whether she did so to protect Anne or Mr. Wynn was difficult to tell. Either was not an unreasonable choice.

Thankfully, Corn and Wall consented to call upon the wyrms instead of following her. Their lack of fondness for Mr. Wynn probably made their compliance easier. But it really was for the best.

Mrs. Frankel invited her in, her face lined with creases she usually did not wear. "Lady Wentworth, it is so good to see you looking so well."

That was not how Anne would have described herself, but the sentiment was kind. "I understand you have been looking after my family?"

"Not only me, to be sure. The surgeon has been calling regularly, and Corn and Wall—"

"The wyrmlings?"

"Yes, I know, it is surprising, but once they knew you were safe, they have been here, tending to their burns."

Anne gasped and reached for the nearest wall to steady herself. "I cannot imagine! How generous, how kind of them! They have no reason—"

"You are the reason, Anne." Balen said softly. "It is a kindness for you, not for them. They are deeply devoted to Kellynch and his Keepers and would do anything in their power for you."

"I fear I have underestimated them." Anne bit her knuckle as she drew in several deep, settling breaths. And that was why they stayed behind. They were not ready to be recognized for their extraordinary gesture. How had she missed them growing in humility like their sire? "How are they? What has the surgeon said?"

Mrs. Frankel frowned. "It is hard to say. We have dosed them both heavily with laudanum. Between the pain of their injuries, the trauma of their experience, and their general disposition, it seems the wisest course. Their injuries are severe, and to be entirely honest, it could go either way at this point. While the wyrmlings are helping to keep infection at bay, that is not the only difficulty facing their recovery. Sadly, they may remain in that neither-here-nor-there state for quite some time."

"I see. I should see them—"

Mrs. Frankel stepped directly in front of her. "I would advise against it. In their state they will draw no comfort from your presence. They will not even remember it. And it will be distressing to you. You have been through enough."

Balen pressed against her leg. "She is right."

"I suppose, then..." Anne sighed, "I should listen. Is Mr. Wynn in?"

"That he is." Mrs. Frankel gave a look of more than mild irritation. "Are you sure you wish to talk to him?"

"I must. There are serious issues that must be addressed." Not that she particularly wanted to deal with those now, but if she did not, then she might never do so.

"I will announce your presence to him. Do you wish for tea?"

"No, I think not. I imagine he will want something stronger when we are finished."

Mrs. Frankel chuckled and trundled off.

"Do you want me to stand with you?" Balen asked.

"Yes, I think so. Thank you." Anne pulled her shoulders back and lifted her chin.

"He is ready for you—well, perhaps not ready, but he is expecting you." Mrs. Frankel walked her to the office.

"Lady Wentworth," Mr. Wynn stood from behind his desk and bowed from his shoulders. He gestured to a plain wooden chair near his desk.

"Mr. Wynn." She nodded, pulled the chair back, and sat down. The extra space might be necessary if she needed to be on her feet quickly. This conversation seemed apt to go that direction.

"Are you sure you should be here, on your feet right now? You had a nasty fall yesterday and a woman in your condition—"

Anne lifted an open hand. "No, sir, pray do not turn this conversation about me. There are far more important matters to consider."

Clearing his throat, Mr. Wynn sat. Surely, he had not expected to get rid of her so easily, had he? "What do you wish to discuss?"

Anne fought the urge to drag her hand down her face and roll her eyes. Neither of which was good for displaying dominance. And now was a time for dominance.

"What is your problem with me, Mr. Wynn? I do not understand. When I first met you in Bath, when I applied for Order membership, you were prickly and unfriendly, but not nearly so—I do not even know a word to describe the disrespect and disregard you display, which I have surely not earned. What exactly is your problem?"

"Those are personal questions I do not appreciate." His face flushed its typical shade of puce.

"And your treatment of me is not personal? Do you believe I appreciate it? You fight me at every turn, though I am a duly-appointed representative of the Order. You treat my input as though it came from a willful child, playing at things it does not understand. Or did you expect I did not see it? That perhaps I was too stupid to understand what you were doing? And your attitude toward the minor dragons is hardly better. I am surprised Jasper tolerates it." She pushed to her feet. "The truth is I have had enough of it. If you cannot or will not cease with your veiled insults and disrespect, I will ask that the Order consider replacing you, both here and in Bath, with someone more suited for the task." She slammed her hands on the edge of the desk. Not just because they were trembling.

"There is no need to make threats, Lady Wentworth."

"What else is there left when common civility is meaningless to you?"

He rose very slowly, walked to the window, and turned his back to her to stare out. "Jasper has been with me a long time. She tolerates me because she understands."

"And what is it that she understands?"

He touched the scar on the side of his head. "This was a gift from my wife."

"You are married?" With his back turned, he could not see her jaw gape and eyes widen, which was probably for the best. It was hardly a polite expression.

"It is a difficult state from which to free oneself, short of resorting to acts in which I am not willing to engage."

Anne bit her tongue. Did she really want to know more? "You have had that since I have known you."

"It is not the only one of her gifts to me. It is more difficult to put away such a person than one might believe." He turned toward her. "Jasper has been instrumental in preserving me from her and her Friend's efforts in the years since you and I have been first acquainted."

"I see." Anne drew a deep breath, then another. Of all the things she had been prepared for him to say, this had never graced the list. And while it was a good explanation, it did not inherently change the problem. "But you would do well to endeavor to direct your scorn to the ones who have earned it, and not liberally splash it about upon all who might resemble them. You do not avenge yourself on them by attacking us."

Mr. Wynn sighed, seeming a little smaller than usual. "A point well taken, that I will make every effort to keep in mind. Shall we sit, Lady?"

Neither an apology nor an admission of guilt. It was the most she could expect from him, at least right now. His sense of dominance was too fragile, and she would gain nothing by shattering it. She sat down, though, because it was a start.

Chapter 29

November 22, 1815

Wentworth set up a small camp for himself and Gillingham near the injured Matlock, and they slept uneasily just out of reach of the high tide. Such torture, having Kellynch called back to shore shortly after he had left. But Matlock and Chesil were not to be denied the services of their subordinate dragon. For now, that service was keeping watch over the injured cownt while the warm-bloods slept.

Sunrise crept upon them cold, quiet and still, as though a momentous, world-changing event had not taken place on that beach the day before. Wentworth cracked one eye open, then threw his arm over his face, groaning. Not yet. The world had nearly ended yesterday. Didn't that mean he deserved a bit of sleep?

Laconia nudged his side and Kellynch bugled. Wentworth was on his feet in a single movement.

"Look!" Laconia pointed into the marcelled sky.

Flying toward them—that could only be Balen!

Wentworth wore a rugged trail in the sand, pacing.

"She is well. The wyrmlings are well. The wyrms are well. It is complicated, but they are well," she cried before her feet touched the sand.

But now he could breathe again. Wentworth fell to his knees in the sand, gasping for breath.

Balen poured out the entire tale in what seemed a single breath.

"But you are certain Anne is well?" Wentworth asked for at least the third time, sitting back on his heels.

"She is uninjured, but taxed by the circumstances, to be sure, Captain." Balen folded her legs to sit and look him eye to eye.

"Those drakes must have waited until I left the territory to make such a move." Kellynch growled, the tip of his tail pounding the sand.

"Probably so, but I expect they would have pressed their attack on Sir Walter somewhere else. It is not beyond imagination that the Royal Lion might have been set ablaze." Balen replied. "Anne is working with Wynn on the matter, but we have little hope that the rogue drakes will be found, at least not quickly or easily. I expect she will need to visit the Dragon Sage as soon as might be arranged."

"She is going to carry out her promise to them?" Laconia's tail lashed across the sand.

"It is only right that she honor that agreement. And this is exactly the sort of situation that most needs the Sage's wisdom and direction. Given all that has taken place ..." Balen flicked sand from her wings.

"Complicated, so damn complicated." Wentworth muttered.

"Has an official decree of death been made? An official statement of Matlock's condition?" Balen glanced at the sleeping cownt.

"Not yet. I think we will have to consult with him on what is to be said. It is too sensitive for us to make such a decision. Matlock should know of the goings-on at Kellynch-by-the-Sea and the extent of Cornwall's influence on the minor dragons. Would you be willing to speak with him directly, Balen?"

"Anne and I thought that might be the case." Balen's ruffled head feathers belied her calm tone. "If I might suggest that Laird Kellynch postpone his return until we speak to Cownt Matlock regarding matters of the estate. He might have specific directions for Kellynch-by-the-Sea. The wyrms, your wyrms as you call them, have established an active defense of the territory. Nothing less than another major dragon will interfere there. Your territory will be safe for another day."

"I am proud of them." Kellynch said.

"They have served you as you have served Chesil and the Order. You gave them an excellent role model to follow." Balen turned to Laconia. "And you should be proud of Corn and Wall. Both of you should. They showed wisdom and courage beyond their years."

Laconia licked his shoulder and purred.

"I am proud of my Friends," Kellynch said.

His Friends? A chill snaked down Wentworth's back. It was easy to forget how unique the relationship was between Kellynch and his Friends. What impact would that have on the Order in the days to come? One could hardly imagine.

Wentworth pushed to his feet, dusted the sand from his hands, and set a pot of coffee on the fire to brew. It would probably be terrible, burnt, and bitter. But it would be hot, which was the whole point. He opened the basket the drakes had brought from the inn. Bread, cold meat, cheese, a pot of jam. A veritable feast.

He sliced off slabs of meat and offered them to Laconia and Balen, who accepted them with draconic zeal. Even without an appetite himself, the sight was off-putting. So, he looked away, tore off a hunk of bread, stuffed it with rough slabs of meat and cheese and brought it to Gillingham, who still slept, cocooned in a blanket, near Matlock's snout. "Here, you need this."

Gillingham groaned, rubbing sleep from his eyes. "Food? You are brilliant." He took Wentworth's offering and set upon it like a ravenous wyrm, with only slightly better manners.

Wentworth sat beside him. "How is Matlock?"

Matlock lifted his head slightly and opened his eyes. "Cross. I am especially cross."

Poor Gillingham nearly choked on his food.

Wentworth was far too tired for that. "Forgive me, I did not realize you were awake."

"And I am hungry."

"Of course. If you will eat from the sea, I can ask Kellynch to hunt for you."

Matlock's lip curled back in distaste. "That will be ... acceptable. Then we must talk."

"I will see to it." Wentworth hurried off while Gillingham checked Matlock's wounds.

Kellynch rallied the serpent-whales and in short order had provided Matlock with sufficient offerings from the sea to clear some of the weariness from his eyes and sluggishness from his thought.

"I have never eaten fish before." Matlock pulled himself into a decidedly feline hunch, tail wrapped around his legs, wings still half-extended, dressed with enormous herbal poultices over the burns. "It is acceptable. I will need warm-blooded prey soon."

Wentworth waved Balen closer, though Laconia kept his distance. He clearly had not forgotten Matlock's ire toward him in

London. "I will see to that. There is news from Lyme that you should know. Balen?"

Balen quickly relayed the tale of the rogue drakes.

Matlock growled, rumbling the sand beneath their feet. "It is a good thing Cornwall is dead." He turned to look directly at Kellynch. "You are certain he is dead?"

Kellynch pulled back, coughing and gagging until he brought up an object on the beach. "His fang, Cownt Matlock, the first of four I carry in my stomach. Examine it, to be sure it is the fang of a firedrake, recently removed from the body. There is no body left to provide in evidence, but the teeth should be sufficient." Kellynch pushed the tooth toward Matlock.

Matlock reached out with his front paw, slowly, painfully, and brought the fang to his nose, sniffing, mouth open, forked tongue flicking. "It is Cornwall's. You could not have taken this from a living firedrake. You have four?"

"It seemed necessary to provide incontrovertible proof."

"Excellent. You will need to deliver these to the Council in London. And you," Matlock looked at Wentworth, "need to be there as a witness to what has taken place."

Damn it all. He needed to see Anne.

"Then you must go to the Dragon Sage. She must be informed, firsthand. Take Lady Wentworth to her. She must be brought to bear on these issues immediately. Tell her she will be needed in London directly."

"Cownt," Balen backed away, bowing, "there may be difficulties. We do not have all the details now, but the Sage's confinement has not had a positive outcome. We do not know what that means yet, but she may not be able—"

"This matter is more important than even that. Tell Chudleigh to go to the Sage as well, then. She has experienced poor outcomes and will be the most sympathetic among us."

"That is most gracious of you." Balen spread her wings and prostrated herself on the sand.

"Yes, it is." Matlock snuffed. "I will remain here until I can return to the Order without tempting a dominance challenge. There is too much happening right now to allow further instability among the firedrakes. You—" He pointed at Balen, "will go to London and deliver a message to my Keeper. I will dictate, you will write. It is confidential."

"Understood." Balen remained prostrate before him.

"By your leave, Grand Dug," Kellynch said. "Chesil waits just offshore, wishing an audience with you."

"I am hardly surprised. As I cannot go out to meet him, tell him I await his leisure." Matlock nodded toward the sea.

Awaiting Chesil's leisure? Pendragon's bones! That was all but recognizing Chesil's dominance. Surely Matlock would never have said such a thing without recognizing the implications.

Kellynch slithered into the waves and disappeared.

"Shall I bring writing supplies?" Balen asked.

"Go." Matlock watched as she flew off and resettled himself on the sand. "What more do you know of this secret treaty Kellynch spoke of?"

"Nothing more than you have heard. As I understand, Anne is still working on those documents. What that means, precisely—I do not know that either. I will need to talk to her myself to know."

"And the wyrms from Lyme, they brought her those documents?"

"Yes, they protected many of the Order documents from the fire." Wentworth held his breath. Speaking well of such lowly dragons could be dangerous.

"That is a good thing. We need evidence of their value to the Order."

"You anticipate difficulties?"

"I would not put it in those terms, but if your warm-blood sensibilities require it, we can use that word." Matlock pulled back his lip to reveal a stained fang, probably as much ire as he could muster right now. "Have Lady Wentworth bring the treaty to the Historian directly at Pemberley. Do not show it at the London office. Its very existence is too damning."

"Londinium is in trouble?"

Matlock slapped the length of his tail along the beach, wincing as though he immediately regretted it. "He may be brenin, and the most dominant dragon, but he would not be dominant over the Council together. The Order was established this way to keep checks on the brenin and ensure adherence to the Accords."

"I had no idea."

"Of course not. Why would we want warm-bloods to have such knowledge?"

Wentworth bit his tongue.

"Tell the Sage she is to take no action until she understands that treaty and returns to London to discuss it with the Council."

"I will convey the message."

"You must do more than that. You must ensure she does what I have asked. I know she is a stubborn warm-blooded dragon, but I have hundreds of years of experience she lacks. Remind her of that—" Matlock chuffed a heavy breath. "—and that we are both on the side of the Order."

"I will. May I speak of this to Anne? She may be able to help—"

"I dislike these warm-blooded sensibilities that require so much coddling. It is weak and distasteful." Matlock rolled his eyes and wrinkled his nose. "Yes, she may know. And Darcy as well. But no more."

"As you say, Grand Dug."

Kellynch slithered back onto the beach, salt water sloughing in sheets from his back and face. "Chesil comes."

Matlock pulled himself up as much as possible, grimacing as he did so.

Chesil thundered onto the sand, stopping only halfway out of the water. His front half alone more than filled the small beach, his presence overwhelming.

"Chesil." Matlock dipped his head.

"Matlock." Chesil towered over them all. "You have survived. That is fitting."

"And the interloper has not. That is fitting."

"We are agreed."

"I have learned there was an agreement between you and Londinium?" Matlock's ears pricked.

"So, it has been recovered." Interesting how that was a statement from Chesil, not a question.

"As I understand. Work is being done to understand the contents, but it may take some time to restore the document and find a translator for it. Old dragon script is not widely read any more."

Chesil shook water from his face and shoulders, showering them with salty rain. "No less than I expected."

"You did not deal with Cornwall yourself. I expect that was because of the treaty."

"Correct."

"And we discovered Cornwall's charter stipulated he must not encroach upon the sea."

"That was another stipulation of the treaty," Chesil said.

"Until we properly understand the contents of the treaty, it will be difficult to abide by it."

"Londinium can tell you."

"Perhaps, but it seems unwise to rely on his memory and interpretation at this juncture."

Chesil grumbled and dug at the sand with his webbed front foot. "I should not be surprised that he would so easily forget such an agreement. Is his continued dominance expected?"

Wentworth held still. Surely Chesil understood the implications of making such a statement in front of a warm-blooded witness, but there was no point in reminding Matlock he was there.

"I cannot say that it is." Matlock cast a warning glance toward Wentworth and another at Kellynch.

Dragon's fire! Was this possible?

"Then the time is better spent negotiating a new agreement."

"Kellynch, you will call the Council here after you deliver your evidence. In the meantime, we may begin the process by establishing the framework of our discussions." Matlock said.

"Acceptable." Chesil turned toward Kellynch. "There is a stipulation I will insist on now."

"What do you want?" Matlock's voice was flat, wary, clearly realizing his lack of dominance in the situation and not liking it.

"I want a representative, an ambassador, an official liaison between me and the Order. It is tiresome and unfitting that I should always have to come to you."

"That is ... acceptable."

Chesil pointed at Kellynch. "You will be my ambassador to the Order and theirs to me."

"It is not a task for a common laird." Matlock said. "Kellynch, here." Matlock slapped the sand in front of him.

Kellynch slithered to that spot and stretched out in obeisance before the Grand Dug.

"Laird Kellynch, for services to the Order I designate you Marchog and the first Order ambassador to the British Coastal Regions. Proper ceremony will take place at the next Conclave." He tapped the back of Kellynch's neck with his fangs, leaving tiny dots of blood, wounds that would form scars, marking him with the newly-made rank.

Was there any other dragon in England to have been so honored?

Chapter 30

November 28, 1815

Anne stood at the dock, Wentworth's ship growing larger against the horizon. She shaded her eyes with her hand against the strong afternoon sun and sharp wind. Soon, soon, very soon.

She held her breath until she could make out his figure on the deck, spyglass in his hand. Then he waved, a broad, energetic gesture, completely lacking in composure and dignity, and so completely right.

She paced until the deckhands moored the craft. Wentworth leapt off and ran to her. How else could she respond, but to do the same? Propriety and all the things that went with it were hardly as important as being in his arms.

His clothes still smelled of that peculiar smoke that firedrakes alone produced, unlike the smoke of wood and thatch that currently permeated Kellynch-by-the-Sea. But underneath it all, he smelt like Wentworth, like the sea, like safety, like home.

He crushed her to his chest, enveloping her in strong arms that assured her there was greater strength than only hers to hold everything together. That the weight of the world did not rest upon her shoulders alone. That she was not alone.

Pressing his cheek to the top of her head, he rocked on his heels with the waves against the dock. "Anne, Anne, my dearest Anne. Tell me you are well. I have heard it from Balen a dozen times, but I need to hear it in your voice, here where I can feel your heartbeat, hear your breath."

"I will not lie to you, beloved, it has been dreadful in more ways than I could have imagined. Dreadful and cold and lonely. I hated every moment of being alone here, without you—"

"And I you. I am so much better with you than apart." He leaned down, stared into her eyes, and kissed her. Not chaste, not proper. As a man reunites with the other half of his soul.

Behind him, the sailors voiced loud approval.

"We best take this home," she whispered. "The carriage awaits."

Jonty Bragg swiftly carried them to Kellynch-by-the-Sea.

THE NEXT MORNING, THEY cuddled together on the worn couch that had been shoehorned into their dressing room. Though faded and threadbare in places, it was the only one in the house that fit the available space, so it was perfect.

Weary lines etched Wentworth's face, gaunt, thinner now than when he had left. The privations of his journey left marks upon him, body and soul. He was changed. Not for better, perhaps not even for worse, but changed.

Those were the sort of marks dragons left and moved one from one plane of understanding to another in ways that could not be explained except to one who was a companion on that journey.

She nestled into his shoulder, under his arm. For just this moment, and maybe this moment alone, all was right in the world.

"As much as I have appreciated Balen's help, there is nothing compared to being here with you." Wentworth found her hand and laced his fingers with hers.

"I would feel more guilty for all she has done except that I understand that she finds those solitary flights restorative and enjoys the excuse for the indulgence."

"And who brought that to your attention?"

"Wall thought I needed to know." Anne glanced about the room for the wyrmlings, but they were probably making Kellynch's lair ready for his arrival. They had sorely missed their laird.

"There are no secrets when one lives with dragons, are there?"

"I am not sure there are any secrets anywhere." At least not once words were spoken aloud. "How is Cownt Matlock?"

"Recovering, but I expect it will be some time before it is wise for him to be around other large dragons."

"It seems so wrong that his injuries could elicit such a reaction. Objectively, I understand it, but—"

"—it is a bit cold-blooded, no?" Wentworth snickered.

Anne pulled back and stared at him. "Did you really say that?"

"You do not approve?"

"After all that has transpired, it is a wonder you can have any sense of humor at all."

"I think it might be all that I have right now." He leaned heavily into the couch.

"And perhaps more than I have." She pressed her cheek to his chest, listening to his heartbeat. "I still cannot believe all that has transpired in so little time, just here in Lyme. The documents, the wyrms, my family, the rogues—"

"You know I would have been hard-pressed to leave if there had been any inkling that things could take such turns. Pray tell me you know that I would never willingly leave you to face such things on your own."

Anne nodded into his shoulder, swallowing hard. "It was more than any of us could have anticipated."

"Yes, but tell me you know. You have been made to resolve situations not of your making on your own too many times. You do not think I would do that to you, do you?" He tipped her chin up to look him in the eyes.

"I am accustomed to dealing with things on my own." She blinked furiously, but it could not hide the burning in her eyes. "But I am so tired. So astonishingly tired."

"I would think you a liar if you said otherwise. It is right and fair for you to be tired. I wish I could promise a time to rest soon, but—"

She pressed her fingers to his lip. "You don't have to say it, I know. We will find a way."

"I expect Kellynch will be here soon, later today, no later than tomorrow."

"His wyrms will be most glad to see him. Although I am no expert, I think his presence in the bay has been missed, too."

"No doubt. With his new rank and role, I imagine he has become one of Chesil's most influential vassals."

"I still cannot fathom he is now a marchog," she said. "I would never have expected such a thing. A new rank among the dragons has not been created in —well, I do not know how long. Do you think it a good idea? Jealousy and spite are so dangerous right now, giving reasons for more seems reckless."

"I understand Matlock's impetus for doing it. Kellynch will need the respect and dominance the rank brings to function as ambassador. It ranks him above all the other major wyrms in the kingdom, and above enough others who consider him lesser by virtue of his type and marine nature. You are right, though, there will be friction."

"I expect he will ignore that fact for a while, enjoying the satisfaction that his new status provides. He has always hoped for recognition, and he has done something to earn it."

"To be sure, there is that. I expect there is some celebration going on, out there under the waves. And for now, I think it is good that he celebrates. Soon enough, the reality of the situation will set in. I think, in spite of all the personal satisfaction of being properly recognized, he is entirely cognizant of the troubled times we are facing. He was witness to Cornwall's demise, planned and participated in it. One cannot engage in an action of that nature, whether one deems it a defense or an execution, without being changed."

All of them had been changed, knowing that such a thing had occurred. "And the wryms on the estate have changed him, too. Rather like my mother told me the birth of a child changes one, makes one see the world in entirely different ways."

"You have not spoken about our little one." He laid his hand over her stomach.

"If you hold very still and quiet, you might feel baby move." She laced her fingers atop his. "Balen tells me he is well. She speaks to him often."

"He? She has already decided that?"

"She tells me it is in the smell. But baby will be what baby will be, and I am not concerned as to that. Balen also declares our heir hears dragons, which is a great relief. A half-Blue family would be one of the worst possible outcomes. At least to me."

He nodded, thankfully not adding his own ideas to the list of possible untoward outcomes. "And when are we to expect this new arrival?"

"In the spring, according to the midwife." She closed her eyes and laid her head back along his arm. "I like the spring, you know. I think it is my favorite time of year."

"Then it is mine as well." He kissed her cheek. "I will look forward to this spring like I have no other."

She closed her eyes, basking in the glow of promise and anticipation.

He stroked her cheek. "I have not dared ask, but I can avoid it no longer. What is the word on your father and sister?"

She shook her head. "As yet, uncertain. They both become so hysterical, a great deal of laudanum is used in their care. I worry it might not be good for them. Still, I do not know what to expect. Even if they survive, will they be able to tolerate the knowledge that there are dragons out there, dragons that could do them harm? I do not know."

"What is Wynn's position? Or do I even want to know?"

"He has changed, too. Or perhaps it is understanding him a little better that has changed me."

"Indeed? Tell me more."

"Pray, later for that. For now, he is in agreement that they should remain in the Order office until the path of their recovery is clearer. After that, I do not know."

The tension in his shoulders suggested he would have liked to press the point. "Something for you to consider, the Order has estates in Scotland where troublesome Order members may be sent. They are not prisons, exactly, those are different facilities, but if they recover sufficiently, that might be an option to keep them safe, and reasonably comfortable, and unable to bring further harm to the Order—or themselves."

"We have been so occupied in managing the present situation I have hardly been able to think that far ahead. It is a good thought, though. A very good thought. Clearly, after what my father allowed to happen to the fairy dragons in Bath, he cannot be trusted to be without direct supervision. Even if Elizabeth's hysteria subsides, which it may or may not, after what has happened, I do not expect she will regard coexistence with dragons in a favorable light, ever. How are such arrangements to be made?—if we need to make them, of course."

"I believe it is the Minister of the Courts, Lord Dunbrook's office, that manages those facilities."

"There is no underling to whom we could apply?"

"Considering the complexities of your father's case, I think it would be best to present the case to the court and let them decide what to do with it."

"And such a presentation must take place in person, I imagine." And that would require a trip to London.

"I do not know that it must, but it seems like it would be a good idea. Even if it were not, since I must go to London on behalf of Matlock, it provides us good reason to travel together. From there we can go to Pemberley. I know I could send you on ahead—"

"No, I would not have that either." They had endured enough separation for a lifetime. "It is a long journey, though."

"Do you think you can make it?"

"For now, I believe so. But we must consider the possibility that by the time we are finished at Pemberley, I may not be able to travel back to Lyme for some time. Kellynch will not be pleased if I must remain away until our babe is born and is strong enough to travel."

"I hope Kellynch's new responsibilities will provide him sufficient satisfaction that he is not so dependent upon you. Matlock released him from the requirement that he remain with his Keepers, so there is that as well. But, regardless, we must do what is best for both of you."

"You will not be disappointed that our heir will not be born here, at our home?"

"All things considered, it may be a good thing. There is no telling how long your father and sister may be here. You do not need that burden."

"There is something you are not saying. I need you to tell me."

"I do not like these rogue dragons wandering about. I fear Sir Walter's presence might attract their attention again, and I would see you protected from them. With only wyrms, for all their valiant efforts, which I cannot appreciate enough, the estate has little protection. Kellynch is not well equipped to protect the land. We will have to look into finding other minor vassals for the estate who can adequately do that. And that will take time. Until then, I would ... I would feel better knowing you were close to Pemberley where the estate is far better established, and managed. I am convinced that Derbyshire will be safer for our family for now."

OTHER BOOKS BY MARIA GRACE

World Wrights Series:
Wrighting Old Wrongs

Jane Austen's Dragons Series:
Pemberley: Mr. Darcy's Dragon
Longbourn: Dragon Entail
Netherfield: Rogue Dragon
A Proper Introduction to Dragons
The Dragons of Kellynch
Kellynch: Dragon Persuasion
Dragons Beyond the Pale
Dragon Keepers' Cotillion
The Turnspit Dragon
Dragons of Pemberley
Miss Georgiana and the Dragon
Here There Be Dragons

Secrets of the Dragon Archives
Dragons at Land's End

The Queen of Rosings Park Series:
Mistaking Her Character
The Trouble to Check Her
A Less Agreeable Man

Sweet Tea Stories:
A Spot of Sweet Tea: Hopes and Beginnings
Snowbound at Hartfield
A Most Affectionate Mother
Inspiration

Darcy Family Christmas Series
Darcy & Elizabeth: Christmas 1811
The Darcy's First Christmas
From Admiration to Love
Unexpected Gifts

Given Good Principles Series:

Darcy's Decision
The Future Mrs. Darcy
All the Appearance of Goodness
Twelfth Night at Longbourn

Fine Eyes and Pert Opinions
Remember the Past
The Darcy Brothers

Regency Life (Nonfiction) Series:
A Jane Austen Christmas: Regency Christmas Traditions
Courtship and Marriage in Jane Austen's World
How Jane Austen Kept her Cool: An A to Z History of Georgian Ice Cream

Behind the Scene Anthologies (with Austen Variations):
Pride and Prejudice: Behind the Scenes
Persuasion: Behind the Scenes
Non-fiction Anthologies
Castles, Customs, and Kings Vol. 1
Castles, Customs, and Kings Vol. 2
Putting the Science in Fiction

Available in e-book, audiobook and paperback

ABOUT THE AUTHOR

Six-time BRAG Medallion Honoree, #1 Best-selling Historical Fantasy author Maria Grace has her PhD in Educational Psychology and is a 16-year veteran of the university classroom where she taught courses in human growth and development, learning, test development and counseling. None of which have anything to do with her undergraduate studies in economics/sociology/managerial studies/behavior sciences. She pretends to be a mild-mannered writer/cat-lady, but most of her vacations require helmets and waivers or historical costumes, usually not at the same time.

She writes Gaslamp fantasy, historical romance and non-fiction to help justify her research addiction. Her research rabbit hole dives can be found on RandomBitsofFascination.com
Contact her at: author.MariaGrace@gmail.com

Acknowledgments

So many people have helped me along the journey, taking this from an idea to a reality.
Debbie, Diana, Linda, Maureen, Patricia, and Ruth, thank you so much for cold reading and being honest!
Friends of the Blue Order, your unflagging encouragement and imagination has been inspirational.
My dear friend Cathy, my biggest cheerleader, you have kept me from chickening out more than once!

Thank you!

Made in United States
Orlando, FL
28 October 2024

53151548R10169